One Christmas in the Sun

Sienna Santerre

Arachis Press 2022

One Christmas in the Sun
©2022 Sienna Santerre

ISBN 978-1-937745-84-4

Arachis Press
4803 Peanut Road
Graceville, FL 32440
http://arachispress.com

Chapter One

Joey

"I'm going out with Russ tonight."

"Russ Penn?" Kris sounded incredulous, and rightly so.

The absurdity of the idea made Joey laugh. "Oh, no. Russ Wesolowski."

Her friend considered this. "I think maybe he's the one Ronnie wanted all along. Not his brother."

Joey thought there might be truth to that. Too late now. Too awkward, after dating and dumping Alan. "Russ is just back for the holidays. Like you."

"Hmm." Kris considered this news as well. "But I'd guess this isn't the first time for you two, is it?"

"Nah. We've gone out a couple times." What with Russ coming home on the occasional weekend and Joey sharing rides with his brother, the two had been bound to run into each other. It hadn't been much more than that. "He and Alan might take off for a surfing trip anytime. I don't know how much we're likely to see of either over the break."

"Ooh, it's waaay too cold to surf!"

"They wear wetsuits." Joey was fairly sure of that. "The water's warmer over where Russ goes to school, you know."

"Yeah, Gulf Stream. Same in Miami, not that I've had time for the beach." Kris sighed deeply and dramatically. "Nose to the grindstone and all that. See, it's almost all worn away!" She pointed to her admittedly small snub nose.

"You haven't even worn the freckles off," responded Joey. "I thought you and Angelica would be partying at the beach and completely neglecting your studies."

"Jelly isn't near as much fun as I had hoped. We hardly see each other."

"I suppose we will see her sometime over vacation."

"Unless she goes off skiing with friends or something. Rich friends, most likely, with cabins in Vermont."

"Cabins larger than our houses, no doubt."

"Oh, sure. Big A-frames with tall windows overlooking the best slopes."

"And best ski instructors."

"Now for that I might be willing to go out in the snow!"

Neither had ever been on skis, other than water skis. Joey had never even seen snow. "All I know about skiing is what I've seen in movies," she admitted.

"And ski instructors," Kris added.

"Them too. They have to be better than college instructors."

Kris nodded an emphatic agreement. "We don't have to look at those again for almost a month. No classes, no exams!"

"I had the last of those today."

"Yesterday for me. I jumped in the bug and drove home this morning."

Which route? wondered Joey. Oh, there was no point in asking. And she didn't actually care, did she? "I don't think we're gonna see Ronnie till the weekend."

"She didn't even come home for Thanksgiving."

"It's a long drive from Gainesville to Naples. Longer than I'd want to drive in her car."

"She'd be better off riding a bus. But not a school bus like you."

Joey ignored her friend's snicker. It was only two days a week she rode the free bus up to the Edison college. Other days, it was her vehicle or Alan's. "Russ's van is practically a bus," she said. "I suppose he'll be along soon."

"Which means I should get out. Very subtle, Joey."

"I'm noted for my tact," she informed her. Both rose from their sticky plastic-seated kitchen chairs and headed for the front door. Joey had lived all her life—or as much of it as she could remember—in this early Fifties 'Florida house' with its bare concrete block construction, flat roof. It even had jalousie windows. Some of them.

No Christmas decorations yet. Her mom was very old fashioned about not hurrying the season. Maybe her Italian upbringing. Joey didn't care that much one way or the other. Of course, the city had begun putting up its lights right after Thanksgiving. She could glimpse some hanging along the Trail, Highway Forty-one, from her bedroom. When Joey was little, there had been nothing built yet in between. Things had filled in, year by year, since.

Her friend got into the black Volkswagen, top up, and waved as she pulled away. Joey could see her roll the window up quickly. It was nippy out. Going home, over on the other side of the Trail, a much nicer neighborhood than this, and closer to the beach.

She assumed Kris wasn't dating anyone. Her boyfriend was far away. Wouldn't Will be out of boot camp by now? Maybe she could ask but maybe she shouldn't. No matter. Back inside. A sweater would be a good idea this evening. And trousers? Hmm, yeah. The corduroys. Best to be ready if Russ wants to do something outside. The boy was big on being outside.

It was beginning to get old already. She liked Russ Wesolowski. He was passionate about a few things, science, the ocean. He could talk about sea creatures endlessly and sometimes did. All that was fine in small doses.

Which was what she had been getting. Over the full Christmas vacation? Maybe not! There might need to be changes. There was his green Ford van, with its surfboard roof racks, pulling up out front. Joey didn't wait but ran out to it.

She plopped into the passenger seat. There were two separate seats up front. Very separate—far enough apart Russ couldn't put his arm around her even if he wanted. Joey wasn't sure whether he wanted or not.

She wasn't sure whether *she* wanted it or not. Maybe she'd find out sometime. "Seafood?" he asked.

"Not yet. I'll point it out when I do."

Russ looked slightly bewildered for a moment, then chuckled. Rather too politely, felt Joey. His brother would have caught the silly joke immediately.

"Seafood sounds great," she told him.

Chapter Two
Kris

It got dark too early at this time of year. Already, she had her head-lights on as she drove along Gulf Shore, heading south toward her home. Christmas decorations hung along the way. They were lit up too, and so were some of the houses.

They had always celebrated the holiday in her family's home. They didn't even bother to call it Hanukkah. Oh, Mom remembered some-times. But there was a Christmas tree alongside the menorah, and Kris didn't remember ever seeing a dreidel in the place.

Carols on the radio. No point in trying to tune in another station. The choice was limited in Naples at this time of the evening. Maybe she'd just load up the portable record player in her room tonight and not stir from it. There was the Summerlin house, rising like a blocky black monolith against what was left of the sunset, palms silhouetted beyond it, at the fringe of the beach. A few lights on. No Christmas decorations. Had Jelly come home already? They hadn't talked before she left Miami.

The University of Miami. She liked it pretty well. She even liked her dorm room. Her mom had urged her to join a sorority—the one she had belonged to, of course—but Kris wasn't sure she wanted to do the sisterhood thing at all. Jewish or otherwise. Too many campus organizations felt like an attempt to continue the high school experi-ence. She was ready to move on. To be an adult.

At least some times! Past the pier. There would be fishermen out no matter how cool it was, huddled over their rods with thermoses of coffee or maybe something stronger. That was very much the old Naples Ronnie would go on about, the Naples that was eroding into the past. Left and then right into her drive. Kris could see lights twin-kling through the front windows. Not the tree; that was in the living room and not visible from here.

How she wished Will were here with her to share the holiday. To share everything. There had been a brief leave for Will at the end of basic training. Kris had been at college but had managed to get home and see him one evening. Only see him. Then he was gone, off to his medical school. That would take months and he was unlikely to get home again before it was done.

After that? She couldn't see that far, couldn't see where he would be, where *they* would be. Will might be sent off to Vietnam. As a medic if he made it through his training. As a regular Marine if he somehow failed. Don't fail, Will! Don't fail.

"Who's that stranger?" asked Donny, as she came in through the kitchen door.

"Not sure," her dad answered. "I think I used to see her around the neighborhood."

"You're going to see too much of me the next four weeks," she told them, taking a seat on one of the tall stools by the counter. "You'll be sick of me and ready to exile me to Miami again."

"You could have come home on weekends a little more often," said her mother. "It's not a long drive."

"Yeah, Mom, I know." Kris had managed it twice during the semester. One of those visits was mostly to see Will.

David Greene allowed, "She's done better than her friend. Preston Summerlin hasn't glimpsed his daughter since September."

"You should say something to her," felt her mom.

"Sure." She hadn't seen much more of Angelica than the girl's father. And she wasn't sure she was her friend. "Ronnie hasn't been home either."

The family accepted that without comment. They knew how far it was to the University of Florida. She would be home soon, though. Maybe tomorrow or Saturday. The triumvirate reunited, however briefly.

"So what special treat are you cooking up there for my return, Mom?"

"I wanted to go out but your father thought you might be too tired." She sounded doubtful. Or maybe hopeful.

Her dad laughed. "Even eighteen year old girls get that way. It's been a long day for her."

She was kind of bushed, wasn't she? "I'd just as soon stay home."

"Okay, dear," said her mom. She didn't look disappointed. "How about something simple, like macaroni and cheese?"

"Or chili-mac," suggested her father.

"But don't mix 'em," added Donny. "That wouldn't be kosher."

Kris squinted at her brother in something akin to disbelief. She wanted it to look that way, at any rate. "Since when has that bothered you? You've never complained about meat and cheese on your pizza."

"Mosaic law doesn't really prohibit that," claimed her father. "It's a later extrapolation."

"Says the lawyer," Donny replied, grinning.

"Your brother has gotten interested in our traditions," said Marge Greene.

Your traditions, Kris said only to herself. She didn't care much about any of it. She wasn't sure she even believed in God.

"Our heritage," added Donny. "Who we are."

"I'm just a hungry girl."

A much fuller girl settled under the covers a while later. Kris didn't feel ambitious enough by then to stack records but only turned on her little radio, tuned to WNOG. Christmas music interspersed with pop. The weather—the announcer promised it would be nicer tomorrow. Sunny and warming up some.

Maybe even warm enough for the beach. She was going to go, regardless. And take her sketchpad. Older drawings were taped up all around her bedroom, around her bed, the light too dim to distinguish one from another. That didn't matter. Kris intended to replace them, to work on her portfolio.

A yawn and another. She reached over, switched off the radio and then the little lamp. Sleep didn't come as quickly as she'd expected, as quickly as she'd hoped. There was a lot of unwinding to do. Things she hadn't thought about for a while were showing up in her head.

Will. All her memories of him, of their summer, of his leaving for the military were fresh again.

Will had made Kris promise not to wait so neither would feel guilty about going on with life. But she was going to wait, wasn't she? And so was Will.

So was Will, she told herself again, and rolled over. She slept eventually.

Chapter Three
Ronnie

The Resident Assistant leaned against the door frame, keys dangling from her hand. "That the last of it?"

She was eager to get out of here too, wasn't she? "It is." Everything else was stuffed into the Simca. Probably more than she really needed to carry home with her. Ronnie did not look forward to that six hour drive.

The RA locked the room, her new dorm room for next semester. She and her room mate—former room mate—had both been in favor of a switch. Not that they hadn't gotten along; they had pretty much ignored each other after the first few days. Sue had found a friend she'd rather room with.

Ronnie didn't care much one way or another. She wasn't very close to anyone here. Anyone would do and she would find out who anyone was when she returned.

Bag dangling over her shoulder, she headed for the parking lot. It was emptier than Ronnie had seen it all semester. Everyone going home for Christmas holidays. She'd be glad to be home too. She missed her friends, her family. Her town.

"Hey!" She turned toward the voice. Did she know that girl? Woman? Which were they now?

"You're Alan's friend, right? The Wesolowski boy?"

She might as well say, "Yes." This was no time or place to explain anything.

"I thought so. Will told me 'bout you. He's my cuz, y' know? Heading home, huh? Me too. We could've ridden together and saved gas!"

A little late for that, wasn't it? Or— "I'm already loaded up but I could fit in a passenger."

The offer seemed to take the girl by surprise. She stepped back, hands on hips, and gave Ronnie a long look. "I wasn't begging for no ride—any ride," she corrected herself. Then she laughed. "You'd have to give me a ride back, too."

"Oh, I intended to strand you in Naples."

"There are worse places. You serious, um, Ronnie, right?"

"I am." And why not? She should do spontaneous things no matter how much it went against her nature. "And I have no idea what your name is."

"Oh! Paulette. Paulette Jones."

Of course. A year older than her. Sister—twin sister, right?— of Carter Jones. The boy who'd lost his leg in Vietnam. Was he back in Naples now?

"Let me get my bag. I was traveling light." Paulette's eyes went to an old red and white Chevy halfway across the lot.

"Hop in. We'll go get it."

Paulette retrieved a large tote and locked up. She gave her vehicle a lingering look before sliding into the Simca, dropping the bag between her feet. "Was thinking about parking it closer to the buildings but I think it don't, um, doesn't matter. Which route you taking?"

"Backwards from the way I came, I guess. The interstate and then Forty-one."

"Oh, you should try Twenty-seven this time. It isn't any further. Not much. And you don't have to drive through Tampa."

That would be nice. "Then you navigate for me." South out of Gainesville she drove on Four-Forty-one and hooked up with Twenty-seven at Ocala. So far, they were paralleling the I-Seventy-five route. She might as well have been over there and making better speed. Ronnie was not going to say anything about it; let Paulette guide her where she would.

Then the interstate veered more westerly, away from their route into the central Florida lake country. This was more pleasant. More scenic. Through Lady Lake, through Leesburg, past the Citrus Tower at Clermont. Past noon, too. "I'd better put in some gas," she decided at Haines City. There was easily a third of a tank but Ronnie was not the sort to run much closer to empty.

She and Paulette watched the attendant fill the tank. "You have to put premium in this little thing?"

"It's finicky. My dad says I can ruin the engine by running regular.

Warp the head or something like that." She assumed a mechanic had told him that. Howard Deerfield knew little more about cars than his daughter.

"Okay. I'm going to pay half."

A nod of agreement. The Simca might use the more expensive gas but it got good mileage. Paulette wouldn't have to spend much and Ronnie wouldn't feel uncomfortable taking the money.

"Would you like a Coke?"

"We could stop somewhere to eat." Ronnie had been feeling empty but hadn't been sure of suggesting it.

"No need. My bag is full of goodies." Paulette headed inside while the attendant washed the windshield and checked the oil. He didn't have to ask which end the engine was in. That happened sometimes with the Simca.

As she went toward the office to pay, Paulette joined her, gripping two dripping bottles by their necks in one hand and a tagged key in the other. "I'll take these to the car," she said, "and let you return the restroom key. The woman inside didn't much like giving it to me."

After popping into the restroom herself, she started up the Simca and they headed south again. Paulette handed her an opened Coke and produced a bag of potato chips. Ronnie had half-expected something 'black' or at least southern, not that she could have exactly defined either one.

They rode along, munching but not talking for a while. Then, "Not so long ago they would've sent me around back to a filthy 'colored' restroom."

"I remember those. It always seemed so—so *stupid*."

"There's a whole lot of stupid in this world." Paulette gazed out the window for a moment. "That's why I'm going to be a teacher. Maybe I can get rid of some of it."

Ronnie had once considered teaching. Or had nightmares about it. "I'm hoping I can do some good too."

"Lawyer, right?"

"That's the plan." If she survived the coursework, the exams, the pressure. She was aware she didn't handle pressure all that well.

"We could cut off to the right up here a ways," Paulette informed her. "Angle down to Port Charlotte.

"I think I'll keep on south to La Belle. I know those roads." This was becoming familiar territory. It was the route Alan had used when he took her and her friends surfing on the east coast. She was not going to say that to her passenger; Ronnie had avoided using the name Alan so far.

"And on through Immokalee? I guess that is the fastest route. Awful lonely roads, though."

Even worse at four in the morning. But she'd had her friends with her. She'd had Alan. No, put that out of your mind, she told herself. Alan was the past. Alan was Naples and summer and she had moved on.

The sun was low when she dropped Paulette at her home in the River Park neighborhood, just west of Goodlette Road, with renewed promises of taking her back to Gainesville. The girl was starting to get nervous about her car being there. "If you need a ride while you're home, give me a call," Ronnie told her. No reason not to be friends. Here and in Gainesville. They had already shared enough on this long ride to feel like friends. Maybe Paulette needed a roommate.

Nah, she wouldn't want Ronnie. She probably had plenty of friends already.

Then home. Dad had the outdoor lights up. Ronnie sat in the growing darkness and watched them a little while before going in.

Chapter Four
Kris

It smelled like pot roast. Pot roast often happened on Fridays at the Greene abode. Mom would have it in the oven early, being just traditional enough not to cook on the sabbath. Or it gave her an excuse not to.

And it would reappear as slices of cold beef tomorrow. That also commonly happened. Kris wasn't concerned about tomorrow's lunch at the moment. She wanted today's lunch.

"Nice at the beach?" asked her mother. Was that potato salad she was making? Dad, of course, was at his office, and Donny at school. The public schools didn't let out till next week.

"Pretty good. I've missed it." Miami was not the same. "I didn't get much sketching done," she admitted.

"It's vacation," her mom reminded her, "but if you want to work, chop some celery."

"Okay, Mom." She retrieved a knife from the drawer. "You want to put the tops in?"

"No, I always save those for cooking."

She hadn't noticed, despite eighteen years of her mother's cooking. She should be more observant. Hey, celery leaves could make an interesting still life, couldn't they? Mom had already separated the ribs and washed them. "Anything around for lunch?" asked Kris. One rib chopped up, leafy end set aside. Was all this going to go into the potato salad?

"Just the usual."

She'd have to forage. It was warm enough for ice cream, wasn't it? Ice cream like she ate with Will at the Summerlins' house. Of a sudden, she found she was crying.

"And I haven't even started cutting the onions," she said, smiling through the tears.

Her mother's only response was a hug. It was the best response, maybe. "How about a grilled cheese?" she asked. That was a pretty good response too.

"Sure. Soon as we finish with this."

A nod. Mom probably understood the need to complete the chore. Or she sensed enough of its importance to Kris, her need to work on something and banish everything else from her mind.

Both went back to their chopping. "Are you planning to carry your bicycle back to Miami this time?"

Kris had just ridden it to and from the beach. She was glad she hadn't tried to take it to Miami with her. She felt unsophisticated enough without riding around campus on a Stingray. "Maybe I need a big girl bike. Even if I'm not very big."

Her mom smiled at that. "Like your friends."

"Yeah. I could go steal the one Jam left with his parents. Hmm, no, I don't think my feet would reach the pedals. Here you go." She handed the bowl of chopped celery over and watched her mom stir it in with the potatoes and onions and hard-boiled egg slices. Mayonnaise from a jar. Joey would turn up her nose at that. She and her mother made theirs fresh.

It was Joey who showed up a few minutes later, as she started on her second grilled cheese. And yes, on her bicycle. "I'll have to peddle back against the wind," she grumbled. "It's picking up."

"Poor baby. You should have just stayed safe at home, what with it being Friday the Thirteenth."

"Is it? Never thought of it. Ronnie should be back sometime today."

"Late, I'd think. She'll be tired."

"Yeah. We'd best not bother her till tomorrow."

And then the triumvirate, as Ronnie had named the trio in elementary school—or maybe it was junior high—would be reunited for the first time since September. "So what are you up to tonight? Not going out with Russ again?"

"No. Um, Sandy asked me to come to the program at the high school. She's in the chorus."

"Sandy?" She might have sounded more surprised than she had intended. Kris hadn't even thought of the girl in months.

"She latched onto me after all the rest of you left town. Or tried to. I think she got tired of boring Joey after a while."

You'll never be able to rival Jelly, Kris said only to herself. Or me, for that matter!

"What are you giggling about?"

"Nothing important. What is it, a Christmas program?"

"Yep. For the school this afternoon, for the public tonight."

"I think I saw enough of those when I was in high school myself."

Joey only nodded at that. Maybe she wasn't serious about going.

"Is her brother home?" she asked.

"Haven't heard. I suppose he will be sometime." The other Russ, Russ Penn. He attended Stetson. Was that further away than Ronnie's school? She wasn't sure. "But," Joey went on, "Ronnie's brother will be here for the holidays. Her dad told me but she doesn't know about it."

"Your Russ will want to know about that. He and Rick used to be best buds, right?"

"Used to be is the word. It's been more than two years since Richard Deerfield joined the navy."

It *was* a long time. Kris doubted the pair would go hunting snakes again—but one never knew, did one? "We'll have to go over tomorrow."

"It will have to be afternoon. I work in the morning."

Still working for Ronnie's architect dad, she assumed. Running errands mostly. "The girl probably needs to sleep in anyway."

"Good enough. So—what's up for the rest of today?"

"I just picked up the new Beatles album. The one without a title on it. Want to listen?"

Joey shrugged. "I might as well. I just got the new one from the Kinks but it seems like I'm the only person in the world who did."

"Undoubtedly," Kris assured her.

Chapter Five
Joey

This used to be her private time, her time to think about things, when Joey walked to and from high school. Around the curve to Tenth, then across Fleischmann and into the woods. It was only a matter of time until those would disappear, until something was built here.

It was dark in the woods, this late. Only scrub grew here, of course, pines mostly. No ancient towering oaks or anything like that! Or did oaks sprawl? The big live oaks seemed to but they got tall too. Not here, just little oaks that would never get the opportunity to do either. She exited the trees right behind the shop class, the covered concrete walkway lying across a narrow strip of grass. It was what, six months since last she came through here? A little more than that.

North she walked past the deserted classrooms, the empty cafeteria with a light burning somewhere back in the kitchen. There was activity up ahead, lights and automobiles and people. She emerged on the circular front drive. To Joey's right lay the auditorium. The parking lot behind it was filling up, the steps and entry were crowded.

Why was she here, anyway? She didn't really care about the Christmas program, the chorus, the band. She hadn't cared about that sort of thing when she attended Naples High. Yet she'd gone to see them sometimes because of Ronnie. Now because of Sandy?

Sandy wasn't her friend in the way Ronnie was and had been since first grade. The Penn girl had tried to keep up the connection they'd made during the summer but inevitably school took precedence, her friends, her activities. Sandy was active in pretty much everything, it seemed. But Joey had been the one who remained in Naples when Ronnie and Kris and—most importantly—Angelica had gone off to college.

Up the steps. She felt a little out of place, not a student, not a parent, by herself. She hoped she wouldn't run into any former teachers. Talking to them would feel awkward. Maybe she should have called up Ronnie and asked her if she wanted to come along. Yeah, she was probably tuckered. Joey wasn't even sure she was home. She hoped she was by now.

She had promised Ronnie she would watch the Swamp Buggy Parade for her, more than a month ago. She'd even written an article about it and sent it off to her friend. As well as a copy to Lin Summerlin. Joey was assembling a portfolio every bit as much as Kris.

She'd see Ronnie tomorrow. And Ronnie's dad first. It was okay working for him. A lot of the time Deerfield had her on her bike running errands, taking plans or papers to someone, picking things up. She answered the phone or did bits of odd work in the office the rest of time. She wasn't a bad typist. But—she was beginning to feel uncomfortable with him. Not that he ever did or said anything inappropriate to her! It was covering for him, lying about where he was, what he was doing, that bothered her.

Joey found a seat near the rear, over on the left hand side. Silly, she told herself. That's the same place you sit in church. Was Ronnie still interested in that? Maybe it was only the Summerlin boy who had sparked it and that—well, that ended up as it ended up.

Still, Ronnie had been seeking something. The band first. Stage band.

James Summerlin. She would know more than her friends about what the Summerlins had been up to because she corresponded with Lin. News by a roundabout route that was. The oldest Summerlin girl wouldn't be coming for Christmas. Salas girl, strictly—Preston Summerlin was her stepfather.

She hadn't seen Russel Penn. Joey didn't think she would recognize Sandy's parents unless Russel was with them. And they certainly wouldn't recognize her. She didn't even know what Mister Penn did. Of course, Myra Penn was a minor celebrity in Naples.

Very minor and one heard on radio, rather than seen. There was the band director. At least he wouldn't have to march the kids around tonight! They found their way through an unsurprising string of Christmas songs. Seasonal songs—not so much carols as reindeer and snow and that sort of thing. An intermission. The chorus next.

Oh, talking about radio—or thinking about it—WNOG was here.

They must be broadcasting the program. She could have stayed home and listened. They did the football games too. Joey had never listened to those but was occasionally aggravated when they came on the air on a Friday evening when she'd rather hear music.

Good reason to have a date that night except sometimes guys would invite her to the game. Those guys rarely got a second date. Here they came onto stage. All in white. Well, the boys' trousers were black but all in white otherwise. Sandy—over there to the left and a bit back. With the altos. For some reason Joey had assumed she was a soprano.

She didn't much like the harmonies. They took all the fiber out of the music. Not that she knew anything about it. Alan might. Angelica definitely would but Joey would not be likely to ask her. They were going to attempt 'O Holy Night'? She did know that was difficult.

And the end and a thank you and people began to shuffle out of the auditorium. Should she try to find Sandy and say hello? Nah, just head home.

"Walking back to your place?"

It took her a moment to recognize the speaker. "Rick! I heard you were coming home."

"Got in this afternoon, only a couple hours before Ronnie."

"She's back, then." That was good to hear.

"Yeah, and too pooped to do anything. I was tired of sitting still after riding a bus all the way from Jax. Decided to walk around and ended up here."

"You're in Jacksonville now?"

"Just transferred. I may run out the rest of my enlistment there."

Rick was in civvies. Joey realized she had no idea of what sort of rank or duties he might have. Nor even how long he had left to serve.

"I'm going to drop by tomorrow," she said. "But now to home and bed!"

"Mind if I walk with you?"

"Through the dark and dangerous woods? Come along."

The woods were rather dark. Not scary in any sense unless one were afraid of tripping over something. They emerged onto Fleischmann. Rick looked up and down the road. "Naples changes a lot, even in two years."

"You're sounding like your dad."

"Heaven forbid." He might have said it jokingly but there seemed to be more beneath that. Possibly even bitterness?

Joey had no idea how things stood between Richard Deerfield and his father. They crossed and walked on.

Chapter Six
Ronnie

Falling into a routine of studies was possibly the best thing that could have happened to her. Ronnie could see that. Now she was home and the routine was out the window. Interrupted for a month. Just maybe that was a good thing too.

"Is Rick already out somewhere again?" She could have come out of her room earlier—crashing early had taken care of any true weariness —but had felt lazy enough to lounge in bed most of the morning. Well, she had come out and poured a large bowl of cereal at one point.

"Went to look up some of his old friends," her mom answered. "We'll have opportunity enough to see your brother. Three weeks leave, he said."

That would be after New Year Day. "Okay. Anything good for lunch?"

"You can find it as easily as me."

Which was true but Ronnie wouldn't have minded just a bit of babying. She ended up with another large bowl of flakes.

Someone pounded on the door. "Police!" came a gruff voice. "We know you're in there, Deerfield."

"I believe that's your friends," remarked Missus Deerfield. "Joey does that rather well."

Kris certainly wouldn't have been able to go that low. "You'll never take me alive, coppers!" she yelled back.

"Dead's fine with us," called Kris. "We're coming in shooting!"

No bullets flew. Hugs to both, Kris being as ever the more demonstrative of the pair, both squeezing the harder and hanging on the longer. "I missed you guys."

"Of course you did," said Joey. "Now, is your handsome brother around?"

"He heard you were coming and ran off."

"Darn, he's the real reason I came over."

"Rick told me he ran into you last night," spoke Patty Deerfield.

Both the girls gave their friend an appraising look. "Should we tell Russ about this?" asked Kris.

"Russ?" What did she mean by that? A picture of Russ Penn came quickly into to Ronnie's mind and was dismissed even more quickly.

Kris appeared suddenly uncomfortable. "Um, Joey's been dating Russ Wesolowski."

Alan's brother. That would explain the reticence. Not that Ronnie cared about him anymore. Best to simply ignore the whole thing.

Joey and Kris seemed to feel the same. "So what are we doing this afternoon? Did you come over on your bikes?" She wouldn't mind riding around as they used to.

"Drove," said Kris.

"Driven."

Ronnie shook her head. "I'm awfully disappointed in you two."

"Not too disappointed to ride in the bug, I hope. It's nice enough to have the top down."

A few minutes later they were cruising south in Kris's Beetle, down Gulf Shore. "All the streets look crowded," observed Joey. "Everyone goes to the beach on a Saturday afternoon."

Even in the middle of winter. Their longtime favorite hangout, Third Avenue, was as bad as the rest. Kris slowed down, looked at all the parked cars, and drove on without turning. "Let's drop in on the Summerlins," she said. "Maybe Jelly is home."

That was only a few blocks further, a little north of the pier. Ronnie would have to walk on the pier while she was home. There was no room for negotiation on that. They found no more open parking spaces here than elsewhere, as they went up the street with its towering coconut palms arching over the pavement, and turned around at the beach. She couldn't see anyone stirring at the Summerlin house.

'No Parking' signs marked the entry to the rear driveway, the gravel one that ended behind the garage. Today, a chain stretched across it, as it usually did on weekends. Other days, they didn't bother with it. "Get that down, Joey," Kris commanded. "We're old friends of the Summerlins. They'll let us park here."

"We won't be blocking the cook's car, will we?" asked Ronnie.

"Has Saturday afternoons off," said Joey, jumping out to do her friend's bidding.

She'd known that, hadn't she? Ronnie felt uncomfortable with it anyway.

"Hey!" Where? "Hey, you trespassers!" An upstairs window. A window in what was James's room when he was here. Her mind couldn't help going back to when she was last in it. The only time she was in it. Angelica had the window open and was leaning out.

Joey only waved in return. The girl disappeared.

To meet them at the back door. "I guess I should have expected you to show up," she said.

"It's good to see you too, Jel," replied Kris. "When did you get back?"

"This morning. Mom had to go over and pick me up, since I don't have a car. And you didn't offer a ride home." She leaned in and confided, "I think that may change this Christmas."

"Maybe your parents would like to purchase my Sixty-two Corvair for you," suggested Joey.

"I wouldn't mind a new Corvair. They're still making them, right? What I fear is I'll end up with something sporty when I'd prefer a practical vehicle." It did not sound like Jelly feared it much at all. "Gonna go down on the beach?"

"Might as well," said Joey. "We didn't have any plans."

"One day back and already bored," Ronnie added.

"Joey will have to bring her boyfriends over. Both of 'em," Kris said. "That'll help."

"Not if I don't share them. I could always tell Sandy to drop by. And bring her brother!" No one seemed to like that idea. The four of them made their way, not hurrying, to the street and then down to the beach.

Ronnie turned left and the others did the same without comment. "Every visit to Naples requires a walk on the pier," she claimed.

"We might as well get it out of the way," replied Angelica, gazing up at the lengthy structure. "Crowded. Would they be catching anything?"

Joey knew about things like that. "The kingfish might still be running but I think it's early for mackerel. Next month."

"How about trout?" asked Kris. "My dad sometimes catches trout from his boat."

"They're more a summer catch. This is the time of year for big redfish but you're better off fishing for them elsewhere."

"Like around the pilings at Third?" Ronnie thought that was right.

"Yep. Everyone up the stairs!"

Up to the decking and into the crowd. Tourists? Winter residents? It could be hard to tell the difference. "The first round of snow birds," announced Kris. "Another flock flies in after Christmas."

"And now me for a little while. I've spent too much time away from here," Angelica said.

"I don't think you had a lot of choice." All through her high school years she'd been off at one boarding school or another. As had her twin brother.

"Oh, if I'd yelled loud enough my parents would have let me stay. Right here with you, Joey! Wouldn't that have been grand?"

"To think I missed out on it. Careful with that rod, man."

"Sorry, miss," said the offending fisherman.

"Use an underhand cast. It's safer on the pier." Without saying more, she walked on.

"Wow," whispered Angelica. "How do you two put up with her?"

"We're happy just to be her loyal minions," announced Ronnie.

Kris added, "She hardly ever beats us."

"Don't count on that lasting," said Joey, over her shoulder.

They walked till there was no more pier, only water stretching toward Mexico. Or Texas if one went straight west. Ronnie had looked at a map.

There was no reason to go straight though, was there? One hundred eighty degrees of liquid possibility lay before one here.

"It feels colder out here," spoke Kris.

"Cold water below us," Joey said. "And a breeze picking up."

"Let's get back. I can fix hot chocolate." Angelica snickered. "Or break into my father's booze." She turned and started away.

"Isn't he home?" asked Ronnie, following in her wake.

"Nope. Mom and he almost always go out on Saturday evening,

what with Missus Cooper being off. You guys gave me an excuse not to go along."

"We could go out too," suggested Kris. She didn't sound too enthusiastic.

"I'm kind of tired. Some other time."

There was nodding of heads and murmurs of agreement. They could all use a day or two to get themselves sorted out. Back to the stairs, down to the gleaming white sand. The sun was sinking through a cloudless sky. They did not spend long at the Summerlin house; soon Kris was driving them to their homes, dropping Ronnie first.

She was a little surprised Joey didn't insist on walking from there. Ronnie waved good bye, went in. Rick had come and gone, according to her mom. He'd be back but he'd miss dinner again! "Fifteen minutes," her mother warned her. Dad read a glossy magazine in the living room.

Time to clean up a little, time to think a little. Think about her friends and all that happened last summer—things largely banished from her mind the past months.

Not a word had been said about James Summerlin. Did all three of them know about what happened between her and James? She wasn't sure but she suspected they did. One thing she was certain about was that James would never have said anything.

Uncertain was whether James would show up for the holiday. Maybe no one knew. Maybe James didn't know.

"Dinner's on!"

Chapter Seven

Joey

She hadn't much expected Angelica to make it to church. Admittedly, it was cold at this early mass. Joey had come close to staying snug in bed herself. It was all the worse when one rode a bicycle.

And she had the Corvair! She didn't need to punish herself. No, not punish. Push. You're pushing yourself, she said to the inner Joey. That's good. That sounds better.

She didn't feel like pushing any more after church, but rode home in a leisurely manner, along the residential streets of Naples. Not the oldest part of town but pretty old anyway. Who was this running up ahead?

Joey only glanced at the man as she went by but then slammed her coaster brake and circled back to him. "Hi, Rick! Don't you know only the crazies are out here at this time of morning?"

He didn't halt so she slowly pedaled at his side. "I run every morning," he panted. "Have to stay in shape."

She hadn't been able to get that good a look at Rick the other night, in the dark, but she could now. He didn't seem so different from a couple years ago. Lost some 'baby fat,' put on some muscle. He was an ordinary looking guy, average height, brownish hair—same color as Ronnie's, pretty much.

"Hey, you didn't tell me you and Russ were together."

Together? "We've just gone out a couple times." Okay, three. And maybe there would be no more. She didn't have to tell Rick that. "Did you intend to steal me away from him?"

"Oh. I'm s'posed to have a girl in every port, you know. I guess I'll have to find someone else for Naples."

"You can always lie. Show my picture to your pals and astound them with my beauty."

He suddenly stopped. Why? Oh, they were in front of the Deerfield house. "I wouldn't do that. Not even in fun."

Richard Deerfield *would* do a lot of things in fun. His sense of humor rivaled his dad's. "I understand," was all she could say, balancing her bike on one foot.

"Wanta come in for breakfast?"

"No, I'd better get on home." She slowly pedaled away, then sped up, and practically flew across the Trail. It was nearly deserted, despite being a national highway. Around the hairpin turn and back down her own street, curving gently between the old houses, the little houses, some thrown up as much as two decades ago. As many places in Naples, the land beneath might now be more valuable than the residences.

Her stepdad was up. "Hey, Wayne. Mom still in the sack?"

"That she is. You'll have to rustle up your own breakfast." His broad, weathered face split in a grin. "And maybe mine while you're at it."

"Hmm. I'll have to think about that. After I stand by this heater a little while." Ah, that was better. "Pancakes?"

"Sounds great. Not if it's trouble though. I can wait for your mom."

"Hey, I have to eat too." Into the narrow galley kitchen. Big pan. She lit one of the gas burners, slid it on. Can of shortening. Damn, she'd love to have some of the French toast Jam fried in butter. 'Pan perdu' as he and Jelly called it. Baking soda, flour, eggs, milk, and, of course, lemon juice. That was how she did pancakes. If someone else used another approach, that was their affair.

Oh, of course they could substitute butter milk. That was acceptable. Where's a decent bowl? The white glass one would do. Soda and flour first. Lumpy soda. Smash it with the spoon, then whisk into the flour. Her mom was one of the few women she knew who had wire whisks in her kitchen. How others got by without them she had no idea. No oatmeal; she liked a little structure—that was a good word—but Wayne wouldn't. Some brown sugar didn't hurt, though.

Wayne Planter was a good guy. Open, even tempered. Maybe Rick Deerfield was like that. A good guy too. She liked him. Maybe he wasn't the shiniest penny in the change drawer but that didn't matter, did it?

Shortening melting. How many eggs? Three? Four? Yeah, four. Mom might get out of bed and want her share. Lemon juice to get that soda working, enough milk for a nice batter. Don't stir too vigorously. Some cookbooks said to let it sit a minute or so but Joey saw no reason. Moreover, she was impatient. Three rounds. Close to rounds.

There should be syrup in the box. Joey didn't use it, as a rule, but Wayne would. She'd let him have these first three. Flip. Jelly for hers. Hmm, apple. That would do. Those are ready. Onto a plate. Wayne could get his own coffee. He'd already made a pot.

She set the plate in front of him on the little Formica-top table and began another batch for herself. Maybe a little coffee for her too. That's mighty weak, Wayne. Oh well. She added some milk. A lot of milk actually. "Will you want more?" she called to him.

"Think this will do, Joey. Thanks." She might as well use up the rest of the batter anyway. Maybe he'd want more, maybe Mom would emerge. She might even be hungry herself.

She carried her plate over and sat across from him. "All your friends home now?" he asked.

"They are. My best friends. I guess they'll be out having fun while I work."

"It's a good job, girl," opined Wayne. "And I'd bet Deerfield would be pretty flexible about your hours." He took in another large mouthful of pancake, dripping with syrup. "'Specially if it's his daughter you're having fun with."

"Yeah. It's a good job." Joey hadn't meant to let her voice trail off like that. It just sort of did on its own.

"Trouble?"

"I—well, I get tired of lying for Mister Deerfield. I don't know where he's off to or what he's doing but I have to cover for him." She hesitated before adding, "Sometimes to his wife." She felt relieved to have finally said this to someone.

Surprisingly, Wayne nodded. "I've heard stuff." He then chuckled. "Construction workers gossip too."

They were likely to see more of the architect than some. "It's too good a job to quit," she decided. She needed the money to continue college. Wayne and her mom didn't pay for that, nor for her car and gas, though board and room were free. Wayne had guaranteed they always would be.

"Then find yourself a better one."

Easier said than done. Despite her—discomfort, she liked the job far more than any she had before. Way better than working in a convenience store! But it wouldn't hurt to look around.

"Hi, Mom. There are—oops." She ran into the kitchen. Not quite burnt, were they?

Wayne called, "You'd best not look for a job as a short-order cook."

"Or stop to gossip with the customers," she called back. "I can fix you another batch, Mom."

"I think I just want toast this morning, dear. Oh, with this apple jelly. And fresh coffee."

Good enough. She stacked the three pancakes on a platter. There was enough batter for two more.

The phone? Who called this early on a Sunday? "One of your friends, I'd bet," said Wayne. She went to answer the plain black desk phone.

"Planter residence. May I help you?" She almost snickered. That was how she answered at Deerfield's office.

"Good morning, Joey. It's James. James Summerlin."

Chapter Eight

Kris

"I don't know whether to mention it to Angelica. Much less her parents."

"I'm never sure of anything with Angelica," Kris replied. Hey, should she put her on her shopping list this year? And what in the world could she get her if she did?

"I do know I'm not mentioning it to Ronnie."

"So only I get to be in on the secret? I am honored, Miss Varney." She tossed another piece of bread to the swans below the bridge. Kris had suggested they ride their bikes into Port Royal. She liked to watch the swans swimming in the pond there but did not intend to get any closer. Some looked as big as she was!

"Not much of a secret. James showed up at his sister's apartment yesterday and intends to stay a while. I think he called me on a whim when he saw Lin had my number."

"He'll be with her through the holidays? I don't think I'd mind spending Christmas in New York City." She attempted to imagine it but found she didn't really know much. Except there was an enormous Christmas tree somewhere.

"Maybe, maybe not. He hinted he might get down here. Hey, did you know he cut his hair short?"

"All that gorgeous hair? We shouldn't have let him out of our sight!"

"Didn't have much say in that, did we? Alan's been letting his grow. It's somewhere between a 'bowl' and an 'Apache' right now. His brother's is even longer."

"We'll have to include Alan over the holidays. Whether it bothers Ronnie or not." On that, Kris did not intend to allow any argument.

"Definitely. Ready to ride?"

"Yeah. We can go back around to Gordon Drive on Treasure Lane."

They pedaled a bit east and then took a right. The homes on either side of the street were impressive but not quite so grandiose as some deeper into the subdivision. They looked more lived in, too, many being among the first built here.

"Did you know Will visited Lin?" asked Kris.

"She wrote me about it. I guess I'm to blame, mentioning Will in my letters."

"They barely knew each other." Lin certainly hadn't seen much of him in Naples. "But she invited him to come see New York and he took her up on it."

"I might have too."

"Yeah, he only had a few days. Not long enough to come home. Then back to his medical training. Want to turn north here?"

"Might as well. Shall we stop somewhere and beg Sunday dinner?"

"My house is as good as any. Or the Summerlins."

"Or pick a random house! Hey, the Rheins live just up ahead, don't they? We could impose on Gordie's hospitality."

Joey might have been joking but Kris took a right at the street. The Rheins' house held all sorts of memories for her. Many of them having to do with sex. "I wonder what Gordie drove to South Florida," she said. Not the little Mini Moke he tooled around town in.

"I think he did like Angelica and had someone drive him up. I haven't seen him back any weekends."

"Oh. Here we are." They both slowed down. Nothing to be seen, not even a car. Maybe someone was off picking Gordie up in Tampa right now. They u-turned and headed back to Gordon Drive.

"Working in the morning?"

"I am. I don't have to work my schedule around my classes anymore, but I haven't talked to Mister Deerfield about changing it. And I'll have new classes and a new schedule in January."

"There's always stuff piled up to do on Monday mornings," said Kris. So it seemed, not that she'd ever had a job. She should be thinking about interning somewhere, shouldn't she? A commercial art or design studio. Maybe even something like a print shop.

"Turning here?"

It was her own street. She would like to ride further. No, best to go home, spend time with the family, eat dinner. The rest of the holiday break remained. "See you whenever," she called, and took a right.

Joey pedaled on north.

Chapter Nine
Ronnie

"I drove over to Flagler Beach once from Gainesville, just to see, um, why you guys like it so much." She should go ahead and say Alan's name. Russ knew what she meant. Oh, everyone knew what she meant. "Anyway," she plowed on, "my old employers are setting up shop over there. The Brookses."

"Another book store?" asked Russ.

"I'm not sure. They weren't open yet." They were sure surprised to see her. As surprised as she'd been to see them. "It looks like a nice place." Could she say anything more insipid?

"I think my brother would live there if he could." He wasn't going to say Alan either but that came close.

"Why doesn't he?" asked Rick.

"He'd be drafted if he dropped out of college." Russ chuckled. "I think he's fairly serious about getting an education too, though he doesn't know what he wants to do."

"That's two of us," Rick said. "No idea what I'll do when I leave the navy. Maybe college."

Russ looked at his diver's wrist watch. "What do you say we go over to your father's office and liberate Joey?"

"Sure." Wesolowski started toward his van. "Hey, leave that here. We can walk over."

"Rick likes to walk everywhere," said Ronnie. "Or run."

"Or I could liberate my bicycle from you. Come on." The two started down the street.

It wouldn't be a bad idea to get on that bike and ride somewhere, just for fun, with no destination in mind. Was the wind picking up? Warm and from the south. That meant another cold front on its way. Ronnie hadn't bothered to check any forecasts.

The streets meandered and curved close to her house before conforming to the grid of most of Naples. Most of old Naples, as it was originally laid out. She pedaled south, then west a block, then south again. Did her dad design any of these houses? Ronnie knew it was quite possible. He'd drawn the plans for the one the Deerfields lived in, the one Ronnie had lived in most of her life.

Howard Deerfield liked to claim he had built it 'on spec' and would sell it one of these days. That seemed less likely with each passing year. That was the Penns' house, wasn't it? She recognized the powder blue convertible as Myra's. She didn't recognize the Volkswagen bus at all.

But there was Russel Penn unloading something from it. He looked up and waved. Couldn't she just acknowledge him by waving back, and ride on? Oh, she should make herself be sociable. She pulled into the driveway. "You were at the wheel of some sort of gray sedan the last time I saw you."

"That's my father's Impala. I got this van before taking off for Stetson."

"And I take it you just got back."

"Arrived late last night but I'm just now awake enough to unpack."

"I drove down from Gainesville on Friday. It's enough to wear anyone out."

Russ gave a knowing nod. Whether he actually knew, she could only guess. "All your friends back?" He lifted a cardboard box from the vehicle and started toward the open garage.

She might as well follow. Ronnie left the bike lying on the concrete. "Mostly. Joey never left, of course, and Kris is here. Angelica Summerlin, too."

"How about her brother?"

Russ definitely wouldn't know of anything that happened between her and James. She wouldn't mind talking about him. Hmm, he might not even know she'd broken with Alan. "Still up north, as far as I know."

"At a seminary, right?" Russel left the box near a closed door. His one time ride, the Solex moped, stood close to a wall. Sandy's ride now.

"No, not really. He's in some sort of religion program at Boston College. It's a path to being ordained as a Jesuit but it's not a commitment to it." That was the way he'd explained it to her last summer.

"That's not so different from me, then. I might or might not be on track to be a minister." He ambled back to the VW. "And almost certainly not a Baptist one, though Stetson is affiliated with them. I did hang around yesterday for services before taking off so people are likely to think I'm serious."

Oh-so-earnest Russ making a joke? That didn't happen often. She picked up her bike. "Hope to see you later. Enjoy the holidays! Oh, and say hi to Sandy."

"I'll do that, Ronnie." On down the street she went. Here was Third. Good place to turn toward the beach.

The usually even-tempered Alan had expressed almost vehement dislike for Russ the last time he'd seen him. Not to his face, of course. She knew that Penn had just brought up memories of school, of a world he thought he'd finally left behind. Alan had not liked school at all. Hated it from the first day on, he claimed.

The Gulf was choppy, with a stiff breeze, a warm breeze, from the south. She should have brought a rod and gone after those big reds Joey promised were out there. Ronnie watched the sun sparkle on the broken surface, as it appeared and disappeared behind the racing clouds. A kaleidoscope being turned too quickly.

She didn't want to go home yet but pedaling south against that wind held even less appeal. Shopping? It wouldn't hurt to finish her Christmas list. Not now.

Ronnie didn't really want to do anything. She turned her bike around and pedaled back toward her home.

Chapter Ten

Joey

"We've come to rescue you from servitude," proclaimed Rick. "We know what a slave driver this man can be."

Howard Deerfield looked from one young man to the other. "This gives double dating a whole new meaning, Joey."

"It's a matter of quantity making up for quality," she replied. "Need me for anything else?"

"Not today. Be in on Wednesday? We can set whatever hours you want over vacation."

"Thanks. I'll think about that. So where are we going? And do I have to take you both on my bike?"

"We're practically next door to the DQ," said Rick.

Russ gave a sigh of relief. "Good. I've walked enough."

Joey slowly rode her bike between the two. Across the highway from the Dairy Queen was a drugstore. The family doctor had offices behind it and further up the street lay the hospital. "When I made an ill-fated attempt at being a candy-striper I'd come over here sometimes. Not since."

"We won't ask you about that," Russ said.

"Good idea. It's warm enough for something frozen today."

"Milkshakes are my go-to when I'm traveling."

"I noticed that about Alan too. But your whole family is vegetarian."

"Nothing against a burger myself," said Rick. "Mmm, or a chili dog? Oh, I guess I'll just get a shake too."

"Chocolate all?" No objections so Russ stepped up and ordered.

She'd kind of hoped they'd fight over who would pay for hers but the boys split the bill equally without a word about it. They sat and watched traffic. The concrete seats were not very comfy.

"Going home now?" Russ asked.

"Unless one of you has a better suggestion."

"Rick made me leave my van at his house so I can't whisk you away and leave him sitting here."

"I know you too well," claimed Rick. "If you don't mind, we can walk you over to your place."

"You'll walk, I'll ride. I could leave you behind, too, if I wanted."

She didn't, though she rode circles around the duo a couple times. "Hey, Wayne's home," she said as they came around the curve. His red pickup was out front. Wayne liked red.

Wayne himself was sitting in a lawn chair, smoking a cigar. He allowed himself one a day and never smoked indoors by agreement with her mother. "Whatcha doing home, Wayne?" she asked.

"Everything's on hold this afternoon. It looks too much like rain."

"You're a mason, sir?" asked Rick.

"Yep. Lay blocks mostly but I'll help out with pouring concrete or whatever else if need be. You're the Deerfield boy, right? Ronnie's brother." He grinned at Russ. "This other one I've seen around here from time to time."

"But more of my brother."

"True 'nuff. I don't see you including him today."

"Oh, he's busy cleaning kennels and whatnot. I'd help him if I were there—but I'm not."

"Not a job I'd want." Then he squinted at Rick. "Joey said anything about her problems with the job she has?"

"Problems? Working for my father?"

"'Having to cover his tracks for him."

"Wayne!" Why did he have to bring this up? And in front of these two!

Rick held up a hand. "Hey, I know about my dad. It's part of what led me to going off to join the navy. I didn't know how to be around him anymore. Or my mom."

Russ looked confused. This would seem to be new to him.

"I reckon the girl needs to find a new job," opined Wayne, leaning back and drawing deeply on his smoke.

At this, Russ brightened. "My parents really do need someone to help Alan. Do you think you'd like to clean cages and mop up dog puke?"

In a veterinary clinic? "Alan would have to be all right with it. He may see too much of me as it is."

"Okay. I'll ask him first. I won't say anything to the folks till you give the go-ahead."

"And now we've solved all your problems," said Rick, "what's next on the agenda?"

"Getting my surfboard ready," was Russ's answer. "I expect waves tomorrow."

Both young men set off down the road, back the way they had come. "I could have shown them shortcuts, what with them being on foot," said Joey. She knew places to cut through when she wasn't riding her bike.

"People let you go through their yards 'cause they know you. You've been doing it since you were a little girl." He nodded toward the duo disappearing around the curve. "They'd be likely to call the cops on those two."

That she wouldn't even joke about. Joey liked them both. She didn't mind hanging around with them, now and then. But was there more than that?

She had to admit there wasn't. Not with either.

Chapter Eleven
Ronnie

Thunder in the night, and then wind-driven rain. It had wakened her before midnight. This was not like the storms of summer that rolled in across afternoon skies and usually away again by night.

Storms were nothing new to Ronnie. After all, she'd been through Hurricane Donna! She had stepped out into the screened-in carport—one of her dad's design quirks—and watched the tall pines bending to its fury. Or was that her fury? Some had come down. She'd been impressed at ten; she suspected she'd be just as impressed at eighteen.

Ronnie could still hear the cry of the wind as she slipped back into sleep but rain no longer beat against her window. Not much light shone through that window when she woke again. After seven. She might as well get up and hope that Rick was done with the bathroom. It had been nice not having to share it the last couple years.

She found Rick a few minutes later at the dining table, scooping hot cereal from a rather large bowl. "Russ coming by today?" she asked, mostly to be sociable. Ronnie tried to be sociable even this early.

"I would guess the Wezzies are out surfing already. Russ wanted to head for the east coast but thought better of abandoning the parents so soon after getting home. Wouldn't bother me!" He slurped up another spoonful. "He claims there are great places to ride within minutes of FAU."

"So I've heard. That oatmeal you're having?" It didn't appeal to her this morning.

"It is, with raisins and brown sugar. Hey, Joey might quit her job with our dad and go work for their parents."

"That's surprising." If her mom wasn't going to show, she'd fry a couple eggs for herself. Saute pan—was it? Yes, it had been slid onto a shelf in the fridge with shortening still in it. Probably by Dad; that was what he did rather than waste that little bit of butter. She might not even need to add any. On a front burner, medium heat. "Any reason why?"

"Who's to say?" her brother responded. That would have to do. She was sure he knew more.

In a couple minutes she was seated across from Rick. He gave her eggs and buttered toast a cursory look. "Broke one turning it?"

"It happens." More often than not. "I don't think it's going to be a good day to do much outside."

"Hey, I already ran while you were lazing in your warm, comfy bed. You should try it."

"Some other time maybe. How did you run when you were at sea? You'd run out of space unless you could walk on water."

"Around and around the deck. It was an aircraft carrier so there was a lot of deck."

Ronnie had no idea what her brother did in the navy. Rick's very occasional letters gave few clues. "Do you spend much time on the deck?"

"Nope. When I'm on duty I'm up above, directing take-offs and landings."

"That sounds hard." She could imagine the pressure.

"There are worse duties. I'll be controlling traffic at Jax, too, but on normal runways." He rose, went into the kitchen, began rinsing his bowl. "I should be able to get a job doing the same thing as a civilian." He did not sound enthusiastic. Rick exited the other end of the kitchen without saying more.

As she rinsed off her own plate—and slid the now-cold skillet back into the refrigerator—the wall phone jingled. For her father, most likely, but she answered.

"Hi, Ronnie. Am I too early? I waited till eight but I wasn't sure."

She didn't have ask who it was. "No, Paulette. I've been up a while." She saw her mom from the corner of her eye. "How are you doing?"

"Oh, I'm just great! But, um, were you serious about giving me a ride?" A giggle. "Or maybe more than one."

"Sure. Today? This morning?"

"That would be great. It doesn't look like a very good day for anything fun but I could get my Christmas shopping done. Or started!"

"I need to do that myself. Shall I swing by your house?"

"No need. My pop can drop me on his way to the station. And he wants to take off right now!"

The station? "Then don't keep him waiting. I'll watch for you." She hung up. That white receiver sure showed any dirt, didn't it? She should remember to wipe it down sometime.

"Was that the girl you drove home from school?"

"Yep. We're going shopping."

"I'm glad you're making new friends." Mom had always seemed to slightly disapprove of her closeness with Kris and Joey. She was the one who urged Ronnie to be in school activities. Not Dad.

No more than seven or eight minutes later a car pulled in out front. A police cruiser. Paulette emerged from the front. Oh, awful weather, thought Ronnie, as she stepped out to greet her. "Let's get inside. It's early to shop anyway."

"Sounds good."

"Your father's a police officer?"

"Yep. So you'd better get me back safe! Good morning, ma'am!"

"Mom, this is Paulette Jones. This is obviously my mom." Why did she look surprised? Hadn't her mom known Paulette was black? Not that she'd mentioned it.

"Pleased to meet you, Missus Deerfield."

"And you, Paulette."

"I'd tell people to call me Paulie but I'm afraid they'd spell it like Polly-wog."

Her mother gave that a faint smile. "I suppose they would. Can I get you anything?" She glanced toward her daughter. "Or I should ask, can Ronnie get you anything?"

"Gosh, I've imposed on her enough—oh, I'm still imposing on her!" She grinned at Ronnie and Ronnie couldn't help smiling in return. "It was awfully impetuous of me to ride home with Ronnie without planning it at all."

"Impetuous of both of us. I'm the one who invited you, remember."

Another odd sort of look from her mom. She'd never really explained that either. Rick wandered back into the kitchen and nodded toward her guest. "Nobody made coffee yet? I guess it's up to me." He found a can of Yuban. It sat on the same shelf it would have two years ago. "How's your brother, Paulette?"

"Not so good, Richard. He just wants to sit around most of the time."

The boy shook his head. "Ask him if it's okay for me to come over, will you? Hmm, eight cups? I'm used to drinking coffee from huge urns. Bad, strong coffee."

"That should do. Your father left early."

"Yeah, I heard him. Okay." He added the water, turned the machine on. "So," he said, taking a seat, "you two going surfing?"

Paulette laughed outright. "Sure, we'll get Ronnie's boyfriend to teach us!" Silence and embarrassed expressions greeted the remark. "What'd I do?" asked the girl. Paulette wasn't slow on the uptake.

"We broke up last summer," said Ronnie. She wasn't going to say she'd broken up with him, but she had. She'd dumped him.

"Oh. Sorry. I've been out the loop too long!" She frowned. "He's Will's friend, right? Jackie shoulda said something."

Her mom and brother looked blank but Ronnie knew she meant Will Booth's little sister. She was a classmate of Sandy Penn, wasn't she? A senior. "It's no big deal," Ronnie muttered. She'd as soon not be the topic of gossip.

Half an hour or so later they were on their way. Most stores would be open now or soon. But first—

"Where are we headed?" asked Paulette. "I don't think we can afford to shop on Third Street!"

"You might be surprised. I know places! But I just wanted to check the water first." She couldn't help giggling. "In case we decide to surf."

She turned onto Thirteenth Avenue, the beach access just south of the pier. There was Russ's green Ford Econoline. She'd half-expected him to be up at Doctor's Pass instead. Not many cars. And the waves?

Even she could tell they weren't much, bumpy, wind-blown. Four—no five—guys out trying to position themselves to catch one of the shifting peaks. "There's a series of sandbars out there where the waves pop up. They build up around the pier." Ronnie had known that even before dating Alan. There were other surfers in the world.

Someone up and riding. Left handed. Probably Alan. He turned back toward the pier and tried to pump himself along but the wave petered out.

"Someone's waving to you," said Paulette.

"It's Russ." He was sitting half-inside his van, a towel around his shoulders. She waved back. Oh, he was going to come over. She rolled the window partway down.

"That was one of the better rides of the day," he said. "But any surf is better than no surf." She'd heard Alan say the same thing. He crouched a little and peered past her. "Paulette, isn't it? It's been some time."

Paulette only nodded a greeting. "I doubt," Russ continued, "there is enough behind this swell for it to clean up into anything decent when the wind shifts." He looked to the sky. "It's already starting to clear. May be bright by afternoon. Tomorrow for sure."

"Will the wind let up?" asked Paulette.

"It should shift around more easterly, which would be great if any waves are left. We may only have ankle-high breakers by then. Looks like Alan is giving it up." His eyes were now on the beach.

"Say hi to him," Paulette told him. To Ronnie, she said, "Hit the gas, girl!"

They laughed all the way to the first store.

Chapter Twelve

Kris

"We should go together and get this for Angelica. Ronnie too." Joey unfolded the ad. "Not necessarily *this* one."

It would be perfect. Not too expensive either, split three ways. "At worst, she'd think it was a gag."

"And at best it could save her life. Or at least keep her from addling her brains."

"She's got pretty good brains," admitted Kris.

"She's way smarter than any of us. Smarter than her brother, even if it isn't always obvious."

Kris snickered. "Obvious to him, I think."

David Greene sat across the living room, attempting to look like he wasn't listening to the girls. Maybe he was actually trying not to. Now he looked up from the newspaper and asked, "Is the Summerlin girl set on a music career now instead of law?" As a lawyer himself, he undoubtedly considered this a great mistake.

"Angelica could do both if she wanted," stated his daughter.

"But," added Joey, "I wonder how much of an intellectual challenge she'll find in music."

"Intellectual challenge? Gosh, Joey, you talk like you've been to college or something."

"Me? I'm jest an ignorant girl from 'cross the Trail."

"It is a valid question, though," said Mister Greene. "Will she be challenged or lose interest?"

"She composes," said Kris. "That takes brain work."

"Like your drawing?"

"Darned right! I'm as intellectually challenged as anyone!" As soon as she said it aloud she had to laugh. Joey wasn't at all slow to join her.

"What's so funny?" came Marge Greene's voice from another room.

"Best you not know," her husband said. "We know you have hopes for your daughter."

She came in, shaking her head. "Donny won't be home for dinner.

Some activity at school. You know tomorrow is the last day, don't you?"

"Yes, my dear. Half a day. I have heard it mentioned around here once or twice."

Joey rose. "If you're having dinner it's time for me to clear out."

"Why don't you join us?" asked Mister Greene. "We can afford to feed you without Donny here."

"I was going to suggest going out," said Marge.

"Even better, and you're invited. The club?"

Both Kris and her mother made disapproving faces. "That's not the place to go for a good dinner, Tom. Lunch, maybe."

He seemed willing to accept that. "Where then? No place I have to dress up!"

"How about that restaurant Ronnie liked?" her mom suggested. "The one her boyfriend took her to."

Kris had to add, "Ex-boyfriend."

Missus Greene breezed by that without comment. "The place has been there as long as I can remember and we've never been in it."

"We've never eaten much seafood at all. But I'm willing to give it a try."

"And Donny won't be there to worry about it not being kosher," said Kris.

Joey seemed hesitant to comment. "That means like no shellfish, right?"

"Right. No shrimp or scallops or crabs or clams or oysters or, um, what else?"

"Lobsters?" suggested her dad.

"Oh, yeah, lobsters! We're not supposed to but you can eat all the lobsters you want."

"They make me break out."

"Ah, divine punishment, no doubt," her father said. "Maybe you're Jewish and didn't know it. Everyone ready?"

So out they went into the dusk and all loaded into the big, dark green Chrysler. "I'm glad you came along," Kris confided in the back seat. "We're not going to have much time before we're heading different directions again."

Joey nodded. Kris liked to think she felt the same.

"A letter arrived from Lin today. I think she wrote it before James got there."

That seemed likely. It hadn't been that long since he called Joey, and mail was slower during the holiday season. "Anything interesting?"

"Mostly no. She passed on some things James had written her."

"I'm surprised he doesn't write you." They seemed a natural pair for that. "I bet if you sent him a letter he'd write back."

"And lose interest a few letters later. I don't need that. He's been active in demonstrations and that sort of thing, she says. He's not at all fond of the new president."

"Even my dad isn't and he's a Republican."

His voice floated back to them. "Wrong direction for the party."

"Yes, Dad. We've heard that. What sort of demonstrations? I still regret you didn't get to march in Miami with those signs I painted for you!"

"Maybe you can send them to James. He did the 'turn in your draft card day' thing. Last month sometime."

"The Fourteenth."

Joey cocked her head. It was a little too dark to make out her expression. "You remember the date."

"Hey, people do stuff at University of Miami too. You don't have to attend fancy-schmancy Boston College to be active."

"At Edison we call it fancy-schmancy University of Miami."

Snickers up front. That could be either parent. "Here's the bridge," said Dad. An immediate right on the other side, down a rather steep slope to the sprawling tin-roofed restaurant. It lay level with the docks, only a few feet above Naples Bay. Or Gordon River. Kris had never figured out exactly where the name was supposed to change. Maybe no one had.

"I should sketch here," she said, tumbling out of the back seat. "I am sooo sick of trying to find interesting palm trees."

"The view is good from up on the bridge." Joey pointed toward it. "The other side of the building is definitely more interesting."

"Or from a boat!" Kris looked around the parking lot. "Doesn't seem too crowded."

"We're fairly early on a Tuesday evening," said her father.

"But," her mother reminded him, "thoroughly into tourist season."

No waiting for a table. A dark-haired woman escorted them to it. "That's one of the owners," Joey whispered. "The wife. I think she pretty much runs the restaurant side of the business."

"Business?" asked Marge. She didn't sound all that interested and didn't raise her eyes from her menu.

"Buying and selling fish. They have a retail seafood place over near the city docks, too, and a private marina of sorts. Shabby and very Old Naples. My father knew them."

Kris said, "Ronnie's father knows them too. I think he might have drawn something up for them sometime."

"Not the same sort of drawing up I do," said her dad. "Flounder sounds good."

"I've never heard a flounder," said Kris.

"But did you ever tuna fish?" Joey asked.

"That joke was old when I was your age," was his only remark.

"Quite a comedy team these two make," said Marge. "A regular Marx sisters."

"Joey is definitely Groucho," Kris stated.

"But we need our third member."

"Yes," Kris agreed. "Ronnie is our glue. We both know we would never have become friends if it weren't for her."

"And now we're stuck with each other."

"Or stuck to each other."

Her mother said, "I hope you aren't leaving her behind."

Were they neglecting the third member of their triumvirate? For a few guilty seconds, Kris considered the question and knew she didn't have an answer.

"Oh, we're going to replace her with Angelica Summerlin," announced Joey.

"She'll be Harpo!"

"Except she'd insist on speaking."

Talk died down while they decided what to order. It smelled interesting in here, didn't it? Rich could be the word. Kris wasn't sure she actually liked it. Maybe for a little while; she certainly wouldn't want to work in the place!

Scallops. She would love some scallops. Oh, best to behave and have fish. Her parents would surely order it. "The flounder," she informed the waitress. Same with Dad but Mom decided to try mullet. None of them had ever had it.

Except, of course, Joey. "Wayne loves smoked mullet," she told them. "It really stinks up the place." She had a rather strong suspicion Joey loved it too, but she ordered shrimp and Kris would have to watch her gobbling them. They were one of the cheaper dishes, weren't they? That was like Joey.

Round tables with seashells under their glass tops. Naples was renowned for shelling once. Not as much as places like Sanibel, true. Everyone said it wasn't like it used to be. Too picked over? Changes in the Gulf? No one was sure. Ronnie had a shell collection, or used to. Kris didn't have the patience for that sort of thing. Any interesting shell she picked up lost its interest after a while and ended up in a box somewhere. She should find some of them and try doing a drawing.

When Will came home on a long leave, she would demand he bring her here and buy her scallops. Shrimp too. Oh, Joey's weren't breaded and deep fried like she'd expected. But swimming in butter. Broiled? She didn't have a menu to look at now and check the specifics.

No one willing to order desert. Kris might have. "Hey, let's walk up on the bridge and take in the view," she said to Joey as they emerged into the cool night. "We'll only be a couple minutes," she told her parents and started up the slope to the highway. Oh, the wind was more noticeable up here.

Lights along both sides of the water. This was one of two channels, the narrower one she thought, that created an island in the bay. "Is there a name for the island?" she asked Joey, waving toward her left, as if that was necessary.

"Almost certainly. Never heard it. There are still commercial fishermen coming and going." They pulled their skiffs in at the docks on this side of the building, behind the restaurant. Lights shone down on them and the water. Some had their outboard motors in boxes halfway up their length. That was so they wouldn't get in the way of the nets. Kris had learned at least a few things. The docks on the other side of the channel were dark, but lights shone here and there further down the shoreline. The water itself was black, below them, in the distance.

Boats and more boats. A few of those had lights too. Did someone live on them? That sounded romantic but terribly uncomfortable. "I am going to come back here with my sketch pad," she proclaimed. And maybe a camera. Hadn't Gordie taken pictures of the bay?

Then heading back into town. Ah, this back seat was comfortable. Kris curled up on one corner of its expanse.

"We're home, Krissie," came her father's voice, soft.

She must have dozed off, even though it was only a ten minute drive or so. For a moment she was again the little girl he would have carried into the house. Only for a moment. She sat up. "Where's Joey?

"Right here. You didn't think I'd leave without sponging desert, did you?"

"Nope. Just afraid you were eating it all up while I slept. Let's go see what we can find."

It had been great to spend an evening with Joey. She really had missed her friend. But the next time, Ronnie needed to be with them.

Chapter Thirteen

Joey

"Mister Deerfield says he intends to close down on Friday and not open again until the new year."

"That will give you a whole week to try out the new job."

Alan had no idea why she wanted to change employers. She did not intend to change that. "You're positive you don't mind me working with you?"

"If I did you can be sure I would have told my parents."

Yeah, he would have. "I guess three months of sharing rides showed we could get along."

"Or at least not kill each other. You realize I'll be the boss, of course."

"We'll see how that works out. Your folks are likely to promote me over your head when they see how marvelously adept I am at doing your job." She took a sip of her drink before adding, "In fact, they just might fire you."

"Wouldn't be surprised." Maybe he wouldn't. She was beginning to think Alan saw life as a series of misfortunes. "You know, my brother's recommendation meant more than mine."

Joey wasn't sure how respond to that so she didn't. She didn't think Russ was a 'favorite' or anything of that sort, but he was the one walking more or less in the parental footsteps. As was an older sister, in veterinary school somewhere.

And she definitely didn't say she might not date the boy any longer. Hmm, older sister. "Is your sister coming home for the holidays?"

"Spending it with the fiance and family."

"He going to be a vet too?"

"Did you doubt it?" Alan gazed out at the water. There were no waves at all now but he claimed to have ridden tiny ones early this morning. She hoped his wetsuit had kept him warm. "Sometimes," he said, "I think I should do like your brother. Join the navy."

"You'd be miserable," she warned. "You detest taking orders from anyone."

"That's true enough. What's worse is I sometimes don't understand them. For some reason I can't always wrap my mind around what someone wants me to do." He was trying to say this without emotion but it got away from him a bit as he finished, "What people want from me."

She could have ignored this statement too and maybe should have. "I've kind of noticed."

Alan had showed up at the office at noon and they had slid her bike into the back of his station wagon, beside the surfboard. The seats were all folded down; they had been, more often than not, when she rode with him to classes at Edison. Why exactly he had come, Joey wasn't sure. Just to say she had the job?

Knowing Alan he might have agonized over any gesture. That he had already driven into town to surf could have made the difference. Rinsed off and changed, too. She wondered where. She wondered a lot of things about Alan today!

"Take you home or somewhere else?" he asked. "I'm free to be your chauffeur this afternoon."

"Anywhere but your place. You can show me all that tomorrow." She'd drive up bright and early, just like when they were going to Edison. "Have you finished your Christmas shopping?"

"Months ago." He glanced into the rear-view. "I thought I heard a suspicious noise."

And a recognizable one. Sandy Penn buzzed up alongside on her moped. "Hey, Sandy," she called. "Wanta go Christmas shopping? Alan has volunteered to take us."

"Sure!"

Alan leaned forward to look past her. "You just got out of school, didn't you?"

"I did. I haven't even gone home yet."

Right, it was the last day for public school. She would have been out riding around enjoying her freedom too. "We need to stop at my house. Why don't we pick you up at yours in about half an hour?"

"Okay! I'll see you!" She engaged the little motor, spun around, and headed back the way she came.

Alan started up the wagon. "I'm supposed to leave my board at your place, right?" he asked as he backed around.

"Yes, Alan. It will be safe." This was one of those times when he wasn't sure, wasn't it? Alan really wasn't that good at understanding people's intentions and it made him leery of assuming things.

As they headed east, he said, "Sandy should meet Ronnie's brother. She'd want to hear all about what he does in the navy."

"But you wouldn't want to go over."

He shrugged. "Wouldn't matter much."

"I know you're not over Ronnie. Not completely." She hadn't ridden with this guy all fall without figuring that out!

"Completely? Who knows when that comes? It just becomes less and less a part of my life, part of what I think about. Less a part of me." Alan sighed deeply and she knew it was a real sigh, not dramatics. It ended almost with a sort of sob. "I only wish that was one of those things I could understand."

They pulled onto the Trail at Central. There was a traffic light there. Alan preferred having a light. She briefly wondered if Sandy had suspected they—or some other of their friends—would be parked at Third. It remained a favored meeting spot.

"I wish you could too. Things happened I—well, I can't tell you about. Nothing that was your fault." Not that she understood them all herself.

"You've hinted that before. Even Ronnie did, sort of."

"It's good you didn't press her on it."

He took a right off the highway and was in front of her house in a couple minutes. They got the board and bike out and into the carport. "I should change," she said. "Do you want to clean up any?"

Alan only shook his head. He seemed distracted. Nothing particularly new there.

A blouse and sweater to replace the tee and sweatshirt she'd been wearing. These trousers were good enough. She thought maybe Ronnie was never truly in love with Alan. A tad infatuated but mostly he was just a new experience, an exploration, a breaking free. A part of summer, of the new life that came after graduation.

Then James had become another part of that new life. Ronnie had handled it as Ronnie had handled it. It might have been better but it could have been way, way worse.

Switch the sneakers for some loafers. Good enough. She emerged from the little house. "Let's go spend money!"

Chapter Fourteen
Kris

"Parties are starting to crowd each other on the calendar," said Kris. "Including the one at the club. Are your parents going too?"

"I believe so."

"I don't know whether I want to go with mine."

"Me neither," admitted Angelica. "They'd probably like to show us off, what with us being grown up and all that now."

"Not that I haven't been been there playing golf or swimming. Or eating. The dining room is the best place to spy Kristine Greene." But not Angelica Summerlin. "Have you been there at all recently?"

"Not since I was fourteen."

And might just as soon keep it that way. None the less— "I could fix you up with a date."

"Only if you have one too."

"Hey, unfair. You know my boyfriend's far away."

"Someone safe. Alan. He's Will's buddy, right?"

Kris had to giggle. "Or Mackie. He's even safer." She wondered if he was in town. She ought to look him up. Harold Macklin was one of Will's friends too. One of hers, for that matter. "I'll ask him," she decided. "And if he's willing to go with me then we have to get Alan to escort you."

"Or we could switch and I'll have the big, handsome gay guy on my arm."

"Too bad your brother isn't home. We could get him to invite Joey."

Not Ronnie. Both knew that wouldn't be a good idea. "That's Monday night. Hey, we could rope them into taking us to a whole bunch of parties." Not that any of the boys would be likely to fall in with their plan.

"Maybe I should have one here. A small one." Angelica looked toward the street. "Is this someone we know?"

Probably just a beach-goer, thought Kris. It was a nice enough day for it, clear and fairly warm again. The air, that is. The water got too cold at this time of year.

It was a nice day to sit outside too. Coffee had replaced the lemonades she and her friend might have shared half a year ago. Her friend Jelly. She didn't quite think of her as a friend before last summer. Things changed, didn't they?

"Sandy. I assumed she'd show up eventually. And her brother." Russel had emerged from the driver's side of the blue and white van. "He'd be another possible safe date, wouldn't he?"

"For all I know, he has a girlfriend. Or a bunch of them! Hi, Sandy."

The Penn girl hugged her. "It's great to have you back!" Angelica had wisely remained seated and avoided an embrace.

Instead her eyes went to the Volkswagen van. "That is just what I need," she said. "Show it to me, Russ."

"Um, okay. Hi, Kris." Angelica rose and followed him back to the street.

Kris wasn't interested enough to join them. Sandy dropped into one of the lawn chairs. "What were you two up to?" she asked. "Making lists for Santa?"

"Making a list of Christmas parties and figuring out how to hit them all. We're even considering using your brother as an escort if no one better comes along."

Sandy snickered. "I think he likes Angelica a bit."

"All the guys like Angelica." And more than a bit. Sandy liked Angelica too.

"There will be a party at the rec center," said Sandy. "You might be too old for that." She craned her head to look at Kris's list. "Country club?"

"Yeah. The Summerlins and my parents belong to the same one. You know, Preston Summerlin quit the one he'd belonged to for years when they wouldn't let us in." Sandy's face was blank. "Because we're Jewish."

"Oh! Gosh, that's awful. I mean, the not letting you join. The Summerlins are great!"

Preston was. His wife, by all reports, had not been happy about it. Maria Morales Salas Summerlin had brought some old school prejudices with her from Cuba. Best to let Sandy assume the best about her.

And, after all, she had never seemed to have the least problem with Kris or her father. Her mom was another matter. That might have been more a matter of personalities. "There are sure to be little parties at friends' houses," Kris went on. "The Rheins always do something for Christmas." She might or might not get an invitation this year, but she could show up anyway. Hey, Gordie would be another reasonably safe escort. She jotted down his name along the margin of the paper.

Angelica and Russel were coming back toward them. "I am definitely going to be dropping hints that this is what I want," the girl announced. "Maybe that will prevent my parents from buying something stupid like a Mustang."

"You could always hand it on to me if you don't like it," Sandy told her. "Or let my brother drive you to parties in it."

"Someone has been gossiping to you, I see. But how about it, Russ? Would you like to be my escort to a big Christmas bash?"

"Um, I—"

"Oh, you aren't doing anything Monday night," Sandy told him, "and it's not like you have a girlfriend."

"Um, I—"

"Okay, then it's settled," said Angelica. "You're going to invite Harold?"

"I think so." Sandy didn't know about Mackie, did she? Nor did her brother, for that matter.

"Looks like another member of your triumvirate is showing up," Angelica reported. "Now we only need Joey."

"She's trying out her new job this morning. Which we probably shouldn't mention around Ronnie."

"Why?" Oh, did any of them knew about the job?

"Because she's working for Alan's parents."

Nods. That they understood. Not only Ronnie but her brother emerged from the Simca. "Ooh, I want to talk with him. Joey told me all about him!" exclaimed Sandy.

"She certainly didn't say anything to me," said Angelica. "I'll have to talk to him too. Just to make your brother jealous."

"He could always take my place at your party."

"You're not getting off the hook that easily, Russel Penn."

"Hook?" asked Ronnie, joining them. "What have you got poor Russ into?"

"He's committed to attending a series of parties. The whole holiday season!" Kris told her. "Hi, Rick."

"Kris."

"This is my brother Rick," announced Ronnie. "Petty Officer Second Class Richard Deerfield, or so he claims. He won't put on his uniform to prove it. Angelica, Sandy, Russ."

"Russ, I remember."

"I suppose you would. So what's this about parties?"

"Yes, just where am I supposed to be taking you or you taking me?" asked Russ.

"Sh," said Karen.

"Huh?"

Ronnie was the one to explain. "She means Sabal Hammock. It's an inside joke for these rich girls."

"Which I haven't used in years," mused Angelica. "Sh. I remember us calling it that."

"There's a bunch of other possible holiday parties, right through New Year's Eve. We're making a list and checking it twice!"

"And lining up guys to accompany us. Looks like Sandy stole the one you brought to us."

Ronnie glanced toward her brother, being pumped by the girl. She didn't appear all that sympathetic. "I may not belong to any country clubs," she said, "but Paulette invited me to a Christmas social at her church. You too, Kris. She specifically told me you were invited."

Will's church. Will's family. That familiar void opened in her heart. "When is it?"

"Friday night."

"I'll see." Maybe if she could talk Mackie into going with her. Or anyone. Damn it, this wasn't how the holidays were supposed to feel!

Angelica picked up her list, looked it over. "Lots of open nights. Hmm, Gordie? What night is his?"

"I don't know but we can find out."

"I'm sure we can."

Chapter Fifteen
Ronnie

"I'm not supposed to touch the animals. Not even to move them from one kennel or cage to another."

"What if they're—oh, I don't know. Puking or eating their tails or something?" asked Kris.

"Call a tech. Always call a tech. Or Alan. I may be trusted to work with the critters later."

Ronnie was glad Joey didn't mind mentioning Alan in front of her anymore. She was also glad she didn't seem to mind them ambushing her when she got home from her new job. Neither her mom nor stepdad was home so they'd waited outside in dilapidated lawn chairs for her to show up.

"I wish I could call a tech when Fluffertail acts up."

"We wish we could call a tech when you act up," Joey told her. "You and Fluffertail are two of a kind."

"Marge Greene's spoiled spaniels," added Ronnie.

"Arf! Arf! Hey, I just got hold of Mackie and he'll come to your thing tomorrow night. He might have been reluctant until I mentioned Carter Jones. Then he was in completely. I still haven't got a commitment from him for the club."

"You should have Rick for your date and let the Mack take Ronnie," said Joey.

Ronnie shook her head. "Rick has already gone over and visited Carter. I think he prefers to keep things that way." Private. Personal.

"So the three of us then. And poor Joey left out again."

"And Angelica," Joey pointed out. "Maybe we'll go party somewhere!"

"With Russel Penn," said Kris. Both girls snickered. Joey looked from one to the other, not sure what the joke was.

"Angelica commandeered him as her holiday escort this morning," Ronnie explained.

"Commandeered! Oh, that's a classy word."

"Better than shanghaied," felt Joey. "But maybe less accurate, knowing Angelica."

Or drafted. No one liked to use that word. It had too many connotations, connotations for them and their friends. "Still no decorations?" asked Ronnie.

"This weekend. Wayne is going into the woods to find a free pine to cut down. We're likely to deck the halls on Sunday afternoon."

"The Summerlins haven't decorated yet either."

"They will," said Kris. "Inside and out. Lights wrapped around every palm tree and all over the house. They have high ceilings, too, for a really tall tree."

Joey pointed out, "Any memories you and I have of Christmas at the Summerlins are pretty old."

"And just glimpses."

Ronnie had no memories at all. She hadn't known the family back then, except through her friends' gossip.

"Want to do anything this afternoon?" asked Kris. "After you wash that stink off of you?"

"You are pretty ripe," observed Ronnie. "It's a good thing we stayed outside."

"You're going to be smelling a lot more of this if I keep up the job."

"Alan never smells that way." There. She'd brought him up in a conversation.

Joey appeared to take no notice, though she probably did. "He stank today. So did Russ. They get to the showers as soon as they can when they knock off."

"They should share them with you!" declared Kris.

"Um, one at a time, I hope," Joey replied. She might have reddened just a little.

Should that have bothered her? wondered Ronnie. It didn't seem to. In fact, she had to keep herself from snickering at the thought of Joey in the shower with the Wesolowski brothers. The Wezzies, as Rick called them.

"I promised to go shopping with my brother," she said. "Or drive him around. It's one time he doesn't want to walk."

"I'd better drive you home then. We'll make plans later," said Kris.

"You're working for Mister Deerfield tomorrow, right?" she asked Joey.

"Last day."

Rick was waiting, ready to go, when Kris dropped her.

"Sandy Penn came by again," he told her, as she made herself a sandwich. She wasn't taking off on an empty stomach. "I'm not sure why. Don't have much more I can tell her about what I do."

"Maybe she likes you. The romantic older man."

She half-expected her brother to laugh or make a face. Instead, he answered seriously. "I'm three years older than her. I know that's not a big difference for adults but it's another matter at her age."

"She's just a year younger than me."

"And it shows."

Ronnie could have said their personalities made more difference than their ages but it didn't matter much. Her brother could think what he wanted.

She was not quite sure she should say what came out of her mouth next. "We're not decided whether she likes guys at all. It was pretty obvious last summer she had a crush on Angelica but that doesn't necessarily mean anything."

"That can be age too," asserted Rick.

"That's what Angelica said." But she might have been brushing the whole thing aside, dismissing it.

"Now if Angelica were interested in an older man things might be different," he said.

Ronnie couldn't think of how to even begin to warn him against that idea.

Chapter Sixteen

Joey

"No, not at all, Joey. People your age tend to try on new jobs for fit every month or two. It was good to have you stick around these past three months."

Well, that went easily. Not that she had expected Mister Deerfield to make it hard. "Thank you, sir." She glanced out the rather small window, with its Venetian blind hanging halfway down. One side always ended up lower than the other. "I think my new boss is waiting for me."

"Alan. Ronnie seems okay with that, doesn't she?"

"It's not much different than riding to Edison with him. And after all, I've been dating his brother."

Deerfield nodded. "I suppose going away to college helped get him off her mind. I know she, um, felt guilty for some reason. Which I'll never pry into. Here's your pay and a little extra." He handed her an envelope, a business envelope marked 'H. Deerfield, Architect.' "Spend it on presents."

Alan was in his station wagon; as before, she slid her bike into the rear. No surfboard there this time, nor in the roof racks. Some days she might be riding with him to Fort Myers in this AMC; others they could be in her Corvair. The two thought they could synchronize their classes pretty well again this coming semester. "I don't know if that will be easier with us working together," Joey had told him but he didn't seem to be concerned one way or another.

Today they were riding only to the Summerlins. Angelica expected them. She stood in the yard, Sandy Penn at her side, watching a crew hanging strings of Christmas lights.

"I'm supervising," she announced. "Sandy is my assistant supervisor."

"And you can be assistant assistant supervisors. Or assistant assistant assistant. You can work that out between yourselves."

"We should be able to light up everything this evening. The inside is mostly done. Come on in."

A cheery 'Merry Christmas' came from the kitchen. "Merry Christmas to you, Sylvie," returned Joey, to be echoed by Alan.

"Will you be coming to the party tonight, Miss Joey?" asked the cook. "The one at the church?"

"Not me. Ronnie and Kris will be there."

That seemed to satisfy her as she went back to her work. A little radio played Christmas music.

"That is quite a tree," she admitted when she joined the others in the living room. Maria Summerlin was overseeing its decoration. "I do love the Christmas holidays."

"Me too," said Sandy, peering toward the jeweled star at the top of the towering tree. "But Russel hates that his birthday is the day after Christmas."

"That's kind of lousy. Any other holiday would be better."

"My birthday fell on Easter once, though it's fairly late. I think I was like five or six," Alan said.

"Mine could too, in theory. I'm April Seventeen."

"I'm the Twenty-first. Russ's is always on Saint Patrick's day."

"I'll have to call him Paddy from now on. Hey, I'll bet Jelly's is the same as Jam's!" At least Sandy seemed to think that was funny. "I remember when it is but I won't tell."

Angelica only shrugged. "It doesn't matter. It's May First. I'm the May Queen. I'm not sure what that makes my brother! Hey, Alan, did you bring your guitar?"

"I did. I'm not sure why you'd want to play with me."

"Don't do that," she said. "Just assume everyone loves to play with you. We're all in awe of your overwhelming talent! And practicing hours on my own every day is already boring me to tears."

I should talk to the boy like that, thought Joey.

"Do you know if Ronnie has been playing?" The question was not directed to any particular one of them.

But meant for her, of course. "I'm pretty sure she didn't take her guitar to college with her." Joey replied.

Maria Summerlin had turned her attention to the group of young people. "It is very beautiful, is it not? I think we need a Christmas Eve party to show it to everyone!"

"Why not?" asked her daughter.

"We have not celebrated the *Noche Buena* here in many years. My Cuban traditions do not fit so well. We had our Christmas feast on the Twenty-fourth."

"With a whole roast pig?" asked Angelica. "Aunt Tina and Uncle Oscar still do that."

"You had meat?" asked Joey. "I remember in the old days we did not eat meat on Christmas Eve. It was like Fridays."

"Not so old. The pope changed it only two years ago," Angelica reminded her.

"My Italian grandmother would fix different sorts of fish," recalled Joey. "Mom doesn't go any further than codfish cakes."

"Those we had. *Croquetas*, yes." Maria nodded with nostalgic pleasure at the memory. "But sometimes with ham instead of cod! But abstinence was only during the day. After sunset we were permitted to feast on anything. Even in the most sophisticated households a roast pig was expected."

Joey couldn't see Sylvie Cooper roasting a whole pig. Nor even Preston Summerlin on his big outdoor grill.

"We would feast and then go to midnight mass. And maybe feast again when we returned!" Missus Summerlin sighed. "It would be impossible here, would it not?"

"Maybe not a pig but there's no reason Sylvie can't put a pork roast or ham in the oven for us. Those Cuban grocers you visit could provide everything else."

"Yes, the pork must be marinated in *mojo*. Plantains, if someone knows how to fry them. You know I can't! And *flan* and *buñuelos* and *turróns* and—oh, it is too much."

"Don't forget the rum cake. We'll put something together. Maybe we can invite a cousin to come over from Miami and show us how to cook it!" She didn't sound too serious about it. "And Joey has to help."

"Me?"

"Yes. Bring your mother. We'll mix Italian and Cuban traditions."

Maria brightened. "Oh yes, your parents are invited to share our dinner. And then we can all walk over to midnight mass together. It has been so long since I did this!" A pause, a consideration. "Your step-father, he is not Catholic, right? He and Preston could entertain each other while we go to the church."

"I'll run it by them," Joey promised. She kind of hoped they'd agree. It would be fun to do something different this year.

"No, no. I want that strand higher," scolded Maria Summerlin, her attention returned to her decorators.

"I think it will be up to me to pull it together," said Angelica. "Now go get your guitar, Alan. And you," she said, turning to Sandy, "will have your own family gatherings but do try to stop by."

"I will! I'd better be on my way right now. I'm supposed to be helping with a toy drive!"

"That was pretty nice of you," remarked Joey, when the girl was out the door. "And not just Sandy."

"'Tis the season. Didn't you know?"

Chapter Seventeen
Kris

"Oh, I know the way," said Mackie. "I've been there with Doughnut. Will, I mean."

"It's okay with me if you call him Doughnut. I did for eight years."

"We all did." The nickname had stuck with the boy since he showed up at school with a jelly filled doughnut in his lunch. One could be called worse things. "This is Ronnie's street, right?"

"Right."

"Left would take me the wrong direction."

"Sheesh, you're sounding like Joey."

Was this Mackie's car? Or one from his father's sales lot? "Too bad you couldn't find Ronnie a date," he said.

"You should have brought Jeff down with you."

"We split. Jeff had problems." Mackie pulled in before the Deerfield house. "He got himself into trouble and was bounced from the team, and then he dropped out."

"Oh. I guess it would be hard to stay together." Though if they cared for each other—

"We were done well before that." She couldn't say for sure how he felt about that. Mackie had always been good at hiding his feelings. And other things. "You know, Ohio has a great art department. I understand they're sort of famous for it, though I didn't know that when I signed with them. I just wanted to be a Bobcat."

"Thinking of switching majors? Hey Ronnie. Slip in the back."

"Maybe, but not to art. I was thinking economics."

"I know that's difficult. I'll bet it's more difficult than the lawyer stuff Ronnie is taking."

"It would be for me," Ronnie admitted.

"And that lawyer stuff would make my head spin. Here we go."

Macklin cut over to Golf Drive. It was early enough there were still players on the course. Preston Summerlin preferred the old course to driving out to his country club on the far side of town. It was where he met all his cronies from the old Naples families.

"You could have crossed the Trail on Seventh," Ronnie informed him.

"Wanted to look at this place first. The scenic route."

"First you sound like Joey, now like Ronnie's dad."

"I missed Naples. It gets pretty dreary in Ohio by this time of year." He took a right on the Trail and then left again at Seventh. "The church is on this side of Goodlette," he said. "Not too far from the road."

The west side. Kris knew Will's home was on the other side. Water-front, in fact, on a canal connecting to the river.

"Why were you at the church?" asked Ronnie.

"There was a convocation for the athletes from the community. Will asked me to come."

"You were a good friend to Will," stated Kris.

"And he was a good friend to me. And you, Miss Greene, are about as good a friend as I've ever had."

"Keep saying things like that and we might have a second date."

"We will if you still want me at that country club affair. And—" He pulled right off the road and around a corner. "Here we are."

Brick. For some reason she'd expected lap-board. A good sized hall beside the church. That's probably where things were going to happen.

"Paulette won't recognize this big whatever-it-is," said Ronnie. "She may be watching for the Simca."

"It's a Dodge Monaco, I'll have you know."

"Pretty much the same car as my dad's Chrysler. Park it some-where, won't you?"

He pulled in beside an older Cadillac. There were only a few people to be seen in the lot, all of them black, most moving toward the church. "There you are!" Paulette Jones was hurrying toward them, a shorter, slimmer, younger girl at her side. "I'm so happy you came, Ronnie. Hi, Kris. Harold Macklin, right? Hmm, just the three?"

"The Mackerel is big enough for me and Ronnie to share," Kris told her.

"So he is! We'll have a service first. That's going to be heavy on

Christmas music. Then the social. You don't have to go to the service, of course, if, umm, it goes against anything you—"

"You know Kris is Jewish," spoke Mackie.

"Everyone knows Kris is Jewish. We all gossiped about her last summer."

"It's the other two we don't know about," said her companion. "Heathens and devil-worshipers, I'd imagine!" She attempted a suspicious look.

"They've been holding me captive!" claimed Kris.

Paulette could only shake her head. "You know Jackie, don't you? Oh, of course you do."

Yes, of course she knew Will's little sister. "I'll have to stay close to Jackie. It's nice to stand beside someone as short as me"

"And I know about your friends. Sandy Penn tells me things."

They would be classmates at Naples High. "You're friends?"

"Pretty good ones."

"More like friendly rivals," said Mackie. "I remember the two of you. The worst sort of popular girls and probably all the worse now you're seniors."

Jackie giggled. "Alpha bitches."

"Jacqueline Booth!" Paulette might have been legitimately shocked.

James had called her something similar not all that long ago, though in less vulgar terms. When? Oh, when he was comparing her to his older sister. Tall, beautiful, successful Lin. Troubled Lin. They walked toward the church's tall double doors, painted white.

"You'll sit with my family," said Paulette. "Are you going to, Jackie?"

"Yeah, Mama said we would. I think—um, maybe I shouldn't say that."

"I suspect you are right."

"But spit it out anyway," said Kris.

"Well, I think it's because Mackie was coming. She likes him and he's a friend of my brother. She still doesn't know what to think of you, Kris."

Kris couldn't help smiling at that. "Nothing new there. Maybe I shouldn't ask what you think of me."

"Honest? I think you're great. You really made Willie happy before he went off and left us."

Will had made her happy too. Before he went off and left her.

Inside. It wasn't all that big. The brick exterior had made the building look more imposing than it was. The seats—pews, right?—were about half full. "Is the congregation all black?" Ronnie whispered to Paulette. Kris might not have asked something like that outright.

Paulette showed no sign of being bothered by the question. "We do have a few white folks in our congregation. Mister Parker over there. His wife is black." So she was, assuming that was she at his side. "Or old Missus Lane who has always lived here on the river and sees no reason she should change her ways or go further for church."

"I've never been to a service at a Protestant church," said Ronnie.

Kris hadn't known she'd been to a service anywhere. "Welcome," came a deep voice. Kris didn't recognize the speaker but her companions did.

"Thank you, sir," said Mackie. "Hi, Carter." Carter Jones Junior was a little behind the man, supporting himself on twin crutches. She tried not to look down at his legs. Leg.

This must be Carter Senior then. "This is Kris Greene," said Paulette. "You got a look at Ronnie the other day. My pop."

"Pleased to meet you sir."

"Thanks for having us, Officer Jones."

"No need to call me officer here. I'm more likely to be called Brother Jones." There was a barely audible, low-pitched chuckle. "You coming along, Junior?"

"In a moment." He and Mackie were conversing, their voices subdued. "Maybe I should switch to the chair." He nodded toward a wheelchair pushed against the back wall. "I try to use these some," he explained, lifting the one crutch a little off the floor, "but I spend more time in the chair."

"Don't spend too much time there, man, or you'll get fat," Mackie told him. "Than I won't be able to get these girls to come visit you." Carter already had tendencies toward it. His family did. Carter Senior was a big man.

"Ha, I can't have that! Okay, then, I'll hobble down to our pew. If I fall over, it's all your fault, man."

"I'll never let you, Carter."

Carter Jones Senior gave an approving nod and followed.

Chapter Eighteen
Ronnie

"On the ride down I saw we were two who can talk outright to each other about things."

Ronnie nodded. "Be serious and say what's on our minds."

"Exactly." The two girls had claimed chairs along the wall. Most were milling about the hall. The place was only moderately festive. There weren't enough lights for the full effect. A somewhat worn artificial tree stood in one corner. "Someone should have brought us plates by now."

"They haven't 'cause we don't have dates. I should claim your brother since he's unattached."

"And he can't run away from you!" Paulette started to laugh, then abruptly shut her mouth. She seemed almost stricken. "Oh. Maybe I shouldn't say things like that."

"He's your brother. You're allowed." Ronnie giggled. "And now he's my boyfriend I can too."

"Of course. That makes perfect sense."

"Here comes Kris. I think maybe she expected dancing."

"Not tonight. We're not one of those churches that are against it or anything, but this is a social, not a dance."

Mackie was following Kris, pushing Carter's chair. "You two," Paulette addressed them, her tones imperious. "Ronnie and I feel neglected. Go get us plates full of goodies."

"Drinks too," added Ronnie.

Kris plopped down beside them. "Will's sister is wearing me out. She's going *all* the time."

'That's Jackie for you. She always has to be doing something. Into everything at school, like your friend Sandy."

"I'm not sure whether she is our friend. More Angelica's," said Kris. "Same with her brother."

Ronnie wasn't so sure about that latter. Angelica didn't pay much attention to Russ Penn either. He certainly wasn't a part of their group.

"Angelica? That's that rich girl, right? With a house on the beach?"

"That's the one. We're besties with her and have the run of the place."

"That's actually sort of the truth," Ronnie felt obliged to add. "Here come our plates. Oh, gingerbread!"

"My mom's. Full of molasses. Thank you, gentlemen."

"Yeah, mm-mm, thanks." Ronnie's mouth was already full.

Mackie leaned down and whispered something in Carter's ear. The young man nodded and was wheeled away. "I think they're going to go outside and talk," said Kris. She reached over and snitched a cookie from Ronnie's plate. "Hey, Jackie." The girl sat down on their other side.

"We think Kris wants to dance," Paulette told her.

"Me too. There will be dancing at the rec center tomorrow."

"Sandy mentioned that. In the afternoon?"

"Mostly. Into evening, I guess. We'll both be there. Organizers! Are you all just gonna *sit* here?"

"It sounds good to me," said Paulette. Ronnie was in agreement but Kris got to her feet.

"Shall we run laps around the hall?" she asked.

"Just around the buffet!" The pair took off.

Paulette watched for a few seconds. "I remember you being active at school too."

"I was but cut back on everything my senior year and got a job." Maybe Joey's example had something to do with that. To be sure, Joey had never been active in anything at school, but she'd had jobs almost as far back as Ronnie could remember. She had caddied as soon as she could at the golf course they both lived near. "Kris was into more activities. Service clubs and all that."

"Girls like me were in the second tier, so to speak. FTA. Yearbook staff. That sort of thing."

Ronnie nodded. She'd always seen herself as being at that top level, like Kris. Her friend undeniably was, just by virtue of being Kris. She was born to it. Ronnie never felt quite like she fitted with that crowd but hung with them anyway. "All of that high school stuff seems sort of petty, looking back."

Paulette snickered. "Looking back a whole half a year?"

"Yep. An eternity!"

It felt like one.

Chapter Nineteen
Joey

She and Wayne had nailed a couple slats to the bottom of its trunk and dragged the pine into the living room. Joey remembered her earliest Christmas—she must have still been two—right here in this room with a tree much like this one. But her father had been here then, not Wayne.

"No problems?" asked Mom. She already had the decorations out.

"Not unless someone saw us," answered Wayne.

"And sends the Pine Tree Police after us."

They all stepped back to admire the tree. Fairly tall it stood, close to seven foot, and its fragrance was already beginning to fill the room. "Do we decorate this evening or tomorrow?"

"I think I want to get cleaned up right now," said Joey. She was sweaty and sandy and uncomfortable. It had turned into a pretty warm day. "And then run over to the Summerlins and let them know you're coming Christmas Eve. You're sure, aren't you? Last chance to back out!"

The couple looked at each other. "We are," said her mother. "Does Missus Summerlin really want me to bring something?" It sounded slightly odd to be carrying food to a celebration there.

"Definitely. And it has to be Italian." Joey disappeared into the bathroom. Although the house had three bedrooms—small bedrooms —there was only one bath. The extra bedroom, the one never used as a bedroom, served to store whatever needed storing.

She emerged feeling considerably less grimy. "As long as I'm clean and going into town I might as well go to evening mass too," she announced. Mom probably wouldn't come but she had let her know her intention. Joey had no idea what she would do when it came time for midnight mass. Her mother remained uncomfortable with church, having divorced and remarried.

The bike? It would be dark by the time she came pedaling home. No darker than some mornings she rode. She walked it out of the carport. Go the other way this afternoon, she decided, north and then cut back on Tenth. The distance was about the same. Ah, it felt good to get her legs pumping, down to the corner, left and then left again. A right on Eighth Avenue? No, go to Seventh and cross the Trail at the light there. Then straight south on Eighth Street, toward downtown Naples.

No need to buzz by Ronnie's. She'd get the story on last night soon enough. From someone. Past the hospital. Past the library and middle school. She hadn't been in the library in a while. Edison had a pretty decent one and she sometimes had time to kill there. Walk the bike across busy Fifth Avenue and then pedal on past the park. Was something going on at the rec center? Lots of kids.

Must be that thing Sandy mentioned. She went another block before turning toward the Gulf, riding past the rear of Saint Ann School, past the convent and rectory, past the new church. Far from finished still.

A minute later she was at the curb beside the Summerlin house. Oh, this was Saturday. The Summerlins always ate out. Maybe Angelica went with them and no one would be home. She looked toward the house and then back to the street. Gordie's Mini Moke was parked just up the way. Another reason it might be best to turn around. Who knew what those two might be up to?

"Are you going to dawdle out there all day?" someone called.

Safe, apparently. She rolled her bike up a way and left it lying in the grass. Angelica and Gordie were sitting on the screened porch, smoking. It wasn't tobacco.

"I haven't noticed that smell since last summer," she said, going in and taking a seat. Not since James was there.

"Want a drag?" asked Angelica, offering her joint.

"Better not. I intend to be back on the bike shortly. Hadn't seen you around, Gordie."

"Lying low. It seems like everyone's moved on, in one way or another. Hey, is Alan around?"

"I see him from time to time." There hadn't been a whole lot in common between Alan and Gordie, other than surfing and the girls. It wasn't to be expected they would have any contact after Gordie went off to South Florida. Gordie wasn't really dedicated to surfing like Alan, either. "We both go to Edison."

"Oh, right." He took another pull on his smoke. "We were talking about parties. My folks aren't throwing much in the way of anything this year. Christmas Eve maybe, but that's about it." The boy stared into space a little while before adding, "That doesn't mean we couldn't have one ourselves."

"Maybe we can fit it into our busy schedules." She turned to Angelica. "I mostly came over to tell you our Christmas Eve thing is on. I suppose I'll have to coordinate between our moms." Joey could not imagine her mother either coming over or talking with Maria Summerlin on the phone.

"Good enough. I'll let Mom know. And Sylvie. And I'm still trying to get one of Tia Tina's daughters to come over but it doesn't look hopeful."

Gordie listened to this like he knew what they were talking about, before asking, "Did you watch the moon launch?"

"No, I was in the woods purloining a pine."

"Now you need to go to confession," Angelica told her.

"Did I say purloin? I meant *rescue*. It was a poor lost little tree and we gave it a good home!"

"Oh, that's different."

"Or between me and my conscience anyway. I am going over to mass in a few minutes."

"I'll come with you. We'll walk over."

"Hey, I'll drive you," offered Gordie.

Why not? They'd still have to walk back. "Okay with me," said Joey.

"Me too. Let me go up and change." Angelica disappeared into the house.

"I suspect," she told Gordie, "she wanted to put on clothes that didn't reek of weed."

He grinned. "Likely enough. I'm serious about having some sort of party at my parent's house. After Christmas, I guess. They're going to head off on a cruise."

She only nodded. There would be one or there wouldn't. A couple minutes later they were in the little open car, Angelica up front, Joey wedged in the back. Neither had ever ridden in it before. "It's fun but I need something more now," he told them, putting it into gear and edging forward. "Hmm." He flipped on the headlights. It was getting toward dusk.

"A Volkswagen van, like Russel," Angelica advised at once.

"Um-huh. Russel who?"

"Penn."

"Oh. Haven't seen him around yet. Here okay?" He'd stopped in the street in front of Saint Ann Church.

"Fine." Both girls tumbled out of the Mini Moke and watched him drive south along Third.

"I don't suppose there is any sort of parish party," said Angelica, as they hurried across the street.

"If there was, they'd have to hold it in the classrooms over at the school. Someday, we should be in the new church and this will become our parish hall."

Angelica stopped at the bottom of the concrete steps and looked up at the old church, the rose window above the door, the little cross at the peak. "I suppose it's a change for the better."

"All I know is, it's a change."

Chapter Twenty
Ronnie

"I'm on the cheerleader squad. I like to do something, um, um, *physical*, you know? Physical, yeah, that's the word. I wish there were more sports for girls. I'll play anything." She threw her arms wide in an all-encompassing gesture. "Even basketball!"

"Someone's liable to dribble you," observed Joey.

Jackie didn't seem to quite know how to take that. Joey took some getting used to. But Sandy laughed and that seemed to make it okay.

"She's had years to practice short jokes on me," said Kris.

The girl nodded and looked Joey up and down. "I know you never went out for any sports but you look pretty darn fit."

"Joey only competes against herself," said Ronnie. She'd never thought of that before but immediately recognized it as true. "I suspect Angelica was playing something like field hockey at her private schools."

"I don't think I'd want to face Jel with a hockey stick in her hands," said Kris. There was general agreement.

"Me? I was always a model of sportswomanship," stated Angelica. "But I didn't much like team sports either. I was a pretty decent archer until my boobs grew and got in the way. I should go use the range at the club."

"Gone," said Kris. "No one used it after you went away. And my father said it was a possible liability. Golf balls are dangerous enough!"

"Not if no one was using it," observed Joey.

"True. Anyway, I shouldn't do anything that might hurt my hands or nails. Guitar comes first now." She turned to Ronnie. "You should bring yours over."

"Russ could," volunteered Sandy. "You know he plays."

Plays at it, Ronnie said to herself. No, that was harsh. He was probably more committed than she had been lately. "I will," she said. "I need to start practicing again."

"Speaking of Russ," Angelica went on, "tell your brother either a dinner jacket or a dark suit is acceptable tomorrow night. When should we meet here, Kris? Six-ish?"

"Sounds good. And Mackie is providing our ride."

"Aw, I was looking forward to pulling up in that VW bus. That's the only reason I invited him, you know."

Sandy grinned. "Should I tell him that too?"

"I'll leave that to your discretion."

"There's your mom," said Jackie.

"Oh, our ride. Later, guys!" Both girls sprinted toward the baby blue Cutlass convertible. It was warm enough for Myra Penn to have the top down. She gave a wave and sped off.

"I think Missus Penn gives both of them a lot of rides," said Ronnie. "They're into so many things. Sandy's on the student council."

"So why did they arrive here with you?" asked Angelica. The girls moved toward the back porch. It had been a while since all four of them—and just them—had been together.

"They came over to talk to Rick. I don't know if Jackie is all that interested in what he does but Sandy still seems pretty set on being a pilot. She knew every technical term my brother does and some he doesn't!"

"I wouldn't expect either to run off and join the navy right away," said Joey.

Kris nodded. "College material. Jacqueline should pick up a decent scholarship somewhere."

Neither girl had said a word to her about where they might be headed after graduation. Well, none of her business. The Summerlins' Christmas tree was lit up. Angelica took a seat on the living room floor. "It looks bigger from here," she said.

They settled beside her. She was right. "Huge," said Kris.

"Makes me feel like I'm three again," Joey added.

"You already act that way," Kris told her.

"There are worse ways to feel and to act," murmured Angelica. "I bet you came over to talk to my mother."

"In part. Nothing too pressing."

"I don't suppose I could get you to stay this time." She turned to the others. "I tried to talk her into sleeping over here last night but she rode her bike off into the dark."

"I wasn't going to miss helping my mom decorate our own tree. And tomorrow I'm up bright and early and off to work. My first solo duty at the clinic. I think they just want to see how I'll do. I'll be working with Alan a lot of the time." She got to her feet. "There's your mom. I'd better talk to her about deserts and stuff."

"Probably our dinner will be ready soon. Either of you staying?"

"We have families too," said Kris. "We should probably see them sometimes."

"Whether we want to or not."

"Or whether *they* want to or not!"

"Heading out?" asked Joey, returning from the kitchen. "I'd better be on my way too."

The long shadows of the palms lay across the grass, the sun almost touching the horizon. Shortly it would sink into the Gulf and darkness would fill the streets. Was this the longest night? Maybe that was yesterday. No matter. The nights were long!

All three had driven over. As they went to their cars, she said to Joey, "I'm glad you'll say Alan's name around me now. There wasn't any reason not to, you know. I would even be okay with being around him."

"I'm sure you would. I'm not so sure Alan would be okay with being around you."

With that Joey went to her Corvair and drove away into the dusk.

Chapter Twenty-one
Kris

Rain and wind. Cold rain and wind. Yesterday's warmth had been the preliminary to another cold front. "I almost picked out a convertible for us," said Mackie. "Good thing I decided to go with the Imperial instead." He'd had the choice of vehicles from his dad's used car lot.

"Here's the gate," Kris said. It hung open between a pair of tall posts rising beside the road. The Sabal Hammock Country Club was just that, a golf course, tennis courts, a club house. No subdivision built around it. Ronnie's father believed those were the future for Naples. Golf communities. He hated the idea. Kris didn't think much of it herself.

"I've never been in here," said Russel from the back seat.

"Me neither," admitted Mackie.

"That's because you weren't hanging around with classy girls like us," Angelica informed him.

"Maybe we would have let you sooner if you'd been driving this classy Chrysler," Kris added to this. It beat riding with their parents.

"As long as it doesn't turn into a pumpkin."

"And these guys into mice."

"You're more mouse-sized than any of us," Mackie told her. "I'll try to let you out as close as possible."

"I've got the umbrella," offered Russ.

"No need. Covered entry, see? Only one of you guys will have to run back in the rain."

"What, no valet parking? You'd better leave that umbrella with me, Russel," said Mackie.

The port-cochere may have kept falling rain off them but plenty was blowing in, misty and cold. They moved as close to the doors as they could and watched Mackie drive off to park. There was no thought of going inside before he returned.

"Speaking of classy, that's a pretty classy tux, Russ," commented

Angelica. "Or classic, I could say. I'll bet it's not rented."

"Mackie's obviously is," Kris said.

Russel nodded a bit self-consciously. "My mother found an older one and had it altered. It's not very stylish, I guess."

"Oh, it will always be stylish. A good dinner jacket is ageless."

"That sounds like something your sister would say," Kris let her know.

"It does, doesn't it? Here comes Harold." He wasn't quite running but Mackie was certainly hurrying, the umbrella almost sideways to keep off the rain driven by the north wind.

Mackie's tuxedo was not classic at all and didn't even fit him that well. Maybe it was hard to get one that did when you were his size. At least it wasn't white.

Kris herself was in a long sheath with a deep neck. She knew that was the best way to make her look taller. Not that it would help when she stood next to Harold Macklin! She took his arm and both couples went into the brightly lit dining room.

Ha, couples. Shanghaied Russ and this good but completely uninterested guy beside her. How she wished she could be on Will's arm instead. That would certainly raise eyebrows at this club. "Hey, I know one of the guys in the band," whispered Russel. 'That's Mike on the electric piano."

They *were* in white dinner jackets. Mike Somebody. She thought maybe he was a student at Edison. "There's Debbie Walker," she said to Angelica. Debbie, as Angelica, had gone off somewhere for her high school years.

"We hate her, right?"

"Absolutely."

A few couples, older all, were on the dance floor. More had settled at tables or stood about eating and drinking. Kris's mom and dad over there, studiously avoiding impinging on her and her friends. Maybe the Summerlins weren't here yet.

"Eat or dance?" asked Russel.

"Always food first," Kris declared. "Then we can find out whether either of you knows how to dance." To Angelica she said, "I suppose you had lessons at one or another of those schools."

"Of course. We sophisty-kates are adept at all forms of dance."

"Sophisty-kates, huh? Joey got that from you, didn't she?"

"She did. The two of us have formed the official Sophisty-kate Club."

"Are boys allowed?"

She looked Mackie and Russ over. "Maybe as mascots."

"But I suppose they could never be true sophisty-kates."

"No, it's just not in them. As proven by the fact they haven't brought us any food yet."

Russ looked bewildered. Mackie laughed. "Let's all go over and see what's available," suggested Kris. She'd rather make her own choices anyway. And it was early. Not picked over yet.

"Those pants are kind of daring," she confided to Angelica as they walked across the room. "You would have been kicked out if you'd worn them to prom." Long and loose. One might have mistaken them for a skirt. Not close up, maybe. A short red jacket over a black buttonless top completed her look. Oh, and one small Christmas tree brooch pinned on her collar.

"I didn't have a prom. In Europe, remember?"

"Well, then this is your official belated prom. I'll crown you queen later."

This didn't bring the expected laugh nor even a smile. "I did miss out on a lot of that high school stuff."

She wondered if Angelica would have even participated. Like Joey, she might have turned up her nose at the whole thing, when actually confronted with it.

"I'm glad they didn't set out any Christmas dinner items," remarked Mackie. "We'll be seeing enough of those."

"No roast pig?" asked Kris. "Jelly's gonna be eating a whole roast pig tomorrow night."

"Just a pork roast, little Kris. And Joey and her family are coming over to help." She perused the buffet. "As can you, if you wish. Any or all of you."

But they'd all be with their own families on Christmas Eve. "Save some leftovers for us," said Kris. "We'd all be glad to help with those."

Or would Russel and Mackie go off their own directions now? They couldn't be expected to hang around with them the whole holiday. Why, Mackie was doing her a big favor just by being here tonight.

She wasn't sure why Russ Penn was here at all. He needn't have fallen in with Angelica's plans. "Who eats salad at a party?" she asked.

"When you're old and fat you won't need to ask that," responded Angelica.

"When I'm old and fat I won't care. I'll eat anything and lots of it!"

This was no serve-yourself buffet. There were waiters on hand to dish out whatever they desired. It made her feel a bit like being in line at a school cafeteria.

Without the Sloppy Joes. Another thing Angelica had undoubtedly missed out on. Debbie Walker too. "I don't suppose we could get anyone to serve us liquor," said Angelica. "A true sophisty-kate needs a martini glass in her hand."

"It doesn't have to have a martini in it," Russ pointed out.

"Quite true! Your *are* useful."

Russ was all about being useful. Even his sister had joked about it. "That sort of thing they can fetch us. Bring me a tonic, will you? Let's claim a table, Jel."

The guys followed them, carrying all four plates. She wondered if either young man knew enough to order something for them. Not that she did, herself.

"Here," said Angelica, seating herself. "Close to the dance floor." A handful of couples were shuffling about. Kris couldn't recognize the tune. Definitely from before her time.

Russ and Mackie set their plates down. "What would you like from the bar, Angelica?" asked Russ. "A tonic in a martini glass?"

"Make it a Cuba Libre, without the rum."

The boy frowned. "In other words, a Coke?"

"But with lime."

"Ah." Off the pair went.

"Foxtrot," said Angelica. "I suppose anyone can do that. Did Mackie take you to your prom? As a senior, that is."

"No, I was sort of between boyfriends." She'd broken up with Gordie by then. "I just went with the first jock who asked me. And never went out with him again. Oh, there are your parents."

Unlike the Greenes, they were entirely willing to come over to greet the girls. "You have to save a dance for me," Preston told Kris. He was as tall as Mackie. She needed to find a shorter guy for a dance or two. Even Russ—she'd have to see how he did on the dance floor first.

The band had launched into a Christmas tune. "Hey, a waltz. Ask me to dance," ordered Angelica.

Russel listened a second or two. "Isn't that a children's song?"

"So let's be kids." In a few more seconds, Angelica and Russ were on the floor. Russel Penn danced fairly well. Not graceful, but precise. Maybe a little stiff.

"Should I ask you?" said Mackie.

"Let me eat first."

Rain beat against the tall glass windows all around the dining room. It almost seemed like it was keeping time with the music for a moment, but went out of sync again. The decorating wasn't too bad. She wondered if the staff or some committee was responsible for it.

"Are you going to be bored this evening?" Kris asked him.

"Not as bored as sitting at home."

"That's honest."

"I'll always be honest, Kris. I deceived you once but never again."

"You know I don't mind that. You were doing what you needed to get by."

"Yeah." His brief moment of introspection gave way to a smile. "I do enjoy dancing with girls, you know."

"Guys are too tall, huh?"

"Something like that." Mackie might have snickered. "And they usually want to lead."

"Just maybe," replied Kris, "I should try that on the next dance."

"Here's your chance to try." He rose and extended a hand. "May I have this dance, Miss Greene?"

Never mind that she only came up to his chest. Kris could have danced all night with Harold Macklin. Her friend. The only thing better would have been for Will to have his arms around her.

Chapter Twenty-two

Joey

"What are you putting in your ears?"

"Olive oil," replied Russ, handing the little plastic bottle to Alan. "Helps protect them from the cold wind and water. You should put in a few drops too."

"I'll have to tell Mom about this. She already thinks olive oil is a cure for just about everything."

"Here." He handed Joey a rolled-up wetsuit. "It should fit you okay. Just pull it on over your swimsuit."

"Or if you want to change in the van, you can skip the suit," added Alan. "That's really better."

She didn't think so. But it was a pain stuffing her trunks inside the tight rubber legs. The top was no problem. It didn't have sleeves, only straps over her shoulders. "That's what they call a short john suit," Russ said.

"Why?"

"Because a long john has long legs." He stood in the open door and surveyed the Gulf. "Way better than we hoped."

Alan agreed. "About as good as Naples gets. Small but clean." He looked at the long surfboard Joey had tucked under her arm. "Should we help Joey with that board?"

"Nah, make her carry it the whole way herself." She didn't think Russ Wesolowski was being quite serious. Neither Wesolowski.

"Is it far?"

"Not very," he replied. "This is as close as we can park to the pass."

To this Alan added, "They make noises about closing off this parking lot. Sooner or later they will."

She could have said he was sounding like Ronnie's father. Maybe it was common among longtime Naples residents. She felt like the place was being ruined herself, sometimes.

"I'll carry your board," Alan went on. "You take mine. It's six or seven pounds lighter."

"And probably the one you should be learning to ride on," said Russ.

Alan nodded to this. He probably wasn't completely happy about relinquishing his ride to her. North along the beach they went, boards under their arms. Alan's 'Hot Curl' was lighter than the big board Russ had sold her in the summer. Or thrown in, basically, when she bought his old car.

All condos along the beach between the parking lot and Doctor's Pass. Sea walls rose to their right, concrete in some places, piled boulders in others. She could see the long jetty at the pass, not too far ahead. Smaller rock groins extended into the water here and there.

"We sometimes surf along one of these," said Russ. "Depends on the tides and waves. At high tide the waves sometimes backwash off this seawall here—" He gestured toward the one they were passing beneath. It was set very close to the high tide mark. Too close, Joey was pretty sure. "And make for a nifty little peak when everything else is kind of shitty."

"Lots of moss washed up," commented Alan. "In the water too." The rusty-red moss was thick on the beach and in the shallow water, being tossed by the foam of the broken waves. The waves weren't very big. 'Clean' the Wezzies had called them and she could see the description fit. They looked almost as if they were made of glass.

"The jetty and the apartment building will keep the wind off of us some. Northeast, you think?" asked Russ.

"East-northeast maybe," felt Alan. "Not that strong anyway. Looks best here by the first jetty. What we've always called 'first jetty.' If it were bigger we'd paddle out up closer to the pass."

"Yes," agreed Russ. "There's a bar over there they'd be breaking on." He pointed further out along the long rock jetty that hid Doctor's Pass from them. The beach curved toward it.

"We would hope. It doesn't always work out!"

"Depends on the tide too."

"There's no one else here," said Joey. "Doesn't anyone else know about this place?"

"A few. Most guys don't bother to walk in and just go to the pier."

"Or maybe Third Avenue. It works now and again."

"Not consistently. You like to hang out there, don't you?"

"Yeah. It's been where me and my friends have met for years." Since they were little kids and first allowed to ride their bikes to the beach.

"We even walk down to Gordon Pass sometimes," added Alan. "That's like a mile from the nearest access."

"But if you're willing to walk, it can be the best spot of all. Better if you have a boat! You bring cold water wax?"

"Yeah. Paraffin would be too slippery," Alan explained. "It gets hard in cold water."

"Works great in the summer. And it's cheap!" The boys applied coats of sticky wax liberally to the tops of all three boards. "You take my board out, Joey. I'll ride the old square-ender."

Russ's board looked about the same size as Alan's. A good foot and a half shorter than the older board. But it had a wide squared off tail where Alan's was rounded. There were undoubtedly all sorts of other differences she couldn't recognize. The three of them waded out to about waist depth. "You could just push off the bottom to catch the smaller waves," Russ told her. "No need to paddle at all."

"Like this one here. Go for it!"

Push? Okay. She launched herself into the little wave. Hey, she'd caught it! Joey only made it to her knees before it fizzled out beneath her. "Next time I stand up," she declared.

"Do it in one motion," Alan told her. "Don't kneel, just pop up."

And she did. Actually surfing at last, after having a board for half a year. "I'll have to try out the other boards too."

"You won't like them as well," promised Russ. "I'm not even that fond of this board I'm riding. It may just be replaced before the holiday is over."

"What's wrong with it?"

"Just a mismatch for me and the sort of waves I'm likely to ride. I want to go shorter, anyway." Russ peered toward the shore. There was enough morning sun peeking over the condos that he had to shield his eyes with his palm. "Is that a camera I spy?"

"Gordie." Joey recognized him at once. "Here Alan. I'll let you play with your own board a while and go talk to him." She switched to the old long board and half-paddled, half-surfed in to the beach.

"Where's your board?" she greeted him.

"Wasn't expecting any waves," the boy admitted. "I just noticed Russ's van when I drove by so I came to check things out." He gave her an up-and-down and drawled, "Wasn't expecting a surfer girl either."

"It's my first day on the job! I'm just a probationary surfer girl."

"Ooh." Gordie had raised his camera and was following a ride. Russ, sliding south. The wave was small but breaking perfectly from left to right. Right to left from where she was standing but surfers figured it from a water perspective. He was tucked tightly into the breaking part. The curl, they called it, right? Oh, that's what the model name of Alan's board meant. She should have figured that out.

She'd heard the motor drive run. He'd taken at least two or three shots. "Cold out there?" Gordie asked.

"Kind of. I may need my own wetsuit if I keep it up. A long john." Wasn't that what the Wezzies called it? Darn, was she going to think of them as the Wezzies from now on? She had Rick to thank for that.

"Sleeves are nice too when the wind comes up. Alan's up." He raised the camera but lowered it without taking a shot. "Alan pushes too hard. It makes him mess up sometimes."

Better than not pushing hard enough, thought Joey. But sometimes neither worked. Sometimes nothing worked. "There was an epic swell on Christmas two years ago," Gordie went on. "Everyone who could hit the east coast."

Alan was coming in. "Is Russ still riding that Frye he bought last summer?" Gordie called to him.

"Yep. He has a new board on order." Alan placed his own board on the sand and pulled out a bar of wax. "I'll replace this one soon. Maybe I'll get a blank and build my own."

"Aw, you two with your short, cutting-edge boards. And I'm still riding my old nine-eight."

"Nothing wrong with that," felt Alan, "if you enjoy it. Like the Duke said, the best surfer is the one having the most fun."

Joey knew he meant the Hawaiian surfer and swimmer, not John Wayne. She ought to learn more about surfing; in fact, she decided, she would research it and write an article. It could be fun. But not until she was back in school!

"You going back out, Joey?"

"Oh, sure. And Gordie has to take lots of pictures of me falling off."

"I'll bet you do it very well. Oh, I was going to let everyone know about it later but I'm going to throw a party at my place on Friday. Afternoon, evening. All invited."

"That's the Twenty-seventh, right?" asked Alan.

"I think so! Today's Tuesday? Christmas Eve." Gordie counted the days on his fingers. "Yep, the Twenty-seventh."

"Okay. Thanks for the invite."

He started back toward the water. Joey grabbed her board—the long one—and followed him. "Russ and I might be on a surf trip then," Alan told her. "I'll see how it goes."

"I'm not sure I'd want to go myself," she admitted. "I'm not thinking beyond tonight's party right now!"

"At the Summerlins. That sounds pretty cool." He climbed onto his board and began paddling. Joey wondered if she could paddle up on her knees, the way he had shown her and her friends in the summer. Alan didn't seem to do that on the shorter board. Neither did his brother.

"It sounds good. How it will actually turn out is anyone's guess. Now, it is time for me to make good on my promise to wipe out for the camera." She pushed into a little wave and the nose of the board dug into the water, spilling her ungracefully.

"Always a problem with that board," commented Russ.

"Yeah, yeah, I know. Give me yours back, Alan."

He exchange boards without comment. Alan was a good guy, wasn't he? Oh, here came a nice one.

She managed to not only to get to her feet but to ride all the way to the beach. Next she had to learn how to turn the thing!

Chapter Twenty-three
Ronnie

"You don't go to any services?" asked Paulette.

"My family isn't religious. We don't belong to a church." She was not going to volunteer that her father was an atheist.

But her friend brought up the subject. "Are you an atheist?"

Ronnie felt she could answer this. She had been reading, investigating. James Summerlin certainly had a role in awakening her interest, but she had already been seeking, hadn't she? "It depends on whether one defines an atheist as someone who doesn't believe there is a god or as someone who believes there is no god."

Paulette frowned, trying to puzzle that out. A nod. "You're the first kind?" She sounded hopeful about it.

"Right. I don't believe, I don't disbelieve. That's why I'm more inclined to call myself an agnostic. I'm afraid my dad is the second kind." Afraid was undoubtedly the wrong word. No matter. She smiled and added, "But it doesn't prevent him from celebrating Christmas!"

"Well that's good. Anyway, the invitation stands. Tonight, tomorrow. We'd be happy to see you at our church."

"Carter would like to see you too," added Jackie Booth. Neither of the other girls quite knew how to respond to that. "Hey, we need to get going. Mom will want her car. She's on shift tonight."

Jacqueline served as Paulette's chauffeur today. "Shift?" Ronnie had no idea what sort of work Missus Booth did. Will and Jackie's father was a house painter; that Kris had told her.

"At the hospital. She's a nurse, you know." Ronnie's expression must have betrayed her ignorance. "Oh, you don't know. That's why Willie decided to become a medic. That's what I think, anyway!"

"Alright, Jackie, I'm ready to go," said Paulette. "Hey, tell Rick he's welcome, too. My brother might be more interested in seeing him." The trio walked out into the sunshine. It was quite a lovely, clear day, and only a tad cool. A modest breeze stirred the trees.

"I think we'll both want to spend the time here with our family."

"It's important to be with your family," allowed Paulette, climbing into the passenger side of the dark blue sedan, "but remember you have a family in Christ too!"

Ronnie watched them back out, drive west. It wasn't really that far from her home to where the two lived. They did live close together, didn't they? She knew the Booths lived on the waterfront but wasn't sure how near it was to the Jones's modest house. They were on opposite sides of Goodlette.

One could walk the distance easily enough, anyway. Was it wrong of her to think she wouldn't want to walk through some of those neighborhoods over off Goodlette Road? Black neighborhoods. Oh, bad stuff could happen anywhere. Her experience in Miami this past summer had shown her that.

All that was as it was. Ronnie had enjoyed going to Paulette's church well enough but it didn't really move her. Not the way attending mass with James Summerlin had. Mass was, well, beautiful. Everything meant something.

Maybe she could go to the Catholic mass tomorrow. Or this evening. Not at midnight but the vigil? Oh, forget it. Too hard to fit in.

James. Yes, he'd helped her with her curiosity about religion, about meaning. Among other things! So had Alan, hadn't he? He sought meaning too, in other places. Those fantasy novels he loved. Even his surfing was a sort of quest.

All too much to think about right now. She would just enjoy the holiday, what remained of it. Thinking could wait till she was back in college.

Chapter Twenty-four
Joey

"I think your mom is actually teaching mine how to cook," whispered Angelica. "No one has succeeded at that before."

Outside of helping Maria Summerlin get the pork roast out of the oven and heat up the various treats purchased at a Cuban grocery, there hadn't been much real cooking. The exception was the fritters they were frying, one of her mother's Italian recipes but apparently not much different from the Cuban *croquetas*. These joined the other food arrayed on the dining table. Black beans and rice, which Maria called *Moros y Christianos*, were fragrant of bay leaf, and of onion and garlic and bacon. Some sort of stew made with eggplant and tomato didn't look quite appetizing to Joey but tasted amazing. Fried plantains. Avocado slices with lime.

And loads of deserts, cakes and cookies and confections, both of Cuban and Italian heritage. It was not always easy to say which was which. They all filled their festively-patterned plates, emblazoned with Christmas trees and garlands and Santas. Then they refilled them! They ate in the living room, around the tall tree, ablaze with lights and with a great golden star at its top, parents in the easy chairs or on the couch, Joey and Angelica cross-legged on the floor.

"We should get there early," said Teresa Planter. "It is always crowded and the choir will sing before mass."

"And dress warmly!" added Maria. "I begin to doubt walking is a good idea."

Angelica scoffed. "Oh, Mom, it's not that far. And not that cold! Joey was out surfing this morning."

"My daughter did not inherit her insanity from me," stated Teresa.

"I blame Preston for my own children's quirks," Maria replied.

Preston Summerlin raised his glass in an amiable salute. "Feel free, my love."

"Don't forget our grandfather," added Angelica.

That grandfather, Conrad Summerlin, nodded just as agreeably as his son. Joey had never seen the elder Summerlin in the house before. He lived alone somewhere over near the bay. Chances were she'd ridden her bike past the house without knowing.

"I do love your home," said Joey's mother. "You've been here a long time, haven't you? Even longer than I've been in my little place."

"Yes, Teri. I stayed here sometimes with my first husband but did not move in permanently until he died. I had nowhere else to go." Forty-seven was the year Enrique Salas was murdered in Cuba. Joey was fairly certain of that. Lin would have been three? Something like that.

"And then Maria came by my law office one day and made the acquaintance of Preston," said Conrad.

"Yes, I met this young lawyer fresh from school and talked him into talking me into marrying him." She gave the lanky lawyer an indulgent smile. "I was the older woman, you know!"

"Only by two years," interjected Preston.

But far wiser, far more mature, at the time, suspected Joey. And far richer. That was not to be forgotten.

"We're past Eleven," said Maria. "Let's get our wraps and start."

A couple minutes later, the four women were ready to go out into the dark. Yes, into the cold too. The three men looked way too comfortable in their arm chairs with their glasses of booze. Joey thought maybe she'd prefer sitting there with them. Even without any liquor.

"Don't get my husband too drunk," warned her mother. "He has to drive me home."

Wayne waved an arm somewhere in her direction. "Oh, Joey can do that."

"And figured I would all along," she said. "Let's go." It wasn't bad at all out. The wind had died to almost nothing and a clear dark sky was thick with stars. It was a good look for Christmas Eve, Joey decided. Her compliments to the designer!

It was three blocks—or two and a half, strictly—east to Third Street. There they turned to see Saint Ann Church rise just a short distance further along. Light spilled from the tall windows and open doors, and the street was already lined with cars. A creche stood in the yard beneath one of the ficus trees. Organ music came from inside. 'The First Noel.'

They stood there a moment, pausing on the sidewalk, taking it in. "Do you think there will be room for another in your pew?"

"James!" His mother threw her arms around him. "How are you here?"

"Plane to Miami, bus to Naples, feet from the bus station. I wasn't expecting all of you here. I just intended to pop in a moment before going over to the house." He looked at Joey's mother. "Missus Planter, isn't it?"

"Yes, um, James." She clearly wasn't quite sure what to call the boy. None of the other Summerlins had intimidated her but this incipient priest seemed to have a different effect. Maybe Joey had talked him up too much!

"Dummy," said Angelica. "If you'd called I would have come get you at the station on the scooter."

"It's a nice night for walking. For thinking, too."

"But you missed out on our celebration," his mother told him, smiling and crying at once.

"There's plenty of food left," said Joey. "The guys can't eat it all."

"They're probably asleep," felt Angelica.

Maria looked her son over before again embracing him. "Now my *Noche Buena* is perfect."

Joey couldn't help seeing the face his sister made.

Chapter Twenty-five

Kris

"Jam! It's true!"

"I take it there have been rumors?"

"Joey called me. I rode over here as soon as was seemly."

He took in Kris and her ride in one nonchalant appraisal. "On a new bike?"

"Yep! Ain't it nifty?"

"Decidedly nifty. A groovy set of wheels." He smirked a bit when he said that.

"You don't do that at all well," Kris told him. "It doesn't sound natural coming from you."

"It isn't natural. Alas, I'll never be a man of the people. Twenty-four inch?"

It took her a moment to realize he meant the bike. "Yep. A three speed like yours. I'm not used to the hand brakes yet. I keep wanting to peddle backwards!"

"A Christmas present, I assume. I took my parents by surprise and they didn't have anything for me." She couldn't tell how he felt about this. "Come on in."

"We didn't get you anything either."

"Meaning your triumvirate?" The house seemed quiet inside. Any Christmas morning activity had subsided but the tree shone in all its glory. Kris's parents wouldn't leave the lights on all day like that. Closed doors surely meant Preston Summerlin was in the library.

"Right. We have a present for Jelly. Joey's going to be bringing it over later."

"Then we can expect all three of you. Soon?"

Kris could only shrug. "Sooner or later. I already spoke to Will this morning so I didn't need to hang around the house any longer."

"He's well?" It only took a nod for James to continue. "I'm sorry I didn't wait for his farewell party."

"We were peeved with you. We also knew why you took off." There was a look of surprise. "Not that we heard anything from Ronnie. Your sister filled us in." Damn it, Jam should know, shouldn't he? She didn't regret having blabbed it.

"I won't ask how she knew. And best I not say anything to her. Angelica, that is. Ronnie—" He shook his head. "I don't know."

"She's not likely to say anything about it either."

"No, I suppose not. Want some leftover Cuban Christmas food? There's some, um, left over."

"Won't there be a Christmas dinner?"

"Not after the feast last night. Plus Missus Cooper has the day off." The boy grinned at her. "Maybe we'll order Chinese takeout."

"I'll have you know that's a cliché and a stereotype, Mister Summerlin." Her family had never eaten Chinese food on Christmas! In fact, there was a turkey in the oven right now.

The phone behind him, by the stairs, rang. It had already stopped when James turned. "Dad must have got it," he said.

A minute later, Preston Summerlin emerged from his library. "Angelica! Maria!" he called at the foot of the stairs. "You'd better get down here!"

Both women, the younger and the older, had knowing smiles as they descended. Kris was baffled. She gave James a sidelong look. He didn't know what was up either, did he?

Jelly mouthed the word 'car' to them. Aha!

Maria Summerlin peeped out a front window and shook her head.

"Soon," said Preston. "Already on the way."

It seemed to be an open secret. Would Jelly get the van she had been hinting she wanted?

Maria took a seat and informed her daughter, "We considered passing the Electra along to you."

"Your mother did. I couldn't see any girl your age wanting a big used station wagon."

Angelica perched on the arm of the sofa. "It would be handy if I took up double bass."

"Yes," said Maria Summerlin. "A musician needs something with room. And something that can be locked up safely. No convertibles!"

"Which shot down my sports car ideas."

"Oh? I could have had street races with Debbie Walker's MG!"

"She in town?" mumbled James. Kris nodded. No one else paid him any attention.

"Of course, we would have preferred to go to the Buick and Cadillac dealer," Mister Summerlin went on. "Skylarks seem like nice cars."

"I'm sure they are," ventured Angelica. She wasn't about to acknowledge her dad's teasing.

A horn honked. Kris didn't doubt that Angelica was ready to jump up and rush outside. Who wouldn't?

"Shall we see what that's about?" asked Preston.

Oh, get to it! These Summerlins were frustrating her with their playing it cool.

"Pretty good idea," said Angelica. She stepped out onto the small front porch when her father opened the door for her.

Kris and James immediately crowded in behind her parents. Red! A Volkswagen but not the desired van.

"A Squareback," said Angelica, walking toward the new car. They all followed behind.

"Yes," said Maria. "We looked at the buses at the dealership but they were so spartan. And the driver sits so far forward!"

"It did seem a bit dangerous," her father said.

"Then we saw this and knew it was just perfect."

"Maybe it is," agreed Angelica. "Maybe it's just what I wanted and didn't know. Oh, thank you!" She hugged mother and father in turn before slipping behind the wheel. Her grin certainly indicated she was not disappointed in their choice.

Kris whispered to James, "See what you've missed out on by not getting a driver's license?"

"I've missed out on complicating my life with things I don't need."

She wasn't sure he completely meant that. Maybe he did at the moment. "Who gets the first ride?" called Angelica. "Mom? Dad?"

"We already test drove it, dear," Missus Summerlin told her.

"Then come on, Kris. You too, James, but you ride in back."

There were no rear doors on the sides. James slid in behind the front seat. "It might have been easier to come in the rear hatch," he commented. "There is quite a lot of space back there."

"Not as much Mom's wagon," replied Angelica, settling behind the wheel.

"Nor Alan's. I don't think you would slide a surfboard in here."

"I hear they're getting shorter all the time. Now—" She turned the key, bringing the engine to life. It sounded very much like the one in Kris's Beetle, but more muffled. "Automatic transmission. That's nice."

"Hmmph. I don't mind shifting *my* Volkswagen," sniffed Kris.

"But shifting her bike's gears gives her some trouble," came James's voice from the back seat.

Angelica ignored them, easing away from the curb, and taking a right at the corner. "I do like it," she announced.

"Wouldn't you have liked anything?" Kris asked.

"Maybe not a Skylark. Let's cruise the pier parking lot and make all the kids jealous. And wish them a Merry Christmas, of course!"

It sounded like a pretty good idea to Kris.

Chapter Twenty-six
Ronnie

"Do you think Angelica will even want our present now?" asked Ronnie.

"She might not have anyway. Who can tell with Jelly?" Joey retrieved a box from the rear seat of the Corvair. The gift wrapping was barely perfunctory to Ronnie's eyes. She should have volunteered to do it.

Or volunteered Kris. She was better at that sort of thing. The pair stood looking over the red Volkswagen. "Someone's been driving it," said Joey. "I can feel the heat from the engine."

"It's in the back, like ours, isn't it?"

"Yep. Angelica can be another member of our Unsafe at Any Speed Gang." They crossed the lawn toward the screened-in rear porch. Ronnie didn't recognize the bicycle propped against one of the outdoor tables. A white three speed.

"Santa brought me that!" called Kris, stepping out of the house. "And you saw what he parked out front for Jelly."

"Yours is so much nicer," asserted Joey.

"I think so too! She's sooooo jealous."

"It's true," said Angelica, appearing behind her. "I really wanted a bike myself. Come on in." She eyed the box under Joey's arm but made no comment.

"So what did *you* get?" Kris asked.

James was sitting in the living room, reading. No sign of the Summerlin parents. Upstairs most likely. It was quite tidy, neither wrapping paper nor unwrapped gifts beneath the tree. Already stowed away. The Deerfield living room was a mess as, most likely, were those of her friends.

Joey said, "My folks gave me a tent. I guess I mentioned the one we borrowed from the Wesolowskis a few too many times. Either that or they want me to move out of the house."

"Be careful about letting Kris use it," warned Angelica.

The joke fell flat, no one knowing quite how to respond to it. They all knew Kris and Will had sex for the first time in the Wesolowski's tent, right there in the Summerlin's back yard. Made love—that was a better way of putting it, decided Ronnie.

As she had made love for the first time in a room just above their heads. And here was James. It was the first time she had seen him since last summer. Well, she wasn't going to make anything of it. It was what had happened and she had moved on. Yes, she'd moved on.

She broke the short silence. "I didn't get anything big. Rick gave me a black lacquer music box he bought overseas. I know it's just a bit of junk but I appreciate it anyway." Ronnie didn't feel like adding anything to that. She wasn't going to enumerate the items of clothing. Oh. "And Santa left me a portable stereo I can carry back to my dorm room." She'd missed not being able to play records.

"Do you give each other presents?" asked Angelica. Her eyes were on Joey's package again. She was seated in one of the arm chairs with it in her lap.

"Oh, we always give each other our gifts before Christmas so we can put them under the tree," Kris told her. "Nothing big. We've known each other too long for that."

"Damn, I didn't get anything for you."

"And we didn't get anything for Jam or your parents or your next door neighbors. Here." Joey handed the box over.

She tore the wrapping paper off, revealing a cardboard box from which she lifted a motorcycle helmet. It was white, with a small black front brim. Angelica at once popped it onto her head. Her long hair flowed from beneath it

Karen nodded in approval. "That's so you don't bash your brains out riding the Vespa. Even though you'll probably drive your car all the time from now on."

"Oh, no, I'll have to ride around on the scooter and show this off."

"I tried to find a red that went with your Vespa," said Joey, "but none seemed an exact match."

To this Kris added, "Just a little off and it doesn't look right. Best to go with a contrast."

"Thank you, all of you. Don't expect me to cry." But her eyes were misting. She sniffled and that seemed to be an end to it. That was a lot from Angelica. More than Ronnie had ever seen, anyway.

"These poor children aren't going to have a Christmas dinner," spoke Kris. "Maybe one of us should invite them to our house."

"Not necessarily both to the same house," Joey said.

"Kris's is closest and poshest. She should have them there," felt Ronnie. She certainly wouldn't want them to show up at her place.

"I think it's better we be with the parents," said James.

"And Granddaddy is going to come over," Angelica added to this.

Joey nodded. "He was gone when we got back from mass."

"Off into the dark in his ancient Continental. Another reason I should stay home. I haven't seen him yet."

Ronnie had never seen him in her life. She should meet the elder Summerlin sometime. Maybe if she did intern or something of that sort for Preston Summerlin in the coming summer.

Joey accepted all this. "Okay, then come over and have leftovers tomorrow."

"Or the next day," said Kris. "They're likely to last a while. Make a circuit of our houses."

"I just may," James said. Angelica made no comment.

The phone jingled. James answered. "Yes. Yes." He put his palm over the handset. "It's Lin."

"I'll get the folks," said Angelica, bounding up the stairs.

"Hi! Merry Christmas!"

"We'd better get back to our own families," Ronnie told her friends.

"Yeah," agreed Joey. "Say Merry Christmas to her for us, Jam. We'll see you later."

"For leftovers!" chimed in Kris.

He waved a goodbye as they trooped out. Home and Christmas dinner. How many more Christmases would she have with her family? With these friends? Ronnie slid into the front seat of Joey's Corvair, giving the Summerlin house a last look before riding away.

Chapter Twenty-seven
Joey

I Heard It Through The Grapevine blared from the radio, tuned to WQAM out of Miami. It was a great song but Joey was getting a little tired of hearing it. She switched it off as she pulled into her drive.

Mom's Valiant was still there. That didn't necessarily mean she was too, as she sometimes walked across the Trail to her cashier job, but Joey knew she had a later shift today. Of course, Wayne had gone back to work.

And there was a bicycle halfway inside the carport, leaning against the wall. A black bicycle. James must have gotten it out, though the last time Joey had seen the bike, Angelica had been riding it. She doubted that was so today.

She entered the kitchen through the door from the carport. Sure enough, James and her mom sat at the dining table, James drinking coffee. Mom wouldn't do that this close to heading off to work. Restroom breaks tended to be few. Damn, she should have a better job than checking out people's groceries.

"Done with work?" asked Mom.

"For today. I'm going to have extra shifts at the clinic. Russ and Alan are taking off for a few days. Surf trip. So I can go clean kennels every morning." Or afternoon, if she preferred. Mister and Missus Wesolowski didn't much care which schedule she chose. Doctor and Doctor Wesolowski, maybe she should say, though they had told her to use their first names.

"Then we can goof off the rest of the day," said James. "And you can feed me Christmas dinner leftovers. As promised!"

"Cold mashed potatoes?"

"Only if there is a slab of cold gravy to top them."

"I can manage that. What are you two talking about?" Joey poked her head into the fridge. She was pretty ravenous herself.

"Catching up on old times," said Teresa Planter. "Until Christmas Eve, I hadn't laid eyes on this boy since you went to the same school."

Why not the mashed potatoes? Joey pulled the bowl out of the refrigerator, along with a carton of eggs. A skillet. Put that on the range to heat up. "He's at church sometimes," she said. At once, she thought maybe shouldn't have brought that up.

"I don't get to church much. Maybe I should but I—I don't feel welcome since my divorce and marrying Wayne."

"You'll always be welcome, even if you're not supposed to receive communion." James became quite serious. "I have little doubt you can get the first marriage annulled, going by what I've heard." He glanced toward Joey. He hadn't heard it from her!

"But that won't make Joey—" Her mother's voice dropped to a whisper. "Illegitimate, will it?"

Joey managed to keep a straight face. So did James but she didn't know if it was as much of a struggle for him. "A misconception. The validity of the marriage has nothing to do with the legality of it." That could have been the end of it but after a pause he added, "Your priest should be able to tell you all this. I'll talk to Father Al if you'd like."

"Well—okay. I'd appreciate that James. Oh, I need to get moving. You feed him well, Joey." Teresa gathered her purse and headed out the door.

She probably felt safe leaving her in the company of a boy who intended to enter the priesthood. If she knew more about James, she might change her mind. "I'm going to fry potato cakes," Joey informed her guest, as she poured a little olive oil into her pan. "Want some?"

"Whatever, Joey. Just set what you want in front of me."

A good idea. She removed a tray of sliced turkey meat from the fridge and set it in the middle of the table. "We can have some of that too. There's bread if you'd like a sandwich. But no fresh mayo." Joey wasn't about to make any right now and her mom wouldn't tolerate the store-bought stuff in the house. Joey didn't care for it herself.

Wayne never expressed an opinion one way or the other. She mixed eggs and bread crumbs with the leftover mashed potatoes, formed firm patties with her hands, and dropped them into the hot skillet.

"That smells good," said James, nibbling on a bit of white meat. Then, "My mom likes your mom. They'd met before, of course, when we were both going to Saint Ann School, but they didn't get to know each other then. I had the impression your mother was a little reluctant to, ah, hobnob with the more well-to-do parents."

"I suppose so. Darn, that one's sticking." She ran the spatula under the potato cake, loosened it, turned it. "I didn't lose enough to matter. So, you think our moms are gonna be besties now?"

"Stranger things have happened. Alan's going out of town?"

"Yeah. Russ will be picking up his new custom board so the two decided to take a couple days. It's at some shop in Indialantic."

"You could have gone with them, now you have your very own tent."

"But who would give tender loving care to the little doggies?"

"You like your job, then." A statement.

"I never expected to admit it but yeah, I kind of do. There's a—I don't know, maybe a sense of purpose I didn't feel working for Mister Deerfield. I'm doing something that is actually useful." That didn't express it right at all, did it? Not the way she wanted it to.

"I think we'd all like to feel that, Joey. Those done?"

"They are." She slid a couple patties onto each of two plates. "Next time, it's your house. You have to make me *pan perdu* again." She grinned at the boy. "Then you really can feel useful."

"I'll try." He ate in silence for a while. "I understand you know about me and Ronnie."

Oh, no. He shouldn't bring that up! Joey only nodded her head. She didn't want to encourage more from him. But, of course, more would come. He was James. He would talk about things.

"I'm not sure whether to say anything to her."

"She'll never say anything to you."

He frowned. "That's what Kris said too."

"But that doesn't mean you shouldn't. And don't avoid her!"

"You're right. I won't. Thanks, Joey."

"Is that the real reason you came over? I'll bet it wasn't my cooking at all!"

"Or maybe I just didn't know what to do with myself."

"I know the feeling, Jam. I know it well. Hey, leave some turkey for me!"

Chapter Twenty-eight
Kris

"I am thinking of getting myself a tape recorder," Angelica announced. "To have here in Naples. I can use a machine at the university when I'm there."

"They have a good studio at Miami, don't they?" asked Alan. "I've heard you can get a degree in recording or music industry or whatever they call it."

"And the one there is free for you to use," said Kris. "Aren't tape machines expensive?"

"Not exactly free. Our parents are paying tuition! But a basic two track recorder isn't at all costly."

For you, maybe, thought Kris. More expensive than her art supplies and those were high enough. "We need Jam to show up and play that pretty guitar of his," she said.

"It's somewhere around the place. He didn't take it to Boston. But I don't know where my brother is. He went riding on his bike but didn't tell me where." She flung her arms wide dramatically. "All my family has deserted me today. Mom at the club and Daddy at his office."

"*My* brother said he'd bring his guitar," spoke up Sandy, the fourth of the group. She had buzzed over earlier on her Solex moped. "It's not very good though." She giggled. "I guess Russ isn't very good."

"Then maybe you should learn to play," suggested Angelica.

"I'd like to!"

And she'd love to have Angelica as her teacher. Kris could see the girl still had some sort of crush on her, despite the three months apart. Undoubtedly, Angelica saw it too.

"I play clarinet in band," Sandy continued. "I read music and all that."

"That's a start. Here comes the birthday brother." Russ's van was turning around at the beach end of the street. He pulled the VW in along the curb in front of the Summerlin house. It was surprising there wasn't more of a crowd on a nice day like this. Nice enough for them to be sitting outside.

He emerged, toting a guitar case. "Happy Birthday," called Kris, waving.

Angelica waited until he joined them before offering her own birthday wishes. "What's in the case?"

He laid it on the table and unsnapped the lid. "A Fender. I bought it used from a guy who liked its look but lost interest. It doesn't really sound very good. Not nearly as good as Daryl's Epiphone."

"Oh, is Daryl home?" asked Kris, not that she cared much. Ronnie's ex-boyfriend, though calling him boyfriend might be an exaggeration. Casual dating in high school, nothing like what she had later with Alan.

"Yeah." Russ didn't seem too interested in the subject. He strummed experimentally across the strings, turned one tuner, then another.

"Close enough," felt Alan. "You know this one?" He launched into Donovan's *Colours*.

Russ listened. "In D? I've never played it but the chords are simple, aren't they?"

"The simplest. Like me!" said Alan before going into the second verse.

The two went on to play a Dylan song. "How about Paul Simon?" asked Russ.

Alan wrinkled his nose in distaste. "His stuff feels frightfully juvenile to me."

"Juvenile?" Russel seemed unsure how to respond.

"Naive."

"I like Simon and Garfunkel," protested Kris.

"And I agree with Alan," replied Angelica. "High school stuff that thinks it sounds sophisticated but is the really the same old banalities."

Sandy looked like she might want to put in her opinion but decided against it.

Russ only shrugged. Angelica gave him a long look and said, "I think I'll go retrieve my own guitar. Come with me, Russel."

He looked a little surprised by the request but followed the girl into the house.

"What's wrong with high school?" asked Sandy.

Kris felt like laughing at the question, or at least the way it was put. So like Sandy. She kept a straight face and told her, "Alan hated school. All school." Both Ronnie and Joey had reported this to her. It sounded silly put that way, didn't it? Almost enough to make her again feel like laughing.

"Maybe if he'd participated he'd have felt differently!"

"I was there against my will. Why should I cooperate with my jailers?" Kris didn't think she'd ever seen Alan so serious and so—so *vehement*.

"Gosh." For once Sandy Penn was without words. She'd probably find some by and by.

Alan strummed the chords to some song she didn't recognize. Possibly country. He might have been singing something under his breath, whispering some lyric just for himself.

"What's keeping them?" asked Sandy, jumping up. "I'll go get them to hurry." She bounced into the house.

A minute later she ran out, her face contorted. Alan stopped playing, mid-strum.

"What's wrong?" asked Kris, coming to her feet.

Not a word. She rushed on to her scooter, mounted it and tried to start the motor. It balked. Sandy started crying and tried again. There. It caught and she sped away, as fast as the little motor bike permitted.

A few seconds later, Russ Penn emerged from the house, his face bright red. "I—I think I should be on my way." He gathered his guitar case and marched straight to the van. A minute later he was gone too.

Alan picked a few tentative notes and then put his guitar back in its case. "Do you want me to hang around?" he asked, after a while. "Or, um, get out of the way."

"There's no need to go," she told him. "We don't know what happened."

"We can guess."

"Yeah." And here came Angelica, casually sauntering out of the house.

She set her own guitar case down next to Alan's. "It looks like our other player fled," she remarked.

"And his sister," said Alan. His voice was even, matter-of-fact. "She didn't look happy."

"She walked in as I was giving Russel a birthday present. And I didn't even get to finish." Angelica snickered. "And neither did he."

"Oh, Jel. Not Russ." Just when she thought she could trust Angelica. Just when she seemed to have become responsible.

Angelica only shrugged. "It happened. And I can tell you Russel did not object at all." She might have smirked a little. "Well, maybe at first."

Alan pretended he wasn't there. Maybe he wasn't. He was good at distancing himself from things.

The Summerlin girl looked from the one to the other, and frowned. "The party's over isn't it? I guess I took all the fun out of it. Ah, I'm such an idiot." She sank into one of the lawn chairs. "Just go, won't you?"

It seemed best to do as she asked. She walked her bike beside Alan as he carried his guitar to his station wagon. "Are you okay?" he asked.

"Yeah. But frustrated with Angelica. How about you?"

He paused for a moment, perhaps hesitant to say what was on his mind. "Honestly, I think the look on Russ's face was about the funniest damn thing I've ever seen. But Sandy—" He shook his head.

"It was a bit funny, wasn't it? Russ will get himself back on an even keel. He's good at that." Sandy was another matter. They could only wait and see. "Are you going to Gordie's party tomorrow?"

"Nope. My brother and I are leaving first thing in the morning. We plan to be gone three days."

"Surfing?"

"Of course. I'll see you all before the new year comes along." He got into his ride and drove away.

Soon everyone would be driving away again, back to college, back to the world outside their little bubble here in Naples. Christmas vacation was half over. It wasn't long enough to recapture what they had once had, she and her friends. They would never again have enough time for that.

Kris Greene got onto her new bicycle and pedaled home.

Chapter Twenty-nine
Ronnie

"What is that racket?" asked Patty Deerfield. She went to the big picture window in the living room. "Oh, it's your friend on her motor scooter."

"Sandy?" She might want to talk more with Rick.

"No, the Summerlin girl. Angelica."

"Just in time for lunch," said Rick. "Hmm."

"You're thinking of asking her out, aren't you?"

"Thought crossed my mind." He shook his head. "Nah."

Ronnie thought maybe her brother underestimated himself. She went out to greet her guest. The morning was overcast and the air almost still. "Hi, Angelica. What brings you by?"

"Oh, everyone but me is going to Gordie's party this afternoon. Then I thought, why, Ronnie isn't going either. We could hang out!"

"In other words, I'm your last resort. Well, come on in." Through the screened-in carport and into the living room they went.

"It's so airy in your house," said Angelica. "Open. Hi, Missus Deerfield. Rick."

"My father would like to hear you say that. Dad claimed he was taking this week off but he went to his office anyway."

Rick gave her a quick glance but didn't say anything, turning his attention back to his lunch. What did that look mean? There was no time now to puzzle out what was going on in her brother's head.

"Chili?" asked Angelica. "And salad. That's an interesting choice for lunch."

"And one that's good for me," asserted Rick. "Roughage is important. A healthy body includes a healthy bowel."

"Eat too much of that and you'll be doing a different sort of running in the mornings," Ronnie told him, and immediately felt embarrassed. These were the sorts of exchanges she and Rick had always had, but only when they were around family. Angelica was barely a friend. Not a close one, anyway.

But Rick had brought up the subject. Blame him!

"I like healthy people," was Angelica's only comment. It could be taken all sorts of ways, couldn't it? Especially by Rick.

That was probably her intention. There were always nuances with Angelica. "Should I fix you some chili too, then?" Ronnie asked.

"No thanks. Let's go get something unhealthy and then ride around. It's a good day for it."

Why not? She was as much at loose ends as Angelica. "Okay. Oh, so I have to perch on the rear of the Vespa again?"

"Yep. I'd take Rick too but there's not enough room."

"I suspect my extra weight would slow you down too much. My sister has told me how you like to speed."

"It's true! Maybe I can give you a ride some other day. Are you going to be in Naples much longer?"

"I have to report in Jax by Five PM on the Second. Thursday."

"Oh, so soon! At least you'll be here for New Year's Eve."

"But I'll be on a bus on New Year's day."

"Then we need to give you a big sendoff! I am going to try to put something together for New Year's Eve at our place. Just for friends but I'm willing to include you!"

"Um, thanks?"

"Don't mention it. It's only because I like Ronnie." Angelica turned to her. "Of course, you're coming too."

Ronnie nodded. She probably would. "Did you just come up with this idea?" she asked.

"Not entirely. There will be a party at the country club but I don't want to go. One holiday affair with my parents' crowd was enough! So it's been in the back of my mind for a day or three. Ready to head out?"

"Sure. Let me grab a bag." Ronnie went to her room for her everyday purse. Not so everyday lately; she'd rarely carried much of anything with her. Best she have something today. She hung it over her shoulder. No, best put the strap over her neck. It wouldn't do to have it flying off while she was on the back of the scooter.

Angelica was already outside when she came out, putting on the helmet they had given her. Maybe she needed one too! "Any place special you have in mind?" asked Ronnie.

"Not really. Someplace to eat first." She straddled the Vespa but didn't start it. "Have you been hanging around with Donna at college?"

"Donna?" Ronnie had no idea whom she meant.

"Donna Forrester. Her cute boyfriend, too, whatshisname."

The couple who had accompanied them to Miami. And sort of rescued her. "Mike. No, I haven't seen either one. They're a couple years ahead of me."

"Oh. If you're serious about being a lawyer someday, you should probably network."

That sounded like the sort of thing her mom would say. "I'm networking with one attorney's daughter."

"Ha! True, though I guess I'm not going into law now. Daddy knows Ben Forrester, of course. We could swing past his house and say hi to Donna."

"Do you know where it is?"

"Haven't the slightest!"

Both laughed. "Some other time then." She *should* look up Donna when she got back to Gainesville. Or even here. And be friendly with Paulette. When were they going to head back? They should get together soon.

Oh, don't start fretting about that, she told herself. There were still a couple weeks of break.

Angelica started off, slowly enough they could converse. "The DQ is the closest place," suggested Ronnie.

"Isn't there a burger place up the highway a bit? I know you and your friends hang there sometimes." Angelica turned north at the first intersection. "Hung, I should say. That was a high school thing, I suppose."

"Sure. *Chris's*. It's pretty good." And not one of those chains. Ronnie disliked those. They didn't belong in Naples. Or maybe not anywhere!

"Okay." Angelica took a right onto Seventh and then left at the highway. They pulled into *Chris's Gourmet Castle* a couple minutes later. It wasn't crowded at all, a mix of kids and adults. Pop tunes rose sporadically from the jukebox.

No one Ronnie recognized. It would never be same. New kids, new music. A new Naples, as the town continued to turn into something alien to her. Burgers and cokes and back out to the scooter. The skies looked darker, the clouds lower. Something of a breeze, a southerly one, was beginning to stir.

"I want to see where you went to high school," declared Angelica. "See what I missed out on!"

"Not much," Ronnie told her. "It's close, though." Shortly, they pulled off the Trail on Twenty-second and cruised east.

Angelica stopped at the Naples High School main entrance. The gate had been slid closed and locked. "Well that's a bummer," she said, peering though the chain-link barrier. "An open layout. That's kind of nice. All the schools I attended felt a bit claustrophobic. Maybe that's why I kept going AWOL!"

"We might be able to get in somewhere else," said Ronnie. "Maybe up by the football field."

"We'll see." She drove the Vespa back onto the street. The student parking lot was closed up too—but there was room enough for the scooter to get in. The gate was to keep cars out, not people. Angelica buzzed around the lot a couple times, taking everything in, and then up onto the sidewalk between the gym and auditorium. She stopped at the edge of the pavement there, the circular drive connecting to the main entrance.

"Is that a lake over there?"

"A pond. With ducks."

"Okay. That's enough." She began to turn the scooter around. "Unless there's something you'd like to visit."

"No. Nothing." Ronnie was not at all comfortable with their tres-passing. The sooner they were out of here, the better.

Back to the street. "Which way?"

"Right," Ronnie decided. The other way would take them back to the highway. They could cross it, go into the Moorings subdivision and on to the Gulf, but she wasn't going to suggest that. Doctor's Pass was over there too.

They crossed a railroad track just before intersecting with a wide roadway. "Goodlette Road," Angelica said. "All right. I know where I am!" She took a right, toward the downtown, without asking Ronnie's advice. "And there is *Caribbean Gardens*. But they call it something else now, don't they?" She slowed down, pulled left into the entrance of the attraction, and stopped there, the Vespa idling beneath them.

"African Safari," Ronnie read from the sign. 'At Caribbean Gardens' it said below the new name. "My first grade class toured it long before the name changed. It was a botanical park then."

"Oh, your elementary school is near here, isn't it? I want to see it too."

"Then go straight across Goodlette on Fleischmann." Ronnie pointed due west. Why was the Summerlin girl interested in these mundane things? There were far more interesting places around Naples.

Down Fleischmann they went. "Turn on Tenth." Angelica nodded. Then a left on Fourteenth and they were at Lake Park Elementary.

Angelica halted and looked it over. "This is where you and Kris went to grade school."

"And Joey through the fourth grade. Then she went to Saint Ann." Ronnie had been upset at the time. More than Kris. Maybe even more than Joey. She had thought it was terribly unfair to take her best friend away from her.

"And met me, poor kid. But I wouldn't know any of you if she hadn't."

Neither would James. None of last summer would have happened as it did.

"Well, no," Angelica went on. "I would know Kris, because of our fathers. But I doubt we would be friends."

"I don't think you were until recently."

"I suppose not. I'd say it was fate except I don't believe in fate." She gunned the motor and started off. "It all hinges on Joey. She lives around here, doesn't she?"

"Yeah. Just go right here."

They did, on one street and then another, curving around the lake that gave the subdivision its name, then left again. "That's the Planter house over there." Ronnie pointed to her right.

Angelica slowed down. "Not quite the hovel Joey describes it as. I think the girl is prone to exaggeration."

Ronnie had to giggle. It was very true of her friend. "Her car is there." The faded green Corvair sat in the driveway, the only vehicle to be seen. "Chances are she's gone off on her bike."

"At Gordie's party. In the company of my brother, more than likely." She started up, then throttled back. "We could drop by the party if you'd like. You know, Alan is out of town."

She hadn't known. Not that it made any difference. She wasn't avoiding Alan! "I don't mind being around him. If I let the past bother me I wouldn't be riding around with you." But James might be there. Ronnie wasn't quite so sure how she felt about that.

"Ooh. I like it when you speak your mind. You should do it more often." She started off in earnest this time. "Where to, then?"

"Doesn't matter." It didn't. Just riding around was fine.

"Where is this church you went to with Kris? Isn't it near here?"

"You'll need to get back onto Goodlette." In truth, Ronnie wasn't sure where to turn to get there. "Maybe at Seventh. Or Fifth?"

"I probably should have taken a right at that last intersection. We're circling back the way we came. Hey, I could ride down the railroad track!"

Fortunately, there was no easy way across the ditch to it. They found themselves only a little north of Joey's house again. "Go right," said Ronnie. "I can find my way there." In short order, they were on Tenth, heading south.

Angelica shot across Seventh before she could say anything. "Go left at Fifth," she told her. Fifth Avenue North. An industrial area, very different from swanky Fifth South, the heart of Naples.

They passed through and across the tracks to again come to a halt at Goodlette. "I'm not sure which way it is to the church," admitted Ronnie. "It's near." She thought it was. Maybe they should have turned on Eleventh.

"What's straight ahead?"

"Oh, that's the neighborhood where Will's family lives. I don't know quite where."

"Then let's explore." Across Goodlette she steered the scooter. It was a nice looking neighborhood. When segregation was the rule, it had been a neighborhood for relatively well-to-do black families. They went all the way to the end of Fifth, to a public park on the river. The kids there stared at them.

"I suspect they rarely see a Vespa here," commented Angelica.

"Red ones, especially."

"Hey, do you know where the Booth family lives?" Angelica called to the youngsters.

The boys appeared tongue-tied but a little girl stepped forward. "On Thirteenth, miss."

"Thank you." She spun the scooter around. "Not that I intend to drop in on them. Just curious."

As was Ronnie, she had to admit.

"Does your friend Paulette live in this neighborhood?"

"Further south." And across Goodlette.

"Okay. There was no reason to assume she did. But I did anyway, didn't I?" They turned right, to leisurely cruise up a street lined with waterfront houses. She could recognize Missus Booth's car, she thought, but she might well be at work. Mister Booth too.

At the end they turned and came back down the street. There was Jackie Booth, waving to them. "I thought I heard your scooter go by," she said, when Angelica pulled over to the street's margin. "Looking for someone?"

"Just cruising around," said Angelica. "I've never been here before. This your house?"

"It is." She giggled and said, "I thought maybe Ronnie was looking for her boyfriend!"

Angelica turned around and looked at her, an eyebrow raised. "Boyfriend? What's all this?"

Ronnie might have blushed despite herself. "She means Carter Jones."

"The Joneses live over in River Park." Jackie waved a hand in that general direction. "They aren't on the water," she said, nonchalantly adding, "but they do have a nice place."

Privileged young ladies come in all colors, Ronnie thought. She hoped she didn't come off as one! "Maybe I'll drop in on Paulette some other time. We need to schedule our trip back to college." She was pretty sure she could find the Jones house again. She wouldn't mention having misplaced the church.

Jackie nodded knowingly. "I don't think she has a whole lot of friends there. I hope you keep up with her."

"I believe I will."

"What are you up to this afternoon?" asked Angelica.

"Nothing much. I went over to visit Sandy but—she was upset about something and I didn't stay long."

Angelica grimaced. "I might have something to do with that."

Jacqueline perked up at once. She obviously wanted to know all about it. Ronnie did too. This was the first she'd heard of something happening.

No need to quiz Angelica, though. Joey or Kris would know something. They all would, soon!

"Water under the bridge, as the cliché goes," continued Angelica. "And maybe under a couple more downstream by now. Hey, you're officially invited to my New Year's Eve party."

Jackie cocked her head. "Is Sandy?"

"She is but I don't have high hopes of her coming." There might have been a touch of—what? Regret? "Nor her brother."

"Okay. Thanks."

Angelica gunned the scooter. "See you later," she said and took off, faster than made Ronnie comfortable. "I doubt she'll show up. I think I'm going to go buzz Gordie's party just for the hell of it," she announced.

Ronnie decided it was best to just hold on and let her go where she wanted.

Chapter Thirty

Joey

"Wasn't that your sister who buzzed by?"

James gave him a languorous nod. "With Ronnie riding behind her."

"Must've decided it didn't look worth stopping," Gordie said.

"You have a good crowd."

"Yeah." There was a crowd, in the back yard, around the pool, standing, sitting, dancing. "Some of them I even invited." The boy wandered off to attend to his guests or maybe just to get another beer.

"Or maybe she saw Debbie's car," said Kris.

Joey didn't know who that was. "Debbie?"

"Debbie Walker. That's her MG over there."

"An MG-B in proper British racing green," commented James. "I don't know when I last saw Debbie."

"I wouldn't know either. Joey's never met her. I really only know her from the country club but I think she attended the same school as Jelly for a while."

"Oh, right."

"One of the ones she was kicked out of?" asked Joey.

"Uh-huh. Hey, that's Mike Kelly in the band, isn't it? I saw him in the dance band at the club. At the Christmas party."

"I see him every day at Edison," Joey told her. "I hope Gordie's paying him in something other than beer."

They had wandered closer to the four man combo, cranking out popular rock tunes. "Where'd Jam go?" asked Kris. "We've lost him."

Joey surveyed the yard. "Over there. That's your Debbie he's talking to, isn't it?"

"Not mine, but yeah. When is his vow of chastity supposed to kick in, anyway?"

"Celibacy. I'll explain the difference sometime. Not until he actually is ordained, I think." It was still a sin, of course. Maybe not that big a one.

She hesitated a moment. Maybe she shouldn't. Oh, if she couldn't talk to Kris who could she talk to? "He confided to me yesterday that, uh, he had some concerns about Ronnie after they—well, about whether she was on the pill."

"What did you tell him?"

"Didn't need to tell him anything. It was obvious that she wasn't pregnant." They listened for a few seconds as the band attempted *Satisfaction*. "It's thanks to you she was using birth control."

Obtaining birth control pills could be difficult, especially for young single women. A prescription was necessary. Kris's mom had made certain she had access and she in turn had helped Ronnie when she asked. That was when she had started getting serious with Alan last summer. Things took an unexpected turn there.

"You aren't," said Kris.

Joey shook her head. She might need to look into getting the pill herself one of these days. Not yet. And the pope said she shouldn't! She might have smiled a little at that thought.

"Well, don't find yourself unprotected when it finally happens," her friend went on. "James is coming back. He must have struck out."

"Um-huh." Kris had taken a cross-legged seat on the grass and was sketching something on her pad. She carried that almost everywhere these days. Joey and James sat beside her.

"So, do you and the sports car girl have a tryst planned under the palms later tonight?" asked Joey. "Or a romantic moonlight ride?" She wasn't sure if there was much moon right now.

"It seems not. I got the impression that being Angelica's brother hurt me. Not the first time, I might inform you." He looked past her at Kris's drawing and then said, "I could tell Angelica was upset about something when we got to the house yesterday. I suppose she confided in you."

"She did and it's not something I'm going to share." Not with James. But Ronnie wouldn't be left out. Kris, of course, had already known. She'd been there when it all happened.

"Aw, I miss out on all the gossip. Our moms are probably going to start keeping secrets now."

"I don't really expect that to go far," said Joey. "Their lives are too different. Too separate. Maria will be at her country club and my mother will be, well, working."

"But you are a link. If you choose to stick around us Summerlins."

"Oh, I might. You're not such a bad bunch. Wayne got along pretty well with your father, you know. They were in the army at the same time. During the Korean War."

"Except Dad never got closer to Korea than San Francisco. He was there when Angelica and I were born." James looked to the overcast sky. "It's going to rain tonight. That definitely rules out any moonlit rides."

"And turn cold again. Only the surfers will like that."

"Aren't you one now?" asked Kris, her eyes not leaving her subject.

"I'm not sure! The Wezzies seem to have adopted me. Hey, that's good!"

Kris closed her sketch pad. "At least it's something. I need to keep at it."

"But it's vacation. Take your four weeks off. I'd like to take a year off like Jam here did!" James had graduated high school a year early and pretty much disappeared from everyone's radar.

"What did you do with that year, anyway?" asked Kris.

"This and that, here and there. I went on retreat at a monastery for a part of it. Thinking about my future, you know? Maybe even praying about it." He paused, perhaps thinking about it again. "Then I went to Europe and just wandered for a while. Busked some." A slight, bemused smile appeared. "Sought the secret of life!"

"And what is the secret of life, oh wise one?"

"If I told you it wouldn't be a secret anymore."

"Will you hit him or should I?" asked Kris.

Chapter Thirty-one
Ronnie

The rain still drizzled, with a fitful wind blowing it here and there, sometimes against one window, sometimes against another. Rick had decided to build a fire.

No one bothered with the fireplace when he wasn't there. It stood in the southeast corner of the living room, sand-colored brick, at first glance barely noticeable against the beige walls. Ronnie wished her father wasn't quite so fond of his neutral pallet. Those sandpaper-like stucco interior walls should be covered up anyway. Wood paneling. That's what they needed.

Howard Deerfield would never go for it. No matter. It might not be her home much longer. It wasn't Rick's at all anymore, not really. That didn't keep her brother from trying to rekindle the blazes he remembered from other winters.

"Some of this pine is rotting," he complained. "It should have been kept drier."

"You're cranky because it was too miserable to run this morning," Ronnie told him. She heard her dad chuckle behind his newspaper.

"So I'm trying to make it better!"

That rarely works, she almost said. It wasn't a morning for optimism. No need to make it worse, though. Rick added crumpled newspapers to the pile of kindling he had assembled, and struck a match. Fire. Maybe he could keep it burning. That would be kind of nice on a day like this.

"It's bound to get nicer later on," said Ronnie. Colder but nicer. "Are you going to run off somewhere again?"

"I have a date this evening." He sort of mumbled this.

"You got up the nerve to ask Angelica?"

That brought a chuckle. "Your friend Paulette. Umm, do you think maybe you would like to come along?"

"Me? Why?"

"So Carter could have a date too. I know you like him okay." Rick pushed some of the wood about with a poker, not looking up at her.

Ronnie certainly didn't dislike Paulette's brother. She barely knew him. Oh, why not? It was something to do. "Okay. But you're the one who has to push his wheelchair," she told him. "Now whose car do we go in?" They certainly wouldn't all fit in her Simca. Ronnie giggled at a sudden thought. "Maybe Carter Senior will drive us in his police cruiser?"

Rick didn't even smile. "The family bought a van to get Carter around in. It has a ramp for his chair."

Their father lowered his paper. "That's the boy who lost his leg in that damned war?" he asked. Dad never referred to it as the Vietnam War. He was and had been outspokenly against it from the start.

"It is," Ronnie told him. She didn't think he'd met Paulette. Always out when she had dropped by. "I need to talk to Paulette about when we leave for Gainesville." She should stop saying that. There was no hurry.

"Oh, right." He probably did remember she would be driving them up. Howard Deerfield folded the paper and laid it on the coffee table. "I see my former employee is here."

Ronnie looked out the big window, the picture window beside the fireplace. Sure enough, there was Joey's Corvair. Even she wouldn't ride a bike in this weather. A moment later, the screen door slammed and a rap came on the front door.

"We don't want any!" she called.

"But this offer won't last!"

Ronnie let her in. "You know you don't have to knock."

"And be shot as an intruder? Hi, Deerfield men."

Rick gave but a sort of half-wave, engrossed once again with his fire-making. "Good morning, Joey," said Ronnie's father. "Still nasty out there?"

"It is. And getting colder! You'd better get that fire going before it snows, Rick."

"That I can guarantee."

"Let's hang in my room," she said to Joey. "There will be less smoke." Ronnie's room was right around the corner, backing up to the fireplace, though no sign of its existence could be seen on her side of the wall. She looked around with a certain dissatisfaction at the room with its frills and pink walls. It looked juvenile to her now. Girlish. Maybe she could change it some, come summer. No time to bother with it now.

"Do you know what Kris is up to this morning?" she asked, taking a seat on the bed.

"She let herself get roped into going to services with her mom. And brother—I think Donny is the one to blame."

Ronnie thought so too. Kris had been keeping them up to date on the boy's sudden interest in his heritage. "I suppose you'll be up bright and early tomorrow to go to church yourself."

"Nope. I'll be up bright and early to clean kennels, so I'll go to the vigil mass. That's the mass this evening," she added. She might have thought Ronnie didn't know what vigil mass was. She did. She'd gone with James once.

"Okay." Now for the question she'd been wanting to ask. "So what's up with Angelica and Sandy? I figure you'll know."

"That's gotten out?" Joey seemed surprised.

"Remember I spent yesterday afternoon with Angelica. And we ran into Jackie Booth."

"I wouldn't think Sandy told her anything." Joey sat quietly for a moment, on the bench by the vanity, maybe pondering how to go on. "I wouldn't think she'd tell anyone. Shall I give it to you bluntly?"

"Do you know any other way?"

That got a smile. "It seems not! Okay—" She seemed to gather herself. "Sandy walked in on Angelica giving Russ a blow job. Ha, it's pretty simple when I actually say it! She ran out crying and Russ followed pronto. That's pretty much all Kris told me, when it comes down to it, and Angelica said even less. Oh, and Alan was there. He would never say anything either."

That was true. "Sandy likes Angelica. A lot." They all knew she had a crush on the older girl. How serious it was, they didn't know. It was likely Sandy didn't know, herself.

"Yeah, sex is part of it. That's obvious, isn't it?" Ronnie nodded. It was. "But also Jelly was sort of her idol, I think, and it shocked the girl to see her idol—well, doing what she was doing."

"And with her brother, no less." It would certainly shock her to walk in on her brother! Ooh, no, she didn't even want to think of that.

"Yes. That might have seemed a betrayal of some sort. I doubt she has it all sorted out in her head."

"You're pursuing the wrong major, Joanna Varney. You should be a psychologist."

"I think," said Joey, "there may not be that much difference between that and being a writer."

"And we're all providing you material! Poor Sandy." She shook her head. "Poor Russ, for that matter. He's really stuck in the middle of it all."

"Don't forget poor Angelica," said Joey.

Yes. Her too.

Chapter Thirty-two
Kris

"I considered attempting surfing solo this morning but the waves were only about ankle high." Joey's long board remained on the roof of her Corvair. "And I don't have a wetsuit yet."

"One of those Wesolowskis should have left you one," Kris told her. "They're due back today, right?"

"Should be. Good morning, James."

"Hi, Joey. You're too late for French toast."

"Make it next week. You'll still be here, won't you?"

"I will. And I intend to leave the next day, the Sixth."

"Epiphany. So we only have you for the twelve days of Christmas."

Kris was a tad baffled by all this. "Can't you fix Joey breakfast any morning?"

"We'd be underfoot. Sylvie isn't here on Sunday mornings," said James.

"Unless I came really early. You should be at Six AM mass every morning anyway."

"It's at Six-thirty," he replied. "And I do that most mornings in Boston. I'm allowed to sleep late here!"

"He's still up way earlier than me," came Angelica's voice from the library.

"Than any of us." Preston was in there too.

"The two of them have the Sunday paper laid out on the floor," said James. He lowered his voice to a near-whisper. "Hmm, the looks you two just gave each other suggest you want to speak with my sister."

Joey shrugged. "No hurry."

"We should talk about her party," offered Kris. "It's soon."

James only chuckled at that. "I'm sure that's all you had on your mind, Kris."

"All you're going to know about, mister," she told him.

He held up his hands. "Okay! You two have a secret you're not going to let me in on, and that's okay. Or three now, probably."

"Hmm. Four with Angelica," said Joey.

"Five with Alan."

"And a couple others we aren't going to mention."

"When you get that many it's no longer a secret. It's a conspiracy."

Angelica emerged from the library. "What are you whispering about out here?"

"We're conspiring," Kris told her.

"Maybe plotting too."

"Let's go plot on the porch. It's turned into a decent day."

James rose. "I think it's my turn to read the paper. Have to keep up with *Prince Valiant*." He disappeared into the library.

Angelica was right. It was a decent day, warming up as the sun rose toward its zenith. Puddles remained here and there on the tile floor where the wind had driven rain through the screens. "And here comes our co-conspirator," said Joey, as the three settled at a table. "We'll have to grill her about her date."

Kris had no idea what she was talking about. She wasn't going to ask, either. Let Joey be mysterious.

But Angelica wasn't going to allow that. "Our Ronnie has a new boyfriend?"

"She double-dated with her brother. The Jones twins."

Ronnie dropped her bike on the grass and came in. Angelica greeted her with, "We're talking about you."

"Gossiping," added Joey. "All about your affair with Carter Jones, war hero."

Her sudden flash of anger surprised all of them. "Don't call him that. Carter was a—a victim and he shouldn't be made light of!" She stood there with her fists clenched at her side.

"Oh, I'm sorry!" Joey got up and hugged her friend. That was a little surprising too, at least to Kris. She was supposed to be the demonstrative one of the trio.

Ronnie wiped away a tear and grinned. "That doesn't mean I actually like him that much." She took a seat and continued. "We only went out to dinner, at the Ho-Jo of all places. Rick claimed it would be easier to get Carter in and out there."

"Did you have a clam sandwich?" asked Angelica.

"Of course! Ah, Rick wants to know if it's all right to bring Paulette and Carter to your party. I told him it was but he insisted I ask."

"They're your dates, right? So they're automatically included."

"Um." Ronnie looked like she might object to the 'dates' label. "Okay."

"Most everyone will just show up if they know there's a party," said Angelica. "A few should actually be invited."

"Mackie," suggested Kris.

A nod. "Definitely. I'll leave that to you. Gordie knows and might or might not bring friends."

"Russ Wesolowski," Joey said, and, giving Ronnie a sidelong look, "and Alan."

"Alan's always welcome. So is Joey's boyfriend."

Joey ignored that statement. Kris suspected the two were no longer a couple, if they ever really were. "I don't think our other Russ is likely to show up on his own again. But he might respond to an invitation."

"I hope he isn't permanently scared off," said Angelica. She sounded sincere. Kris had to admit she didn't care whether she ever set eyes on Russel Penn again. Joey and Ronnie probably felt the same.

"Sandy will definitely not drop by," Joey said. Maybe never? "She really should be invited anyway."

"I sort of did that, via Jackie. She's invited too." Angelica looked toward the street for a few seconds, watching another beach-goer's car pulling in to park. "But I'll make sure she gets a personal invite. Russel too. Maybe I can guilt James into doing it. I'll undoubtedly think of some other people."

"You could ask James about that too. Maybe he'll want to bring Debbie Walker as his date." Kris couldn't keep from snickering after saying that.

"Debbie? I don't think I want to know what my brother's been up to! Why don't I invite Donna? Your law student friend, Ronnie."

Ronnie only shrugged. Then she said, "I can talk to Russ Penn. No need to get James involved."

"Great. Enough plotting. Let's go down to the beach."

"Too cold to swim," Joey reminded her.

"I know. I just want to walk around a little. Oh, my mother has invited your mother to come to the New Year's bash at the club. Whether any of them will be able to stay awake until midnight is anyone's guess."

"I'm not sure I'll be able to myself. I should bring my tent in case I fall asleep."

"Better bring blankets too," Kris told her. "It will be a lot colder than the last time someone pitched a tent here."

Angelica smirked. "I won't say anything this time about putting it to good use." The joke had fallen flat when she made it on Christmas.

"I think you just did."

The four emerged from the porch. Right back there, beneath those palms, was where the tent had stood that summer night. The night she and Will had finally consummated—oh, that was a good word—consummated their love. Both had known it was coming.

And Will was far off now, learning to be a medic. To save men's lives! Who knew where the marines would send him when he finished his training? "Keep up, Kris," called Joey. "I know your legs are short but make an effort!"

She started after her friends but suddenly her legs didn't want to work. Kris Greene sat down on the grass and began to cry.

Chapter Thirty-three
Joey

The Wesolowski brothers were back, of course. They'd gotten in late sometime yesterday. She'd seen no sign of them this morning.

Let them sleep in. And let them take over tomorrow morning! Joey hosed off the concrete floor, the last task in her routine. More than the usual number of pets had been here these last few days, boarded while their owners went off to holiday somewhere else. It didn't really make much more work. Broom this water away. Good, that would do. The last of it went down the drain with a faint gurgle.

"See you guys later," she told the dogs and cats. That's all that was here right now. Nothing exotic. Joey coiled the hose, hung up the push-broom, put away her yellow rubber boots. Her very own, bought for her by Doctor and Doctor Wesolowski. Vicki and Jim. Not that she couldn't have worn Alan's. Her feet were about as long, if a bit narrower.

"Decent job," came Alan's voice. "Want to come in and have some breakfast before you go?"

"Nah, she can eat the dog food," said Russ. He was pushing a large bag of it along in a wheelbarrow. Joey did not feed the animals; that was not among her duties and might never be. He poured some of it into a tall plastic bucket. "You feed the ones in the runs," he said to Alan. "I'll tend to the patients up here. Maybe you could help me with the water, Joey."

Why not? She decided to follow Russ. "You're invited to the New Year's Eve party at the Summerlins," she informed him. "You and Alan both."

"Both, huh?" He was looking over a chart before dolloping out the food.

"Yep. They like Alan. You they'll tolerate as my date." She chose not to look at Russ as she filled the water bowl. That could be done from outside. "Though I'm not sure we're actually any sort of couple." There, she'd said it. She knew she should sooner or later.

"Neither am I," admitted Russ. "That doesn't sound too promising for us, does it?"

"Oh, you can always be my fallback guy. Never know when I'll need one!"

"And vice versa?" He filled a dish, latched a door. "But that should be Alan."

"Alan?"

"It's kind of obvious you two have something."

It wasn't obvious to her! She topped off another water bowl, paying attention to the chore and trying not to let her face betray her thoughts. Her surprise at Russ's claim.

"Obvious to everyone but you two. Some of these bowls need cleaned, I think. That's for the techs, not us."

She knew about that. The veterinary technicians did most of the feeding too. The Wezzies were just filling in this morning.

"That's the last of it. And here's Alan coming around the corner. All done?"

The younger Wesolowski brother nodded. They did not raise their voices in here, nor move quickly, nor anything else that might upset the animals. They were good at it, weren't they? A lot better than she was. Growing up in a veterinary clinic must have made them so.

Their natural temperament too, maybe. Especially the decidedly low-key Alan. Not that Russ wasn't even tempered. What was that phrase she'd heard? Laid-back. That was Russ.

And where the heck had she heard it? From Gordie? Maybe. "Are you still feeding *me* breakfast?"

She had grabbed a little breakfast here before so she knew what to expect. Wholesome and vegetarian. Granola and all that. "I could go fix some coffee," offered Alan as they passed into the kitchen.

"Alan has his own coffee maker in the garage. I don't know where he picked up the coffee habit because we never have any in our house. We do have tea."

"The fast food places we visited on surf trips," replied Alan. "So you're actually to blame."

"At least you didn't pick up a cheese burger habit," commented Joey. "I wouldn't mind a cup of tea, Russ. Is that granola, Alan?"

"Yep. Pour you a bowl? This is with coconut. We have other varieties."

"That would be fine." Joey had sampled his granola before, on their surfing trip last summer. His coffee too! Her and Alan and Jam and Ronnie. Five months ago? Or a tad more. It seemed forever, right now. She hadn't really known Alan before that day, when he was in his natural environment, so to speak.

"Hey, Russ, did you get your new surfboard?" She'd almost forgotten about that. She hadn't asked about their expedition at all.

"I sure did. Come on out and get a look." They carried their bowls into the garage. It was shorter than the one she had last seen him with, and with a rounded tail—she knew they called the rear of their boards the tail—like Alan's. But a little shorter and subtly different. She could tell it was another Gordon and Smith. It said so on a rather large floral logo.

"Is it, um, narrower in its, I don't know, hips? Is that the right word?"

"It is the right word. You're also right about it being narrower there. This is the Magic model and its wide point is moved forward a tad. I liked the way it rode."

"Then you found some waves."

"Sort of," said Alan.

"And what's this?" asked Joey. "It looks like a naked surfboard."

Russ snickered. "The perfect description. Alan's going to make it some clothes."

Alan only smiled. "It's a surfboard blank. I'll plane it down to the shape I want and then glass it. Um, put fiberglass on it."

"Cool. I'd better get on my way." She handed her empty bowl to Alan. "Remember to show up at the Summerlins tomorrow night. Both of you! And be prepared to stay late to see the new year in. Hey, you could bring your tent and pitch it next to mine. Did you know Santa brought me a tent? See you later!"

But with any luck, not until New Year's Eve. She'd had enough of the kennels for a while. Joey got into her Corvair and headed home.

Chapter Thirty-four
Ronnie

She had to admit to herself she was not entirely comfortable doing this. Ronnie half-hoped Russel wouldn't even be home and it wouldn't matter. She pedaled her bike up the Penn's street. It was really a great day to be on the bike. She should go somewhere else when she finished talking to the boy.

His van sat in the drive. She'd better be ready if Russ was here. Don't let him know that she knew what happened. Be nonchalant and just let him know he was invited, that his friends would like him there. That wasn't very honest, was it? Ronnie didn't think anyone truly cared that much and Angelica just felt guilty.

And maybe not all that guilty, really. Russ emerged from the house. It was nice little house, wasn't it? About the age of the one she lived in, Ronnie guessed, but the yard was more open. It looked a lot like every other ranch house along the street.

"Hi, Ronnie." He sounded a tad wary. Maybe he should be!

"Good morning, Russ. I dropped by especially to make sure you know you're invited to our New Year's party at the Summerlins." *Our* party. Yes, that was the way to put it.

"Oh. Well—" he began.

Best to cut him off right now, before he put his objection into words. Dismiss it before it took form. "I know something happened but that shouldn't keep you away. We'd all like to see you there." You liar, Ronnie.

He gave her a long look. "You know what happened. There's no way your friends wouldn't have told you."

So much for that. "Then it matters even less. It's past and there's nothing to hide."

He looked at the ground. "Except myself. Myself and my shame."

"Shame?"

"Shame. Guilt maybe, but I think I've squared that with my conscience. With God, if you'd like. But I'm ashamed, Ronnie. I've been planning to be a minister, to help people do what is right, and I fell down the first time I ran into a real temptation."

"So you don't fall the second time. Or third or however many it takes." You're spouting clichés, girl, she told herself.

"Oh, sure, I know that. That's fine for me personally, to deal with my own weakness, but how can I—" He only shook his head without finishing the thought. "I envy your friend James. He seems so dedicated. And he's so darned smart."

She had to choke back a laugh. "James is far from being a holy man. He is much more complex than that, anyway."

"Maybe I should talk with him."

"Maybe you should. Another reason to go to the party, before he heads back to college."

"Before we both do." Russ stood there a moment, thinking about it. "But maybe not with Angelica around."

"Maybe. But maybe it's not good to run away from her, or from your shame or embarrassment or whatever you want to call it. She's never going to bring it up, you know." Ronnie hoped she was right about that. She wasn't really certain.

Russ said nothing. It was as good a time as any to ask, "Is Sandy all right? She's invited too, of course."

He shook his head. "I can't make any sense of her. I mean, sure it was a shock." He blushed at the memory of it. "And a terrible embarrassment for both of us, but I don't understand her moodiness. It's like she's mad about something. Mad at me? I don't know."

If he didn't know, she wasn't going to enlighten him. It was Sandy's business anyway, not Russ's. "Mad at Angelica maybe. Her heroine turned out not to be as perfect as she thought."

"Maybe." Russ nodded in something close to satisfaction at that answer. "I don't think we could get her to go to your party."

"Well, make sure she knows she's invited. Jackie Booth was invited too. You might mention that." Anything else she should say? Oh, yes. "And you can bring someone along, of course. Or a bunch of someones. Even Daryl Sterne."

He smiled for the first time. "That's a bit of a concession from you."

"I've nothing against Daryl." She'd never really had anything for her high school boyfriend either. "He can even bring his guitar." She straddled her bike, gave Russ a farewell wave, and set off.

That went well, she told herself. Well enough. It had been a chore she set herself and saw through to completion and that was good. Now just to ride around and forget everything for a while. It was a good day for it.

But Ronnie found herself pedaling toward the Summerlin house. She might as well stop, mention that she'd talked to Russ. Then maybe drop by the Greenes, and see if Kris was home and feeling better.

She should be. She should be back to her cheerful self, all her feelings about her boyfriend again below the surface. Ronnie sometimes wondered if Kris and Will's infatuation might have been as much an attempt to hold onto the summer, their last summer as kids, as anything else.

But what did she know? She'd never been that thoroughly in love. She wasn't sure she could be. A boxy little car of some sort was parked on the street in front of the Summerlin house. Ronnie paid it no attention. Probably just someone on the beach.

"Just the person! Hey, Ronnie!"

Where? Oh, at the back of the yard, where a fringe of sea grapes and tall grasses separated it from the white sand of the beach. Angelica was sitting on the concrete bench there, in the shadow of the palms, with another woman. Donna Forrester, she realized, as she walked toward them.

She hadn't seen Donna since their ill-fated trip to Miami in August. Ill-fated. She'd have to remember that and use it in conversation some time. Not that she ever talked about what happened then! Donna was in black slacks and a sweater. She had improved her hairstyle some. It still looked like it belonged on a middle-aged housewife.

Rather than squeezing onto the bench beside them. Ronnie took a seat on the grass, a little to one side. "Hi Donna."

"Donna is coming to the party tomorrow night," announced Angelica. "It seems I am rescuing her from a holiday of overwhelming boredom."

"In truth, I was very much at loose ends. Mike is with his family and I don't really have a lot of friends in Naples now." Donna amended that to, "Close friends." Ronnie suspected the original statement was closer to the truth.

"That's something we're all facing," Ronnie said. "The people we used to know have scattered and some will never be back."

Angelica shook her head. "Gosh, what a pair of bummers you are. You have me! And now you have connected with each other."

"So we have. We could have done that anytime the past three months," said Donna. "I should have looked you up."

"We both had lots of other things to think about." Ronnie couldn't imagine why this older girl would want to have anything to do with her. "And you have a boyfriend."

"Yes, Mike does cut into my free time! Anyway, I am going to make an effort to connect with you when we get back to Gainesville. And you can drop by my house here in Naples anytime."

Wherever that might be. "You're welcome at my home, too."

Donna rose. "I'm going to be on my way. It was great to see you again, Angelica. You can expect me tomorrow night."

Angelica did not bother to walk her to her vehicle. Ronnie sat and watched Donna for a moment, wondering where she needed to be on her way to. "You just called her up and invited her?"

"I had James do it. They knew each other already." Oh, right. He had been in Miami too. "Maybe she hopes to replace Mike with him."

"At least for one evening, maybe. I made sure Russel Penn knows he is invited to your party."

"Oh? And did he RSVP?"

"He gave a definite maybe. I think it was a maybe."

"I suppose you heard what happened, what with both Kris and Joey knowing about it."

"Just like Kris and Joey know about what happened with me and James last summer. Thanks to you, it seems." She tried not to make it sound like an accusation though it was, more or less.

Angelica didn't miss a beat. "You're welcome. And your triumvirate knows all the sordid details of me and Gordie. It's hard to keep a secret around here!"

"But they don't know about you and me." Ronnie almost didn't mention that. It was very much of the past and didn't seem at all important anymore.

Angelica sobered. "They might. Joey does, anyway."

Ronnie didn't know what to say to that so she said nothing.

"I needed to talk to someone and she was the best choice." Angelica sat silently long enough she thought she was done with the subject. No. "I made a pass at her once, you know. Or maybe you don't know. That was long ago, before I went away. I guess I haven't outgrown doing stupid things."

"Does anyone?" Ronnie got onto her feet. "I'm going to ride over and see if Kris is stirring."

"Hold on a minute. I'll steal James's bike and go with you." Angelica rose beside her. "Won't she be happy to see our smiling faces?"

Maybe she would.

Chapter Thirty-five

Kris

The bike, Kris decided. The new one. She must figure out some way to get it to Miami with her. Then the Stingray could still be here at home when she visited. She went to get it out of the garage.

Her brother was in there, maybe waiting for her. "Hey, I'll ride over with you," said Donny.

"You can stay for the whole party if you want." No one would mind. But he wouldn't get any of the beer that was sure to be there. Nor any weed, which also might show up.

"Nah, it's just another night. It's not like it's the real new year."

There he went about their Jewish heritage again. It truly was getting old. Donny had a new bike, too, practically identical to hers but blue instead of white. They rolled both out into the drive. It wasn't late, mid-afternoon by the clock, but it would be getting dark soon. Kris missed those long, late evenings of summer.

Well, Daylight Saving had something to do with that, didn't it? They rolled west, toward the beach and the sinking sun. Will had called again earlier. It was so good to hear his voice. It had been good of Ronnie and Jelly to come over yesterday too. Jel did care when she remembered to.

A right on Second. It always felt safer to bike on than Gulf Shore. Or Third, for that matter, with its shopping. Then left at Twelfth, the pier. Might as well see what was going on there. Donny asked no questions but followed her lead.

Not much doing. Not even any kids hanging out beneath the big banyan. Maybe getting too late, too cool. She hoped she'd dressed warmly enough. If not, she'd have to borrow one of the blankets she'd told Joey to bring. Maybe she'd even try camping there in the yard, as Joey and Ronnie had.

No, not with a warm house and comfortable bed so near! And not with no Will to share the tent.

Right on Gulf Shore, then left to the Summerlins' place. "There's your old boyfriend," said Donny.

Mackie. Donny didn't know about Mackie and that was just as well. Not that it would matter much; he was certainly mature enough to understand. More mature than she was at his age. Maybe more mature than she was now! Harold Macklin had just pulled in across the street in a bright yellow Mustang.

They rolled up beside him. "Is that your car?" asked Donny. He was obviously taken with it. Understandable. Kris rather liked it herself.

"Just another one borrowed from my dad's lot. I don't really want to drive a car to Athens so there's be no point to owning anything."

Kris imagined icy northern roads. She'd never driven on one but they seemed terrifyingly dangerous.

"Season's over, right?" asked Donny, as all three crossed the street, the Greenes pushing their bikes. "Are you playing anything else?"

"Sticking to football and studying. There will be spring drills eventually."

Kris wondered if he'd decided to switch to economics. This wasn't the time to ask. They were here to party! "Not much of anyone around yet," she commented. "We'll probably get roped into helping set things up."

"It will make you feel useful." He surveyed the yard. "What's with the tents?"

"Let's find out." She recognized the larger shelter as the one Alan had set up here in the summer. The other must be Joey's.

"Welcome to Camp Summerlin!" called Angelica. She was watching Joey pound stakes into the ground.

Joey looked up. "The Wezzie Scouts are about somewhere."

"Yes. I like Alan's big brother! I went for the wrong Russel, I think."

"He's yours if you want him." Joey moved to the next stake.

"Russel?" whispered Mackie in Kris's ear.

"Um, yeah. We'd better talk about all that somewhere else. Have we lost Donny?"

"Over there." Her brother had gone to greet Gordie Rhein, who'd just pulled up in his Mini Moke. There was a girl beside him but she couldn't make out who she was. And she was *not* going to put on her glasses.

"Okay." They walked to the rear fringe of the yard. How could she put this, without saying what actually happened? "Angelica put the moves on Russel Penn. We think it may have scared him off permanently." They might find out this evening.

"Oh. And Alan's brother is named Russel too?" He nodded and then said, "Maybe it's his turn to be scared away."

"Somehow I think he may be a little better equipped to deal with her. Let's sit." Both dropped onto the bench there, and looked back up the yard, to the tents, the barbecue grill, the tables, the Summerlin house, all striped with the long shadows of the coconut palms.

"How are you doing, Mackie? I could tell you were hurting though you try to hide it."

"You may be the only one who can tell." The large young man sighed. "It's Jeff, of course. Or was Jeff. He cheated on me from the start. Then he got arrested for soliciting someone at a public park. That was the end of his athletic career. Of his college career." He stared at the ground. "God, I wish I wasn't gay. That's not the kind of life I want."

"It doesn't have to be. I'm sure there are good guys out there, and one good guy you could love and he'd love you." Guys like Mackie himself.

"I hope you're right."

For a moment she felt like bashing Jeff Yoder with something large. Then came the thought that he was likely to be hurting too, wherever he was. But Mackie didn't deserve it.

Nobody deserved it, yet the world kept on making people miserable. Good people. She didn't know why it was that way. Probably nobody did. But she should demand that James explain it!

"Oh, that's Debbie with Gordie."

"Debbie?" Mackie didn't sound at all interested.

"Debbie Walker. I don't think you know her." Different circles.

"I know of her and her family. Filthy rich. Way richer than the Summerlins. They own loads of land here in Collier County. All around the state."

Kris got up. "We might as well go say hello."

Mackie followed without a word.

Angelica waylaid them at the tents. "So Deb has latched onto Gordie," she drawled. "She's welcome to our leftovers."

"Ooh, Jel, that's harsh." But true. Kris had dated Gordie in high school. He'd been the first guy she had sex with, the only one other than Will. Angelica's encounter had been somewhat briefer.

Hey, how would Angelica know about her and Gordie? If he'd ever said anything to her, he'd be the one she'd bash with a heavy object.

"I'll try to be nice to her for at least a while," said Angelica.

"I think you can if you really, really try."

Mackie wisely withheld any comment as he followed in their wake.

Chapter Thirty-six
Ronnie

"Pull right into here," called James, unfastening the chain across the drive. Rick drove in, not too far.

He leaned out the window. "Is there any better place to put the ramp down?"

"Where you are should be fine."

Carter announced, "I'm going to try to walk down on my crutches. Be prepared to pick me up if I make a fool of myself."

"Are you sure?" asked Paulette.

"Let him make an impression," Rick advised her, climbing out of the driver's seat.

Carter chuckled. "One way or another!" He leaned over and slid the door open. Ronnie pushed the ramp out to Rick, who fixed it in place. "Here goes." He levered himself out of his wheelchair on his crutches. Carefully, slowly, the young man descended. Rick stood close—but not too close. Ronnie released the catches that held his wheelchair in place and rolled it down after him. He might not need it, if he took care not to tire himself on the crutches, if he found a place he could sit comfortably. She would park it somewhere unobtrusive, ready if Carter wanted it.

She followed behind as they crossed the lawn to the front walk. "Watch out for the extension cords," Ronnie warned. "They're all over the yard, ready to trip you up."

"Must've known I was coming. Thanks for the heads-up."

Paulette nodded an appreciation too. It just seemed sensible to Ronnie to be aware of any hazards. "Sure. You could go in this way if you wanted. There are some steps up into the house."

Carter stopped and looked both ways. "I'll go on around. It appears that's where the party is. Hey, and there's Mackie. The only one big enough to pick me up if fall over." He made his way across the grass. "You know we were on the football team together. Golden Eagles. His wings carried him further than mine."

Mackie was a year behind Carter, but he was already a star in his junior year. Ronnie honestly had no memory of Jones playing. But he was a pretty big guy. She would definitely let Mackie be the one to pick him up!

Angelica had joined James. "Summerlin twins," Ronnie said, "meet the Jones twins. Paulette and Carter. Angelica and James." Some of them knew some of them already. She wasn't going to try to sort out which.

"Thank you for inviting us," said Paulette.

"Yes. We appreciate it," Carter added. "I'd also appreciate finding a place to sit down." He looked around at the selection of lawn chairs and concrete benches.

"Let me get a more comfortable chair from the porch," said James. He disappeared, to return a few seconds later toting one of the rattan seats. "We should have thought of this earlier," he told them. "Where would you like it?"

"Wherever you'd like me to stay for a while. Not too far from the food."

"Good thing we did think of that." James set the chair down in a likely spot and Carter lowered himself into it.

"That's good," Carter said. "Not too low. I don't think I could get up from one of those lawn chairs." He nodded in their direction.

"You are getting better on those sticks," spoke Mackie, who had come over to join them.

"Some. The doctors—the ones at the VA—say maybe I could be fitted with a fake leg." He patted his right leg, the one that was missing from above the knee.

"Don't call it fake," scolded Paulette. "Artificial, maybe."

"Get a wooden peg leg. You could be a pirate!" Angelica suggested.

There was momentary silence, uncertainty how to react to that, but Carter laughed loudly. "Finally someone with a good idea. Long Jones Silver!"

Ronnie thought it best not to tell him Long John Silver used a crutch, not a wooden leg.

Rick sniffed the air. "I smell smoke."

"Joey and the Wesolowskis are getting the grill started up. It normally wouldn't be used until around Memorial Day," said James. "What those vegetarian Wezzies are going to eat, I don't know, but there are burgers for everyone else."

"It's going to be warm enough we can eat outside," said Ronnie. "I wish we had Will's hibachi. Someone should have told Jackie to bring it." They had toasted marshmallows over it on that summer night. She had smoked pot for the first time as they sat around it, a tiny camp-fire. Oh, there would be no point with a fire in the big brick grill.

Jackie might not show up anyway. No one made a comment. Maybe they thought she was just thinking aloud. Maybe they weren't paying any attention to her. Where were her friends? Joey at the grill. There was Kris, talking to Gordie and some girl she didn't know. She reminded her of Lin. Shorter, to be sure, but with that same air of stylishness. Of sophistication. Very tanned and rather athletic looking. But the face under that brown bob was forgettable, really. One didn't notice that right away, taking in the rest of the package.

As forgettable as her own face, maybe, but she didn't have anything to draw attention away from it. Suddenly, unexpectedly, the entire yard lit up in yellows and reds, greens and blues. Someone had turned on the strings of Christmas lights, still wrapped around the palm trees and all along the eaves of the house.

"Wow. Someone must have noticed I'd just arrived! Hi, Ronnie. Oh, hi Joey."

Donna Forrester. Joey had sauntered over. "Hi, Donna. I assume someone invited you. Not that it matters!"

"You can blame James for it."

"Oh, we blame him for everything." Joey looked toward the house. "Though I suspect his father is the one who flipped on the lights, before heading off to his own party."

"I think Kris's parents are skipping this one," said Ronnie.

"Yeah. But mine are going as the Summerlins' guests. In Mom's old Plymouth, I assume. That will make some sort of impression."

Ronnie almost missed that Joey referred to the couple as her parents. She usually said Mom and Wayne or something of that sort. Just how long had it been since she'd seen her father, or even heard any word of him?

Oh, Paulette. She waved for her to come over. "Paulette, this is Donna. Paulette is another of us from the University of Florida."

"Paulette Jones. Certainly. I remember you from high school." Paulette would have been a grade behind Donna, as Ronnie was a grade behind Paulette.

"I hope you don't have intentions of being a lawyer too," said Joey. "Enough of those about."

"Not me! I'm going to teach school."

"Something useful," Ronnie said.

"I hope so!" said Paulette, missing the joke. Donna was willing to give it a smile but not to comment. She undoubtedly thought being a lawyer was useful too.

Ronnie sometimes had her doubts, though that was the reason she chose her career. Her intended career. It had seemed like a way she could make a difference.

She had also been caught up in Angelica's wake and now the Summerlin girl had gone off in another direction and jettisoned her own plans to study law. There would be no Summerlin and Deerfield partnership. Ronnie hadn't taken that fantasy, Angelica's fantasy, too seriously.

But she had liked it. Maybe she had always followed along with other people's ideas. Joey and Kris—Joey had been the one to hatch schemes when they were little girls but Kris was more likely to implement them. It was time for her own schemes. Time to imagine her own future.

A new trio of friends? Donna and Paulette and herself? Her imagination couldn't extend quite that far.

"The coals should be ready shortly," Joey was saying. "We'll have burgers and hot dogs and such."

"Need any help?" asked Paulette.

"Sure. Come help me prep. I'm afraid Angelica's contribution ended with bringing it all from the grocery store."

Not only Paulette but Donna followed her. No, there would be no new trio.

"Everyone desert you?" came Angelica's voice.

Ronnie turned to her. "I might have deserted them. It's hard to tell."

"That it is. But I'm going to conscript you into my service. I need to bring my record player down and set it up. We need music!"

"I thought you'd entertain us with your guitar all evening."

Angelica only snorted at that. She followed her into the house. "We can put it on the porch but it's up in my room right now." A sudden halt at the bottom of the stairs. Angelica turned to her, seeming suddenly unsure of herself. "You don't mind going up with me, do you? I'd understand."

Ronnie could have been just a bit short with her answer. "I thought we'd worked all that out already, Angelica. None of it bothers me now."

Angelica gave here a long look before turning back to the stairs. "I think you might be a little miffed at me for bringing it up."

"Annoyed, maybe." Both had to giggle at that.

They entered Angelica's room. It faced west; the fading hues of the sunset could be seen out over the Gulf, a smudge of red in the darkening sky. "Here it is. Hmm. I can fold it up like—this and then swing the speakers in and latch them. Okay. It will be a two-woman job to get it down the stairway."

"We could have drafted Mackie."

"Never! We don't need no men-folk!" Each took one side of the stereo. "Though James and my dad carried it up here. Let me go first. I'm taller."

"I think there's enough room to go side by side."

"That would be safer, wouldn't it? Don't want to go falling backwards down the stairs."

Frontwards wouldn't be so good either. A minute later they emerged onto the porch. "James. Run upstairs and pick some albums," demanded Angelica. "You don't need to stand around gossiping."

"Yes, ma'am. Jazz or classical?"

"It had better be loud, stupid rock. Let's get this plugged in. Over there. Hey, a couple of you guys slide a table over that way."

James returned with a stack of records. "Some of these will do," felt Angelica. "But maybe I'd better not make you our DJ."

"I'll do it!" offered Donny. "For a while."

"Good enough. Play 'em loud. I see we have more arrivals."

"Jackie," said Ronnie. "That isn't—no, I don't know her." Jacqueline and another girl emerged from the twilight.

Jackie looked around at the party, such as it was. "There should be more boys," she stated.

"Unclaimed boys," added her friend. "And older than Donny Greene." She waved to him. He studiously turned his attention to an album cover.

"Sandy didn't make it?" asked Jackie.

"Not yet," Angelica told her. "You've brought a friend. Welcome to the party."

"Yeah, this is Maxie." Maxie was more a Mini, not much taller than her friend. Long dark hair was pulled back from a tanned, boyish face.

"Maxine Hall," said the young woman. "We're classmates."

"And both on the cheerleader squad."

"Maybe we'll call on you to lead some cheers later. There's food— or will be in a few minutes—and music and even some boys. My brother is unattached, you know." She nodded in the unsuspecting James's direction. "Tell him to dance with you."

As the pair wandered off, Angelica turned to Ronnie. "At least a few people are showing up. Who knows? Maybe we'll get more."

"I don't think anyone expects Sandy to come."

"Probably not. But, hey, whether he shows up or not, I do thank you for going over and inviting Russel."

"And I have no idea why I did it."

Chapter Thirty-seven

Joey

"Russ. Hmm. I'm going to call you Rusty so I don't confuse you with Russ Penn."

Tall and blond and even sort of handsome. Good natured and smart, too, if a little narrow in his interests. Joey liked Russ Wesolowski, yes. She liked his brother too but there was definitely nothing between them. She was sure of it.

She was also sure Angelica had better treat Russ nice or answer to her.

"That might be acceptable," Russ replied. "If Russ Penn happens to be around."

"Probably not going to happen tonight," said Alan.

"We'll see," Angelica replied. "He may not be able to stay away!"

Alan only shook his head. It was an effort for Joey to keep herself from doing the same. "Russ is going to be a marine biologist," she said. "Right?"

"Yep. That's what I'm studying at FAU."

"Surfer U!" said Gordie. "Maybe I should have gone there. There are good breaks nearby, aren't there?"

"Some decent ones. The inlet up at Boynton is a fairly short drive. The set up there is a lot like at Sebastian." The surfers all nodded. Everyone knew Sebastian Inlet. "I'm more likely to surf at Yamato Rock when it's small. That's a little point at the north end of the beach at Boca Raton."

"Is that the place they call Jap Rock?"

"Some do." It was obvious from his tone that Russ did not. "It's popular for divers too. I'm thinking of getting into scuba."

"That would be useful for a marine biologist," felt Angelica. "Practically a requirement, I would think."

"But an expensive new hobby at the moment."

Surfing took up enough of his money. Alan's too. Joey wondered if he had started working on his do-it-yourself surfboard. She would ask sometime. Maybe after another hamburger. The poor Wezzies were missing out on these!

Here came Kris. "You escaped from Debbie," remarked Angelica.

"Yeah, at last. God, she is one boring girl! How did you happen to end up with her, Gordie?"

"She invited herself along. Doesn't seem to understand the word no."

Kris nodded sympathetically. "I should rescue you from her clutches. Distract her while you make your getaway!"

"She'll go home sometime," said Gordie. "I can survive."

"Okay. But I owe you plenty, Mister Rhein, for all you did for Will and me."

"No problem, Kris," he mumbled, maybe a little embarrassed. Then, "My father loves the idea of me being friends with Debbie. I wouldn't be surprised if he had dreams about me marrying her and all her money."

"Her family would be likely to call that a nightmare," said Joey. "Hey, late arrivals!"

The car looked sort of familiar. The others headed over to see who it was but Angelica put a hand on her arm, a wordless request to remain a moment.

"You're okay with me flirting with Russ? You're sure he's not yours?"

"Absolutely. Friends only."

Angelica smiled a knowing little smile, before stating, "You seem closer to Alan."

Again? What was it with people trying to pair her with Alan? "Nothing there either," she said. "Oh, that's Daryl's Falcon."

"Want to bet whether he brought Russel?"

It was a pretty sure thing he had. Someone else too; at least four figures climbed out of the car. Yeah, there was Russel. Daryl. The other guy? Mike Kelly. Why did they bring him? And a girl. Reggie. A fellow NHS graduate last year and now a fellow Edison student. Must be with Mike. No. Daryl put his arm around her.

Letting everyone know who she was with. Staking his claim. She almost laughed at the thought—and reminded herself to jot it down for future use. Maybe she should carry a pad for that sort thing. Like Kris.

"I think," said Angelica, "I won't go over and welcome them. Better to let Russ be for now. And I don't care one way or another about the others. You know the girl?"

"Reggie Dozier. Regina. We went to school with her." Did Angelica mean she *did* care about Russel? That was sort of implied. "She's okay."

"Big praise from you, Miss Varney."

"Yeah, wasn't it? That's my quota for being agreeable today."

The newcomers had joined those by the porch, the Joneses, Ronnie. Most everyone. The Rolling Stones blared. Through the screen, she could glimpse someone dancing.

Angelica headed for the grill, where her brother held court. Mostly for Debbie Walker at the moment. Joey had biked past the Walker house in Port Royal a few times, though it was on one of the streets with no outlet, culminating in a cul-de-sac. Maybe the sprawling place should be called a mansion. Her father moored his lengthy boat in the canal behind. Ha, and maybe it should be called a yacht!

"Hi," James greeted them. "Debbie and I are comparing notes about our colleges. Both prestigious old places for rich kids!"

Debbie looked unsure what the boy meant. She might have thought it was a joke at her expense. "I attend Wesleyan," she said.

"In Georgia, right?" Joey asked. "What are you studying?"

"Liberal arts, officially," came the breezy reply. "Which means nothing in particular."

"I suspect that is all you'll need," observed Angelica.

The young woman missed any undertones to the remark. "Oh, yes. I don't see why I need a degree at all but Dad insisted."

Not for the country club life she must envision as her future. If she envisioned anything.

Debbie rose to her feet. "I should go find Grubby. Maybe I can get him to dance with me. Do you dance, Jam?"

"I've been known to. Maybe later."

"I actually had to think a moment who Grubby is," said Angelica, as the girl walked away. "We've been calling him Gordie so long now."

"All of six months."

"Oh, you would count them up, Joey. As long as we're here, you can fix us more to eat, brother mine."

"Burgers?"

"Didn't I see some sausages?" asked Joey. "I could go for a spicy sausage on a bun. With plenty of brown mustard."

"Joey the gourmet. Maybe you should be a food critic." He lifted the lid on a large cooler, and retrieved a burger and a couple sausages from bowls resting on the ice.

"Yes. Restaurant reviews," agreed Angelica. "Write one up for this party!"

"Three stars? No, maybe only two. The service has not been good at all. Hey, you'll have to take me to your club so I can review it."

"Your mom can give you a report," James informed her.

True. "Debbie's family are members, right? Kris told me she was there."

"Oh, her father built the place. One of his many projects and developments," said Angelica. She turned to her brother. "If you were headed for almost any other career, old Walker would consider you excellent marriage material for his daughter."

"I can imagine. Maybe I should lie about it and get invited to his place."

"Take rides on his yacht," said Joey. "With a few of your closest friends as guests."

"I suppose you could come along to cut bait."

"And I'd do it very well, mister! You'd better fish out some more meat. Looks like hungry customers are coming."

"They might be more interested in your other cooler," said Angelica.

James gave them both a determined look and a shake of his head. "The good stuff's in it. They can drink the cheap beer up on the porch." He looked in that direction. "Despite it being New Year Eve, we might want to turn the music down a little. The last thing we need is a visit from the police."

"Let's hope it would be Officer Jones. Y'all hungry?"

Joey had heard Angelica turn on her southern accent a couple times before. Her brother did it better, in perfect mimicry of Preston Summerlin—though his voice was not quite so deep. There weren't that many true southern talkers among her friends. Families in Naples had come from all over, creating a sort of homogeneous accent of nowhere-in-particular among the kids who grew up here.

Her father, Joe Varney, had been southern, but Wayne was midwestern and her mom's accent had come with her from the northeast.

Russ Penn was at last daring to be in proximity to Angelica. With the support of his friends. "Hi, Reggie," said Joey. "Good to see you here. Maybe I should have invited you myself!" She might have, had she thought of it. She was friendly enough with the girl, shared a couple classes. She had absolutely no idea what Regina's plans might be for a major, for a career.

"Instead I got it, what, third hand? You invited Russel and Russel invited Daryl and Daryl invited me." She gave her date a sidelong look. "Maybe as a last resort."

Daryl looked a little uncomfortable with the remark. There might have been truth in it. And despite being smart, Daryl was not quick-witted.

Regina was smart too. Also, well, homely. Not ugly. Plump and plain. Ha, she could say the same of Paulette. "James will feed you," she said. "You all know your hostess? Angelica Summerlin herself. Take a bow, Jel!"

Angelica only deigned to give her a scornful glare. It was almost enough to crack Joey up. "May I present Reggie. And Mike. You don't have to remember him as I'm sure you'll never invite him again." James struggled not to laugh this time. "And you know Daryl and Russ. That's Russ, not Rusty." No one understood that joke except Angelica herself.

"Burgers?" asked James, jumping into the first gap she allowed him. "Hot dogs? Most of the other eats are over there." He waved an arm toward a nearby table, spread with buns and condiments and chips and stuff. It was safe to leave pretty much anything out on a cool December evening.

Soon to be a January morning, and Nineteen Sixty-nine. About an hour yet? Here came Kris and Mackie. Paulette too.

"My brother had to resign as DJ," Kris reported. "He's on his way home."

"You'll have to fill in for him then," Angelica told her.

"Okay. But I will not dance with Jackie and Maxie. Hey, sausages? Why didn't you have those out before, Jammer? Fix me one! Fix Mackie one too. Or maybe two, too. He's big."

"So I've noticed. Let me just slap some more of everything on the grill."

"I think I need to stand closer to your grill," said Paulette. "It's getting chilly."

"Hey, I have blankets in my tent. Come on and I'll get you one," Joey told her. "I might need to wrap up a little myself." This sweater was not quite cutting it.

The girl put the blanket Joey handed her around her shoulders. "That's better!"

"Does Carter need one?" There were a couple extra. Might be more in the Wezzies' tent too.

"He might. I'll take one up to him." They started back to their friends. "Someone should have thought things through before giving my brother so much beer. He has to attempt to hobble in and use the restroom."

"Did he manage okay?" Joey could imagine all sorts of disasters in the Summerlins' bathroom.

"Yeah. He doesn't like being dependent on someone but he knew he'd better let Rick help him." A smug little smile came and went. "Rick's a great guy. I hate to see him go."

"He'll be close. A lot closer than he was the last couple years, anyway. And closer to Gainesville than to Naples."

"That's true. Not that it helps Junior any!"

No, it wouldn't. Paulette herself would be gone too. Maybe she and Alan could go over and visit Carter sometimes.

Not that she needed to do it with Alan! Where was that boy anyway? Or his brother, for that matter. She doubted they'd be hanging with Ronnie. "What are you guys talking about now?"

"Angelica's quizzing us about our prom," reported Kris. "She's pissed because she didn't have one."

"Only curious. Did you do like in the movies and decorate your gym?"

Mike answered. "Nah, they blew their money to rent a hall. In a resort over by the bay."

"It was a pretty nice hall," Daryl said. "I took Ronnie."

"And I was with Mike," added Reggie. "That was, um—"

"A matter of convenience," Mike supplied.

Reggie shrugged and let the statement stand. Joey guessed the same could be said of her date tonight.

Russel didn't volunteer anything, nor did Angelica ask him. Someone must have gone with him; Joey had no idea as she had avoided prom and all other school-related events.

"It's cool that you're studying music," said Mike.

"I think so," came Angelica's reply.

"I may. I'm not sure. I'm in a band, you know."

This received only a languorous nod of the head.

"And you're going to be a priest?" he asked James. "Russel's planning to a minister. We have some good talks."

Going by Russ's expression, Joey wasn't sure how good they were. But polite Russel Penn would never say anything.

"We'll have to talk sometime," Mike went on.

"If you'd like." James looked up from the grill. "Maybe Russel too."

Russ nodded his head, slowly, barely perceptibly.

"Half an hour to the new year," announced Angelica.

Chapter Thirty-eight
Kris

"We should bang on things," said Maxie.

Jackie concurred. "And set off firecrackers."

"Or just have another beer to toast the new year," suggested James. "But not for you young ladies. You'll have to stick to cokes. Like Rick has been doing."

Jackie accepted this with equanimity but Maxie protested, "Hey, it's illegal for you too!"

"But only I would get in trouble if I got caught. If you did, I might be charged with contributing to the delinquency of a minor."

"Oh." The girl considered this. "We don't want to get Jam in trouble, do we?" she asked her friend. Jackie shook her head.

Angelica was looking at her watch. She'd appointed herself official timekeeper. "Four. Three. Two. One! Happy New Year!"

There were cheers but no fireworks. Kris wouldn't have minded a skyrocket or two. She'd watched them launch from the pier, explode in showers of color over the Gulf, last Fourth of July. Right here in this yard, with Will.

Beer bottles clinked together in toasts. Then no one was quite sure what to do. Go? Party some more? Sing 'Auld Lang Syne'?

Maybe kiss someone. Not Mackie, not that he'd mind. Kris kissed her hand and blew it north. North to Will.

"We'd better take off now," announced Jackie. "We had lots of fun!"

"We promised to go right after midnight."

Kris had absolutely no doubt the pair had liked the idea of partying with college kids. It was also likely they—or at least Jackie—had been permitted to do so by their parents because Paulette would be here.

But they had spent more time in the company of Kris's brother. Donny was two grades behind them, in part because of when his birthday fell. He was not two years younger. The Greenes had tried to get him accepted a year early but the schools had been obstinate about sticking to their cutoff date. Maybe it was just as well, what with

Donny being on the short side. Like her, like their father.

"I'd tell you to drop by anytime," said Angelica, "except that I'll be off to Miami again soon. Me and Kris."

"But you can pester our parents if you want," James added. "We won't mind."

The pair traipsed off into the dark. One of them had a car out there, Kris assumed. It looked like the Joneses were going to be going too. Rick Deerfield was bringing the wheelchair.

"No way Carter is going to walk up his ramp at this point," murmured Paulette. "I'm glad he had a good time."

Ronnie was assisting her brother. Mackie too. "I hope you and Ronnie had a good time, too," said Angelica, joining them.

"She's been hanging with the Forrester girl most of the evening." Paulette sounded just the slightest bit sour, or maybe even sorry for herself.

Angelica caught on at once. "Ah, it's like the popular girls in high school. You were one, weren't you, Kris?"

"I'm afraid so!" But Ronnie? She was more on the periphery. Chances were Donna had been the same. "I'm sorry if they ignored you. I'll give Ronnie a good talking to!"

She tried to look determined but Angelica snickered and that ruined it. "Okay, you do that, Kris. Donna was just someone new to talk to this evening but I'll have her for six hours on our way to Gainesville. No getting away from me then!" Paulette yawned. "Oh, excuse me! It looks like we're ready to roll."

Carter Junior was ready to roll anyway. Mackie was pushing his wheelchair toward the van, the ramp already in place. The three girls went to join them. Russ Wesolowski fell in beside them.

"Best to take him in backwards," Rick was telling Mackie. "Lean the chair way back so you don't dump him on his face."

"It might improve it," claimed Carter.

Shortly, they had the young man inside the van. Why was Ronnie down on her knees? Oh, fastening the wheelchair to the floor. She waved to them and slid the door shut, as Paulette slipped into the front seat. "Hey, Rick," called Russ. "I'll be by in the morning to see you off."

"I'll expect you," came the answer, as he went around and got behind the wheel. Then they too rode off into the night.

"Are you going to hang a while, Mackie?" asked Angelica, as they crossed the lawn, back to the porch and what remained of the guests.

"I might as well. Looks like you're about to lose Russel and his friends." They were unmistakably getting themselves together to depart. "Sort of friends."

Kris agreed with that assessment. "Daryl is his friend. The others happened to be on hand."

"And he needed some support," added Angelica, her voice low.

Mackie gave her a curious look but didn't say anything about it. Kris had clued him in a little about the situation earlier and he would have noticed the way the two were acting around each other. The tension—yeah, that was the word. It sounded good, whether it was accurate or not!

Joey's arms were full of blankets. "The ones I lent the Jones twins," she explained. "I'll get them back into the tent. Unless one of you is cold." Another was wrapped around her own shoulders.

"Do you plan to sleep out here?" asked Angelica.

"Haven't quite decided yet. I could give the tent a test run."

"If I drink any more beer, I may need to stay off the roads," said Russ.

"Oh, you know your brother won't have overdone it, Rusty."

"I can't complain about the name, can I? Penn is still here."

"I'd complain anyway." Kris looked about. "Where *is* Alan?"

Not with the group up here. "Back by the grill," said Mackie. "With Gordie and the Walker girl."

The Christmas lights made it easy enough to see three figures, though Kris couldn't have identified them. The coals still glowed faintly. "Better him than me," spoke Joey. "You guys taking off?"

"We are," answered Daryl. "Thanks for having us."

"Whichever one of you we should thank," added Mike. He was speaking very precisely, the way someone would who had drank a little too much and knew it.

"Ones," said Russ. "Angelica and James. And I think their friends helped them."

"Damned right we did," Kris told him.

"They couldn't do it without us," said Joey.

"But I'm the one who will say 'you're welcome' and 'we must do this again' and all of that," Angelica said. "And I do hope you will come over, Russel. I promise to behave."

"Um, okay, Angelica. Thanks." He practically scurried away.

Reggie raised an eyebrow but said only, "Thanks again for having us. I'll see you around, Joey." With that she followed the boys toward the street.

"She probably will," Joey said. She looked about. "Hey, did we lose Donna?"

"Her car is still out there." Mackie nodded in its direction. "Studebaker Lark. Can't hardly miss it."

"Maybe she's in the bathroom."

"Maybe she was kidnapped!"

"Maybe she walked down to the beach," said James. "And here she comes walking back."

"Oh, hi Donna! We were sure you'd been nabbed and would be held for ransom."

"But they really meant to grab Debbie and were going to cut your throat."

"It's a good thing you got away!"

"Uh, yes, I guess it was. Everyone gone?" The place did look deserted.

"Not quite. Wanta come sit by the grill with us?" asked Angelica

"Sure."

"Well I'll be damned," muttered Russ as they drew near. "It's not like Alan to be the center of attention."

Sure enough, Debbie and Gordie were sitting quietly, attentive to Alan's words. "Usually the good listener type, isn't he?" Kris whispered.

"Yeah." When they got within earshot, Russ broke into laughter. "Hiawatha."

Hiawatha? Sure enough, Alan was reciting poetry. "He learned big chunks of it when he was a little kid. I guess he still remembers them."

Thus the wedding banquet ended,
And the wedding guests departed,
Leaving Hiawatha happy
With the night and Minnehaha.
"And that's the end of the wedding of Hiawatha."

"How did you get him to recite for you?" asked Russ. "He hasn't done that for years for us."

"I found out about it when we went on our surf trip last August," said Gordie. "Alan was going on while he was driving and thought I was asleep. Said it helped keep him awake."

A nod. "I don't suppose he gave you any Shakespeare."

"Some other time," Alan said.

"Is that to be or not to be?" asked James. To be rightfully ignored. The group settled on the grass in a rough semicircle before the big brick grill. "Any more food anyone? Or beer?"

"James kept his private stash of greenies back here," Angelica informed them.

"Share it now," commanded Debbie, "and we'll forgive you."

The Summerlin boy duly passed out the last Heinekens. "I have a little something to smoke too, if anyone's interested."

"It's about time," said Angelica. "Go get it. Is it in your bedroom?"

"No, I don't keep my stash in the house. Right now it's in the Wezzies' tent."

"So we'll be the ones arrested if a cop stops by?" asked Russ.

"Better you than me," said James, already on his feet. "I'll be right back."

A moment of silence, sitting there gazing at the embers, sipping at their beers. "I'm glad Russ did show up," said Angelica. "The other Russ, not Russ-that-I-can't-call-Rusty-now."

"Nope. Not allowed," he told her.

"Okay. Anyway, I'm glad he wasn't scared away permanently." Those who didn't know the why of that gave her curious looks. Even Debbie. "You don't like Russ much, do you Alan? Ronnie told me that."

"I may have, um, spoken harshly of Russel Penn once or twice, but I know he's a decent guy. A well-meaning guy. Just a bit pretentious at times. And just a little too earnest for me to take!"

"I get that," said James, taking a seat.

Gordie nodded. "Even I get it."

"But Kelly is way worse when it comes to spouting pseudo-intellectual crap."

"Oh? I think I got a sense of that too." James's attention seemed focused on the joint he was rolling. "Thanks for the warning. Are you and Mike inclined to argue? There." He passed his creation to Gordie and started on another.

"There's never any point to it." Alan shrugged. "And he's glibber than I am."

"We could set James on him," said Angelica. "He's an ace debater."

"He probably wouldn't recognize it when he'd been out-argued."

"Um-huh. Want one, Mackie?"

"I'd better not, what with being in an athletic program and all. They haven't been testing for it but I'm not taking the chance."

Seemingly conservative, Young Republican Donna didn't hesitate to take a drag on the joint that was passed to her, before handing it on. Kris had decided she wasn't so bad. But she still didn't like Debbie.

No one was saying anything. They were all too tired, all too mellow, too willing to just sit there. "Are you ready to go, Deb?" asked Gordie.

"Not yet."

"I could ride Debbie home if you want to take off, Gordie," offered Angelica.

He hesitated, his eyes flicking for a moment toward Debbie. Maybe he'd like an excuse to get away from her. "Okay. If it's all right with you, Debbie."

"Sure. Whatever."

Gordie rose. So did Russ Wesolowski. "We'd better hit the road too," he said. "Okay, Alan?"

"Oh, I thought you guys were going to spend the night in your tent," spoke Joey. "I am going to try sleeping out here. If it gets too cold, they'll find me curled up on the couch in the living room in the morning."

"We'll leave the door unlocked," said James. "If only so you can use the restroom."

"What? I'm not allowed to pee on your lawn?"

Debbie snickered at that. The pot might have made it sound funnier than it was.

"I guess I'm ready to go too," Alan said. "Need to help my brother in the morning, so Joey can sleep in. But we'll expect her bright and early the next day."

"I'll be early," promised Joey. "No telling how bright I'll be."

The three boys headed off to their vehicles. Mackie remained, sipping his beer from time to time. Kris suspected he was staying mostly because of her. Mackie being protective.

She was feeling pretty sleepy herself. Mackie and James were talking about something, their voices low. Debbie sat listening, taking an occasional drag on her joint. It was down to no more than a nub. So was the one she'd been sharing with Joey. No more of that tonight.

"It's getting cold. Let's go sit in the tent," suggested Angelica. "The Wezzies' one. Joey's is too small."

"You too, Donna" said Joey. "More bodies will keep us warmer."

"I'd better get going too," the girl said. "I'm—I'm awfully grateful to you for having me over. To all of you, I think."

"Our pleasure. Sorry about the kidnapping earlier," Joey said.

"But at least you got away. Maybe you'd better bring that handsome boyfriend to protect you next time."

"Okay, Angelica, I'll see what I can do! Bye, James. And thanks!" She gave him a wave as she headed for her car. The three girls ducked into the tent.

There were more blankets in it. A couple sleeping bags too, apparently in case the brothers had decided to stay. "I'll have to steal these blankets," said Joey. "Oh, and a lantern." She switched it on. "I'll take it too."

"We'll leave the Christmas lights on all night," Angelica said. "Unless you think it would keep you from sleeping."

"Dunno. It might." Joey sometimes had trouble sleeping. Kris knew that well. She couldn't say how long her friend had been complaining about it. All her life maybe.

"We must get Alan to recite for us," said Angelica, sliding around, attempting to find a comfortable spot. "Hmm." She pulled a sleeping bag over and sat on it.

"Good luck with that," Joey replied. "I suspect it will be hard to get him to do it again. But I get Alan memorizing poetry. He likes structure."

"Uh-huh." The slightest furrow appeared between Angelica's dark eyebrows. "He and Ronnie seemed so much alike when I first met him. But they aren't at all, really. Alan's like you, Kris. An artist."

Kris couldn't come up with anything to say about that.

But Joey agreed. "I think you're right. Like with him making his own surfboard."

"We must get him to make boards for us too. Or shape boards. That's what they call it, right?"

"I think so. Maybe we'd better see how the first one comes out."

"Or the second or third," said Kris, "and find out if he improves. Hand over those chips, will you?"

Joey passed them to her. "Good point," she said. "Just like your drawing or my writing."

"Oh, are you still sending stuff to my sister?"

"I am. I think she even reads some of it."

Someone scratched at the canvas flap. "I'm going to take off now," came Mackie's voice.

Kris got up. "Me too. Great time, Jelly." She went out into the night. Where were Jam and Debbie? Had they deserted poor Mackie? Both walked to where her new bicycle leaned against a palm tree.

"Would you like me to drive you home?" her companion asked. "I'm sure it would be safe to leave your bike here."

"No thanks, Mackie. I can ride. I even have lights!" She switched them on to show him.

"Okay. I'm sure I'll see you before we both leave town again." With that, he crossed the street to his temporary ride.

Kris turned and surveyed the Summerlins' yard, still illuminated by the strands of Christmas lights. The forms of Jelly and Joey were silhouetted on the wall of the tent but she couldn't tell which was which. And beyond them—was that Jam kissing Debbie Walker back there at the beach end of the lawn? No concern of hers. She wasn't even likely to gossip about it.

Kris got onto her bike. Second gear. She'd be home shortly, long before dawn. The first dawn of a new year.

Chapter Thirty-nine
Ronnie

"You know you're not going to be able to make a clean getaway," Ronnie told her brother.

"No slipping quietly out of town?" Rick still wore civilian clothes; he had not once donned his uniform during the holidays. His gear was packed, all in one duffel sitting by the door. "I said goodbye to pretty much everyone yesterday."

"You know Russ Wesolowski will have to come by."

"Said he would." Both stood at the window. The new year looked a lot like the old one. "But that's someone else arriving."

"Sandy." On her scooter. Ronnie thought it likely that would be replaced by a car sometime soon.

"And Russ right behind her." The green Econoline pulled into the Deerfield's oyster shell drive. Russ Wesolowski. Alone. Ronnie didn't know whether she had expected Alan to be with him. Just as well he wasn't.

She followed Rick out into the carport to greet them.

"So you made it home safely," said Russ.

"Yeah. Carter Senior told me it wasn't a good idea to walk so he brought me in his squad car."

"Good. As ideas go it was a pretty idiotic one."

Rick only shrugged. "I've walked through worse neighborhoods. Far worse. Hi, Sandy. Haven't seen you in a while."

"I know." She might have sounded a tad guilty. Sandy certainly wasn't her normal ebullient self. "I couldn't let you leave without coming to say goodbye. You've been so nice to me."

Rick grinned. "Nice to the silly little high school girl?"

Sandy couldn't resist a smile of her own. "Something like that! Do you have to run off and catch a bus now?"

"No bus this time. My parents are going to drive me up to Jacksonville and take a few days of vacation."

Ronnie couldn't resist saying, "Escaping their fast-paced, hectic life."

"Oh? Then you'll have the house to yourself. Your turn to throw a party!" Russ told her.

"Okay. Then you're invited. You too, Sandy." She thought it might be a good idea to add, "But not you-know-who." Or maybe it wasn't a good idea.

"Oh, you—could I talk to you about it later?"

She answered, "Sure," but she wasn't really. Russ and Rick appeared mystified by the exchange.

"Here comes someone else you'll need to invite," said Rick. Joey, on her bike, coming up the drive. "Another girl who hates to see me go."

"One in every port, right?"

"It looks like two for Naples. Are we about ready, Dad?"

Howard Deerfield had emerged from the house with a couple of suitcases. "I am. Your mother will be eventually." He surveyed the trio of visitors. "It's good of you to come say goodbye to my son."

"I wasn't going to let him sneak away this time." Russ didn't get the chance to say goodbye when Rick suddenly joined the navy a couple years ago.

"Me neither," said Joey. "And he's not avoiding a hug goodbye." Which she gave him right then. Sandy did not hesitate a second before doing the same.

Russ took his hand to shake, but Rick pulled him in for a hug too. "Take care of yourself, man. And maybe cut that hippie hair."

"It will be even longer next time you see me," Russ promised.

Here came her mom with a small travel bag. "Oh, Sandy. Thanks for dropping by. Will you tell your mother I'll be by to talk about some things when I get back?"

"Sure, Missus Deerfield. I know you two have been plotting!"

"You might say that. Are we ready?"

"We are," said her father, settling behind the steering wheel of the Fairlane. Rick tossed his bag in on the rear seat and turned to embrace Ronnie, before getting in. Then they were gone.

Russ turned from the street and said to Joey, "I was about to go over and strike Camp Summerlin. Did you get your tent down already?"

"Nah, I went over to church instead when I got up this morning, and then home. I can get it later."

"Church?" wondered Ronnie.

"It's a Catholic holy day. Were s'posed to attend mass."

Did she attend with James? Or maybe even Angelica. Ronnie still intended to go again sometime.

"Ride over with me and we'll get both of them," offered Russ. "I can fit your bike in the van."

"I can leave it here. Won't be the first time. Oh, do you want to ride along, Ronnie? Russ wouldn't dare object."

"I know better."

"I'm going to hang here with Sandy for a while."

The girl looked—what? Grateful, maybe? She might have expected to be brushed off in favor of Ronnie's friends. Joey certainly noticed there was something between them but made no remark.

The pair rode off in Russ's van. They weren't a couple anymore, were they? That seemed pretty apparent last night. "Want to come inside?" she asked Sandy.

"Sure." She followed her into the screened carport. They almost never pulled a car into it but treated it more like a porch, with rattan furniture. The large lift-up screen door was rarely opened. It didn't really open that easily anyway.

Sandy took a seat, fidgeted a moment, and blurted, "Does everyone know what happened?"

"They do not. Kris and Joey and I share pretty much everything, but it doesn't go beyond us."

"Alan was there. I know he wouldn't blab."

No, he wouldn't. The only witness Ronnie wouldn't completely trust was Angelica.

"I wanted to go to the party last night," Sandy went on. "But I just couldn't, you know?"

"I think I do. It's about Angelica, isn't it? Not your brother."

"I'm used to Russel doing stupid things."

"All guys do."

That brought a smile. Briefly. "I'm not even sure why I'm mad at Angelica. I thought at first because she took advantage of him but that sounds stupid when I say it."

"A bit," admitted Ronnie. "That doesn't mean there isn't some truth to it. Angelica can be, um, thoughtless sometimes in dealing with people."

"Yeah. She's kind of reckless. That's one of the things I thought I liked about her."

"Me too. But she sometimes jumps into things without thinking of whom she might hurt."

"I suppose Russ isn't the first guy she's, um—" Sandy seemed to search her vocabulary. "Come on to." Ronnie didn't think she was completely satisfied with that phrase. She wouldn't be either.

"Believe me, he isn't." She was not going to say she had been one herself. That would complicate things more than necessary. "Reckless and self-centered. But you know she means well, don't you? Angelica is not a bad person."

"Maybe that's what made me mad. Angelica doing stupid things when she—she is so much better than that."

Ronnie knew there was more to it, much more. It seemed just a little glib, but she had told herself similar things last summer. Had she ever truly satisfied herself with her explanations or had she simple buried it all?

As she buried too many things. "I need to warn you that Angelica would probably want to talk about it."

"Oh, no. Really?"

"She may be having as much of a problem understanding her feelings as you."

"I'd better make sure we're never alone together!" Sandy got up. "I guess that means I intend to visit the Summerlins, doesn't it?"

"It sounds like it," admitted Ronnie. "You're heading out?"

"Yeah. Thanks for talking with me."

"Anytime." Maybe she had actually helped. Sandy could work on things from here.

They both could.

Chapter Forty

Joey

"I'll go help him in a while," said Joey. "I can't have him saying he did it all himself." She and Angelica sat atop one of the tables in the Summerlin yard, feet on a bench, watching Russ strike his tent.

"Oh, let him. It will make him feel more important."

"Most guys have too high an opinion of themselves already."

"So true! I wonder how they'd feel if we wrote performance reviews about them."

Joey felt it not a good idea to go further with that topic. "It's not a review but I am writing an account of the party to send to your sister. I thought she might like to read about your shenanigans."

"I behaved! I can't say the same for my brother."

"I am quite sure I shouldn't ask about that." But she was curious. "Debbie?"

"Yeah, They were still smooching when I went inside. I could see them from my window—I had to peep, you know—but, uh, I had to stop watching when she went to her knees." There was the obligatory pause. "Not that I could really see anything from that distance."

"I would hope not." And it was going on right outside her tent. Joey was thankful she fell asleep quickly for once. "I don't think that will go in what I write."

"Better not. Lin still has a good opinion of her little brother." Angelica sighed. "He went down a notch for me. Debbie Walker." She shook her head. "If it was someone like you, I could see it."

Joey could not see it. And what of Angelica and Russ Penn? She most definitely was not going to bring that up. "Did you ride her home on your scooter then?"

"I did and I didn't say a word to her about it. But I did drive rather fast around the turns in Port Royal."

Joey approved. She wasn't altogether sure why. "I suppose James will behave himself when he's back in Boston."

Angelica slowly nodded. "I believe so. He'll remember his vocation or something, and not give in to temptation. Or not so easily."

Joey hopped down from her perch. Time to go help Russ finish packing up the gear. Angelica fell in beside her. "I'll be honest," the girl said. "I'd probably fool around with Debbie too."

"But you didn't." The opportunity had surely been there.

"Nope." Angelica giggled. "Maybe some other time!"

"You're hopeless, Miss Summerlin."

"I suppose so. Did you know Paulette slipped in and cleaned up the bathroom a little before she left? I'd never clean up after my brother."

"Unless you count taking Debbie Walker home."

"Oh, that's wicked, Joey! I wish I could repeat it to James."

"What are you two laughing about?" asked Russ.

They looked at each other. "Debbie Walker," said Angelica. That was true. More or less.

"Understandable," Russ said. "Help me fold my tent, will you? Then we'll get Joey's down."

"You mean you aren't attracted to Miss Walker?" asked Joey, as the three of them knelt down.

"Truth? Not a whole lot. She does have a nice body. Athletic. Try to keep it straight, Angelica. Good. Now we'll roll it up."

"Okay. I guess I need to play more tennis."

"Or surf," suggested Joey. "Guys like us surfer girls."

"That's good. Into the bag with it." They worked the rolled-up tent into a sleeve that seemed just slightly too small for it. But it did go in. "Better get all the stuff out of yours, Joey."

Yeah, her blankets. A few other things. "Oh, your lantern is in here." Joey handed it out to Russ. Some of these blankets belonged to the Wesolowskis too. She'd needed them last night.

"So, if not Debbie, and apparently not Joey or me, just who are attracted to, mister?" Angelica was asking him.

"Oh, I'll admit to being attracted to you two. Scared of you too! But—" There was a long pause. She poked her head out the tent to see what was going on. "I kind of like Ronnie. Always have and being around her these last couple weeks, well, reminded me of it."

"But it's awkward after what she had with your brother," Joey said.

"Don't I know it? We're going to be awfully far apart too."

"Not this coming summer," said Angelica. "It's not all that long till it rolls around, you know."

"Unless you decide to take off and go surfing all summer again."

"Which is a possibility," he admitted. "Or I might get the chance to go into the field with my studies. There's talk about Belize."

"And that would come first, wouldn't it?" asked Joey. "No need to answer."

"Because you wouldn't really have an answer right now," finished Angelica.

True enough. She sometimes forgot how perceptive Angelica could be. "Let's get these stakes out of the ground."

An hour later, Russ delivered her and her tent to her home. "You sure you don't want me to drive you over to the Deerfield house?" he asked.

"I'll walk over and get my bike sometime. I do that a lot." And had been since she was a little girl. Her mom was letting her cross the Trail on her own by the time she was eight. If she hadn't, Joey probably would have done it anyway.

Mom undoubtedly had recognized that. No one home right now. No work for Wayne, it being a holiday, but her mother had a shift. Early enough for some lunch. She made herself a sandwich, peanut butter and sweet pickle relish, and went into her room. Maybe a nap. She'd stayed up pretty late last night, after all.

And rose early this morning, early enough to hit the first mass at Saint Ann. It had been kind of fun last night, but not the equal of some of the times they'd had in the summer. Maybe nothing would ever equal those. They'd still been kids then, her and Ronnie and Kris, putting off the inevitable for one last season.

The three of them and their friends, old and new. The Summerlins. How different that summer might have been without them. Maybe some of what was could be held onto. Maybe there would always be a welcome at the house on the beach. Maybe the triumvirate could still come together from time to time, there or at the pier or at their old favorite spot at Third Avenue.

Joey lay back on her bed, closed her eyes. She had to admit, if she'd been in Angelica's room last night she might have found a pair of binoculars. Not admit it to Angelica! Only to herself. She would have been curious and probably turned on. Her hand slid across the front her jeans. She was turned on right now, thinking of it.

But she fell asleep before thinking any further.

Chapter Forty-one
Kris

"My parents said they would be back Saturday or Sunday."

"That gives you plenty of time to get into trouble," said Joey.

"Enough time for a party. Just a little one. I can't compete with the Summerlins!"

That sounded good to Kris. "Okay. You know we're also having a farewell party for James. Probably Sunday."

"Or maybe Saturday night. That should be small too."

"So before then," said Ronnie. "We'll have to have a farewell party for the rest of us too. We'll all be split up again by the end of next week."

"Mackie leaves the day after James. On the Seventh," Kris announced. "And all the high schoolers will be back in class."

"A good excuse not to invite any," asserted Joey. "You've already invited Sandy to yours, Ronnie."

"I did. And I told her Angelica would not be here." She seemed to consider that a moment. "I'm not sure she would mind now, though."

"But you'd better stick to it. So not James either, I would assume."

Kris said, "Maybe he'd welcome the opportunity to get away from his sister."

"I don't think I want him here anyway."

Not surprising. Not simple, either. She doubted Ronnie completely understood why she wouldn't want James to come.

"Maybe the whole idea of a party is stupid," Ronnie went on. "I could just call it off."

Maybe it was stupid. Maybe they didn't need one more party.

"You may never get another opportunity like this," Kris told her.

"Strike while the iron is hot," added Joey. "And press your clothes while you're at it."

Ronnie only thought on it for a moment. "Okay. Tomorrow night? Hmm, no, I'll make it Friday. Friday afternoon and evening."

"Then you need to start inviting people. *We* need to start inviting people," said Kris.

"Yeah," Joey agreed. "It will be our party. We'll chip in on the expenses."

That sounded like a good idea to Kris. Ronnie might have the least ready money of any of them. "And best not to have any beer at this one if high school kids are coming. It's expensive anyway."

"So this can be our farewell party, whether there is another later or not," Ronnie said. "I should invite Paulette. But maybe not her brother."

"The logistics of getting him here would seem daunting."

"Oh, Joey, where do you come up with those sorts of words?" Kris asked.

"My trusty thesaurus. Anyway, Paulette might welcome the opportunity to get away from him a little while."

"Not that she won't when we head back to college. I've been thinking we ought to encourage Carter to enroll at Edison. I'm definitely going to mention it to Paulette."

A giggling Kris told them, "The logistics of getting him there would seem daunting too!"

"And you two will be gone," Joey pointed out. "Which would leave things up to me and Alan if he needs help. Speaking of Alan, you should probably include him since you already invited Russ. Want me to say something to the Wezzies?"

Ronnie did not seem the least fazed by the mention of her former boyfriend. "Sure. Should I tell Sandy her brother is invited? We need some guys and he sort of qualifies!"

"I don't know that we actually *need* guys," stated Joey.

"But a few nice ones wouldn't hurt," felt Kris. Should she invite Mackie? For that matter, would he want to attend James's goodbye party? They ought to do something for him, too.

"Why, what's the matter, Kris?" asked Ronnie.

She sniffled just slightly. "I was just thinking about Mackie. He'll be all alone again when he goes back to Ohio."

"And cold too, I suspect." Joey smiled after delivering her quip but then spoke seriously. Fairly seriously. "He'll have his team. That's almost like being in a family, from what I've seen."

For a moment, Ronnie looked like she wanted to add something but thought better of it. Instead, she veered away from saying anything serious herself. From offering any thoughts. "We'll certainly invite him. I think right here in the carport should be party central. Keep it to here and the back yard."

"Aw, and we looked forward to trashing your house."

"No need for anyone to go inside at all," Ronnie declared. "Not even for the bathroom."

There was a little one that opened onto the screened-in area and only onto it, around the corner from where they were sitting. Around two corners, actually. "Your dad knew what he was doing when he designed this place," said Joey.

"Though I think it was mostly so he could clean up outside. I'll leave it up to you two to invite whoever you want and I'll do the same."

"And none of us should mention it to Jam and Jelly," Kris said.

Joey gave an emphatic shake of her head. "On the contrary. It could never be kept a secret so we'd better be open about it. I'll tell them it's just a few school friends getting together."

Kris had an idea her friend might say more than that. That was up to Joey. She was certainly the closest to James of any of them. Maybe to Angelica too. "Hey," she said, "didn't you get a new record player for Christmas? Bring that out here and let us listen to something. Even one of those dreadful records you like!"

"And make sure," Joey added, "to have it out at the party." She gave Kris a wink. "But we'll make sure to bring along some proper music."

"As you wish," sniffed Ronnie in mock umbrage. "Maybe some of our guests will want to make their own music."

"There is always that danger," Joey admitted.

Chapter Forty-two
Ronnie

"That used to be a high school, didn't it?"

Paulette glanced out the window of the Simca. "George Washington Carver High. It was finally shut down last year and any students still attending there went over to Naples High."

Ronnie wondered what the rather small building would be used for now. Maybe her father would have heard something.

"Before it was built," her passenger went on, "black kids had to either ride a bus to Fort Myers or drop out. Back in the Fifties."

They continued down Eleventh Street to Fifth North. Ronnie was still not quite sure where that church was! "Did you go there?"

A momentary reticence. Maybe Paulette was gathering herself, trying to formulate just the right answer. "For one year. My pop had mixed feelings about letting me go to school with a bunch of white kids. I think—I think he was afraid I wouldn't be safe."

"But you had your brother."

"That's true. And I protected him as best I could!" Both chuckled at that. It occurred to Ronnie that maybe Paulette was still protecting her brother. "He couldn't have had any sort of athletic career in high school if we hadn't switched over."

That helped explain a few things. "Will Booth wouldn't either, then."

Ronnie knew that integration had taken a long time. It was a subject her dad was all too willing to go on about. A decade or so had elapsed from the time the courts ruled in that Brown case until this school finally shut down. Black students had shown up in the schools before then, of course. Will had been among the first at Lake Park Elementary.

It had been hard for him. She could see that looking back. It had made Joey awfully mad at times.

"The Booths were all for getting their kids into the integrated schools as soon as they could. You know where they live, right?"

"I do." Ronnie had turned right on Fifth Avenue. "Angelica and I visited. On her scooter."

"Oh, the famous red scooter. Is it Japanese? I know a guy with a Honda bike."

"Italian." Brown versus the Board of the Education. Was that the name? She should read up on the case. She should be familiar with that sort of thing if she was serious about a law career. That still seemed nebulous. Ronnie had a hard time visualizing it or any other future. Across Goodlette Road, left on—this street.

Jackie came running out to the car, firmly muscled arms and legs protruding from shorts and a tee. She threw a beach bag into the rear seat before climbing in. "It's a great day! Nice and warm."

"But getting breezy," said Ronnie. "And the clouds are rolling in."

"We could just hang at the park instead," ventured Paulette

Jackie would have none of it. "No way. I'm all set for the beach!"

Ronnie felt the same. "It is supposed to turn a lot colder in a couple days. This may be the last chance to enjoy the beach till spring."

"Definitely for us," said Paulette. "We'll be far off in Gainesville."

Ronnie pulled out of the Booths' drive and headed back the way they'd come. "It's not that far from the ocean," she said. "Lots of students drive over." Flagler and other towns. She did intend to go again. Right now, she turned west on Fifth.

"Anywhere on the beach okay with you? Or should we go up to Lowdermilk, where they have restrooms?" She wondered if maybe that was where Alan and Russ showered and changed out of their swimsuits

"I thought you liked Third Avenue," piped up Jackie. "Sandy Penn told me that's where you and your friends hang out."

"Sometimes. We could even park by the Summerlin house." Not that she felt like intruding on them again. They saw too much of her, Ronnie was sure.

"I'd rather go to Lowdermilk Park," said Paulette. The girl didn't offer a reason why. Maybe she felt more comfortable in a public park.

"Okay." Ronnie turned right on Goodlette. "I'll go through the Moorings."

"Oh, no, not past the high school," moaned Jackie. "I didn't want to even see it till next week."

"I'll warn you when to close your eyes."

"I thought you liked to see all your friends," Paulette said.

"Sure. Just not at school! I should have called up someone else to come with us today."

Ronnie wouldn't have minded. Or she didn't think she would have. "Not much room for anyone else in this car."

"I could have invited Maxie. She's almost as small as me." Jackie giggled. "That's why we sometimes call her Mini."

"Is her home anyplace near?" They could stop, if Jackie was serious about it.

"Oh, no, the Halls live out east, across the river. Maxie didn't go to Lake Park Elementary like we did."

"Like you did," Paulette reminded her.

Shadowlawn, most likely. That elementary school wasn't built yet when Ronnie started school. In fact, Lake Park hadn't been finished and they moved to it during her first grade year. Way back, grade school had been in the building downtown that was now the middle school. High school shared the campus, too.

The athletic field came up on her left. "I'm not looking!" proclaimed Jackie Booth. "Let me know when it's safe."

A couple minutes later it was, and they crossed the Trail into the Moorings subdivision. Most of these houses on either side of Mooring-line Drive had sprung up in the last few years. Ronnie did not approve of the winding streets here and the man-made canals. Or maybe her father didn't and she just went along with him.

But she did prefer the neatly laid-out ways of the older Naples. All this seemed somehow unreal. Or at least not the real Florida, but someone's slightly tawdry dream of how Florida should be. Over the high bridge—high for Naples—and down toward where the street met the Gulf and curved south, becoming Gulf Shore. Doctor's Pass was right over there, hidden behind the tall apartment complexes.

Then Lowdermilk Park to the right, with its big half-full parking lot. Ronnie remembered the man for whom it was named. Her father knew him. She could also remember when the park was opened, providing access to an area of beach becoming increasingly closed off by new construction. It wasn't enough but it was something.

"My senior class had our Skip Day here," she said, pulling into a space and shutting off the Simca's engine. "It wasn't much of a party but there was a decent band." The lead singer had been kind of cute. What was the band's name, anyway? She couldn't recall.

Palms stood all around the park, both coconut and sabal—or cabbage palms, as Ronnie and her friends had always known them. Yuccas. Something like yuccas, anyway. Their colors were subdued in the half-light of this increasingly gray day. "Do you need to change?" she asked.

"Not me," said Jackie, peeling off her tee.

"I wore my suit, too," said Paulette. As had Ronnie. They might want to change out of them later. She would just as soon her companions did rather than get her seats wet and sandy.

Paulette's suit was quite conservative, one-piece with a skirt. Jackie wore a two-piece not unlike Ronnie's own, pretty run of the mill for girls their age. It looked better on Jackie, with her tight midsection.

She wondered if either got to the beach that much. "I'll race you to the water!"

All three ran toward the Gulf. It would be cold, yes, but who could know when they might plunge in again?

Not surprisingly, Jackie won the race.

Chapter Forty-three
Joey

"Oh, I know where the Forresters live. They're across the river in Oyster Bay."

Joey considered this. "A longish bike ride." Not that she wouldn't be willing to tackle it, even with this wind.

"Too long for me!" said Kris. "We can go rescue Donna in my bug. I did mean to drive over that way and sketch."

"Rescue?"

"From boredom. Our fascinating and witty conversation would lift anyone out of their doldrums!"

"And you accuse me of using fancy words. So get your artist stuff and let's go."

A few minutes later they headed east. Mostly east as Kris zigzagged from street to street. "I stopped by the Summerlins' before riding on over to your place," said Joey, "and explained to Jelly why they weren't invited tomorrow. All I really had to say was 'Sandy' and she understood."

"How about James?"

"He wasn't there and I didn't ask about him." She did know the boy tended to go off on long solitary walks or bike rides. Sort of like she did herself. "And I called up Reggie Dozier. Maybe I felt a little guilty for overlooking her before."

"She's kind of boring."

Maybe so. Joey didn't know her well enough to say. None of them did, despite years of school together.

Kris had found her way over to Tenth Street, following it to the highway. A smallish grocery store, one of the oldest in town, stood on the corner to their right. Across Forty-one was the railroad depot. The end of the line. They took a right.

The first bridge. The gray-green water lay choppy beneath them, with a stiff breeze blowing up the river. "Your sketch pad is liable to fly away if you try drawing on the bridge," said Joey.

Kris only nodded. "Gordie showed me some photos he took of the bay last summer. Black and white, with an older camera. I'd have to admit they were pretty good."

"From the water?" They sped across the second bridge.

"Yeah. The Rheins have a nice boat. He took me out riding in it once." She paused only a second or two before saying, "I didn't invite him to the party."

"Me neither. Is this the turn?"

"Uh-huh." Kris took a right at the landscaped, divided entry to the subdivision. Joey didn't think she had ever been in this neighborhood before. Maybe she should ride her bike into it someday and give it a better looking over.

Going by the signs, they were on Sandpiper Street. "Not all the way to the end," Kris told herself. "Yeah, right here." Joey was not at all surprised that the house in front of which they stopped was on a canal. "It is entirely likely Donna isn't home."

It didn't look like anyone was home, in truth. Kris pulled into the empty concrete driveway. "One of us should try the doorbell."

"Just honk your horn," Joey advised. But she hopped out and rang it. The door was set into an arched alcove, potted plants beside it. It was probably intended to look Spanish. Give them time, she told herself. Someone might be busy or in the shower or something. She waited half a minute. No answer.

With a shrug, she turned back to the Beetle. Kris stood watching her, standing in the car's open door with one foot inside, one on the pavement. "We might as well go," she said.

"Not without looking around," replied Joey. "We're Donna's friends. We're allowed."

"I hope the police buy that." But Kris followed her around the house into the back yard.

Not surprisingly, there was a dock, a narrow wooden one attached to the low seawall. More surprisingly, Donna stood on it, tying up a little aluminum jon boat. She looked rather different from the Donna they'd seen before. A khaki fisherman's cap was pulled over her normally carefully-coiffed hair, and rather dirty shorts protruded from beneath a loose long-sleeved shirt. She tossed a couple oars atop the sea wall and climbed up after them.

Joey was sure she had noticed them but Donna gave no sign of it until she stood on the grass, the oars over one shoulder. She lifted her free arm in greeting.

"Home is the sailor," called out Kris.

"But not from the sea, I'm sure," Joey added.

"Not hardly," Donna said. "Not past the end of the canal today. It's a little too rough on the bay."

"Do you go out there in that boat?" Kris asked. "It looks awfully small."

"I sometimes row it up to the bridges. Around the island and back, sometimes one way, sometimes the other."

"That's pretty far."

"Far enough for me. Especially if the tide is flowing strong!" Donna's smile settled into something more pensive. "I miss being able to row when I'm at college."

"You should ride a bike everywhere like Joey does."

"I just might. Let me get these stowed." She entered a metal door, its frosted jalousies cranked partway open. Probably the back way into the garage. "Come on in."

Joey thought rowing around the bay sounded almost as good as riding a bike. Shoot, it might even be better. She would have to try it.

Donna's Lark was in the double garage, along with the usual other stuff people accumulate. "My father doesn't much like my junk car sitting outside," she said, stowing the oars in a rack. "He'd rather the neighbors looked at his Lincoln."

"I think it's kind of cute," Joey told her, "in its own odd way. Sort of like Kris."

"In other words, it's a quite sexy automobile," Kris said.

"The third member of your trio isn't with you today?" They followed Donna into the house. The utility room. And a restroom off to the side. Joey didn't get a chance to peek inside and see if it included a shower stall. She would want one handy if she came in dirty from the garage.

"She and Paulette went to the beach. Ronnie is ditching all her old friends." Joey attempted to sound as mournful about this as she could.

"But she'll come back," stated Kris. "She knows she'll never find anyone as classy."

"Or as sassy." Kitchen. Very open, like the Deerfield house. Those ivory-colored drapes were pretty blah. "That's sort of why we came over here. Aside from alleviating your boredom."

"Or maybe our own. Party tomorrow at Ronnie's place and you're invited."

"Nothing big like the New Year thing," Joey assured her. "Sort of an end of vacation goodbye."

"And you can bring someone if you want. We promise not to tell Mike!"

Donna seemed uncertain how to respond. She stood regarding the pair for a moment. "It's good of you to think to include me."

"Oh, that was just a last minute thing when no one else would agree to come," Joey assured her. "Drop by in the afternoon or evening. And now you have to give us a tour of this place."

"Yeah, we really came just to case the joint."

"Where do you think the jewelry might be?" Joey stage-whispered to her friend.

"I think," said Donna, "you two just might be in need of my services when I become a lawyer."

Chapter Forty-four
Kris

Her sketches weren't too bad. Some she had drawn in the Forresters' back yard, not that there was much of interest there. Then she had imposed on Joey's good will and stopped at the bridges to sketch some more. Yes, the wind had been bothersome.

Kris stowed them in a folder. These she should take back to Miami with her, rather than hanging them on her bedroom walls. Part of her portfolio, the portfolio on which she did not really need to work yet. She wanted to get a start on real art classes at the university, instead of the required coursework she was taking now. Those felt like a rehashing of high school.

Out into the kitchen. Her bedroom was close to the kitchen; she could have had the bigger one Donny occupied but she liked being closer to both kitchen and front door. Not to mention the bathroom. "I'm going to be on my way," she announced to her mom.

"It's early," said Missus Greene.

It was. "I should help Ronnie set things up." Not that there was much to do. The food was already in place. "Donny knows he's invited if he wants to drop by."

"It's not good weather for him to ride his bike."

Kris could only shrug. "If he wanted a ride he should be here." Instead he was, in fact, riding his bike. Somewhere. She went out through the door into the garage and then to her Volkswagen, parked in the drive. She definitely was not going to ride her bike!

She still needed to find a way to get it to Miami. Kris looked to the low, black cloud sheet, rushing from the west. There hadn't been much rain yet. It would come. She slipped into the front seat and placed the stack of LPs she'd carried under her arm beside her. Every Beatles album was included. Kris liked the Beatles.

Straight down Third Avenue she drove, through the shopping area, across Fifth. It was the quickest way to the Deerfields. Turn on Fourth North, a couple jogs, and she was pulling up before Ronnie's house.

Howard Deerfield's Datsun sat to one side. The Simca was the only other car.

But Ronnie didn't seem to be home. The front door was locked. Kris deposited herself in one of the rattan chairs on the porch. Or car port. At least it was on the east side of the house and protected from the wind. Still, it might be necessary to move the party indoors. Even over Ronnie's objections.

No sense in just sitting here. She went to the rear of the carport and turned left into the screened walkway that followed the contour of the L-shaped house. The door by the utility room? Nope. Locked too. Right, past the restroom, the workbenches, and to the rear screen door that opened onto the back yard. No point in stepping out there. Gusts of wind bent the tops of the pines, only slightly darker than the sky against which they stood silhouetted.

It was getting colder, wasn't it? Doors slamming. She went back to see Paulette climbing out of Joey's Corvair. Ronnie got out of the back and waved. "We had to go pick up Paulette. Everyone else is on their own!"

The three girls hurried into the shelter of the car port. "Gee," commented Kris. "You could have brought at least a guy or two."

"Weren't you going to invite Mackie?" Joey asked.

"He opted out this time. We'll see him on Sunday, at James's farewell."

Paulette gave her a long, appraising look. "You don't have a thing with this Macklin boy, do you? I thought you was, er, were Willie Booth's girlfriend."

Joey snickered. Even Ronnie went so far as to slightly smirk. There was no way Kris was going to let her in on Mackie's secret. Secret? She couldn't think of a better word for it. "We're just old friends. We dated a little in high school but there's nothing now."

Paulette nodded. She didn't look completely convinced. That was her problem!

Ronnie unlocked. "Come on in. I think we may need to let the party spill into the living room."

"We can roast marshmallows in the fireplace!" Kris enthused.

"No way am I cleaning it up along with the rest of the place," came

Ronnie's reply. "I expect this rowdy bunch to make a mess of it."

"We'll help," Paulette assured her, quite seriously.

"Thanks," said Ronnie, just as seriously, though she probably had the urge to laugh. Kris certainly did. "I may need to limit food and drink to outside."

"Maybe dancing too," Joey said. "It will help keep us warm!"

It might well be getting too cold to hang out there. The wind would come around more northerly too, sooner or later, and there would be less shelter from it. Later, Kris hoped. "Not that any of us have ever seen you dancing," she said.

"She only does it in the privacy of her room," asserted Ronnie.

Joey nodded. "Naked."

Her friends only smiled. They were used to that sort of crack from Joey. Paulette looked like she didn't know whether she should laugh or not. Maybe she even believed it. Kris was half-inclined to believe it herself.

She did not intend to investigate. "Let's get things set up."

A couple card tables. Ronnie's new stereo. Set out the snacks. Ice could go into the coolers and the drinks too, so things would be cold when guests began to show up. Guests would show up, wouldn't they? There would be an awful lot of food and drink for the four of them if they didn't!

"No grilling, I guess," said Ronnie. "It's way too windy to set up the charcoal grill outside." Or even in the carport, probably.

"Oh! I can fix that," Joey informed them. "We have a camp stove at home. I'll run and get it. With me, Paulette?"

"Sure."

No sooner had the Corvair backed out than a blue and white van appeared. Joey waved to it and sped away. The side door slid open even before the van rolled to a stop. "Where's Joey off to?" called Sandy.

"She's getting some things from her home," Kris called back. "She won't be long."

Ronnie came out to stand beside her. "So, at least one guy," she said, as Russ Penn emerged. "No, two of them." A boy they did not recognize hopped down after Sandy, to be followed by Jackie Booth.

"Donny isn't here?" complained Jackie. "We wanted to dance with him again!"

"Hey, you have me," said her companion.

"But you can't dance worth a darn," Sandy informed him.

Kris told them, "Donny might show up later." She wasn't going to count on it. Especially after sunset; her brother might well be headed to services this evening.

Wherever they were being held! There were plans to finally build a synagogue in Naples, her parents said, but the Jewish community had been meeting in various halls and centers in the mean time.

"Is your friend Maxie coming?"

Jackie snickered. "Maybe she'll ride up on her horse."

"She lives kind of far out," Sandy said. "I wouldn't count on her showing. This is Jerry."

"Hi," said Jerry. "Thanks for having us." Kris could tell he didn't know which of them he was thanking.

But Ronnie said, "You're welcome. Drinks in the cooler over there. Snacks." She pointed to one of the card tables. "We hope to have something hot in a while. And," she continued, "if you need to use the restroom, go to the one around the corner, not one of those inside. Okay?"

"Anything beyond the living room is off limits," Kris added to this. It should be made plain and simple to them. "In fact, I'm appointing Sandy and Jackie as our security guards to keep everyone where they belong."

"That means we get to thump you if you stray," Sandy informed her date. Jackie's date?

"Who chose that music?" asked Jackie. "That's another reason we need Donny here." The three went into the house.

Russel had held back through all of this. "I'll thank you too. Both of you, and Joey when she gets back. I know you three are a team."

"But I'm the captain," announced Kris.

"Nope, that would be me," came Ronnie's immediate retort.

"At least we agree it isn't Joey."

"I might not have come," Russ went on, pretty much ignoring their exchange, "except Sandy wanted to. I'll admit that. It was good of you to, um, think of her."

"I'm glad both of you came," said Ronnie. "And Jackie too and that boy—"

"Jerry," Kris supplied.

"Right, Jerry. I was afraid no one would show up with this weather." She looked out through the screens at the stormy skies. "And I'm not sure anyone else is going to."

Ten minutes later, someone did show up. Joey and Paulette, with the stove, green and a bit rusty, with two burners. They also had a cardboard box containing tongs and other instruments of grilling.

Kris stood watching Joey and Ronnie getting it all set up in the middle of the space. She wasn't going to get in the way, particularly as she would have absolutely no idea what she was doing. A flame? Oh, Joey had struck a big kitchen match. She cursed under her breath, pumped something a few times, and struck another. They'd get it lit eventually, Kris was sure. Her attention went elsewhere. Ah, someone had put on the 'Rubber Soul' album. That was better. She would just stand here, listen a while, watch the scudding clouds.

Paulette sidled up to her a couple minutes later. She didn't say anything for a few seconds and Kris's attention began to drift away again. "I didn't know about Harold Macklin," Paulette blurted. "I mentioned him to Jackie and she filled me in."

It did not surprise Kris than Jackie would know. Maybe it didn't surprise her she would share the knowledge too. "It's kind of his own business."

"I guess so. But my family would consider it a sin."

Maybe Paulette did too. If so, she wasn't going to dwell on it.

But at least she would no longer suspect Kris of cheating on Will.

Chapter Forty-five
Ronnie

"It burns kerosene," Joey told her. "I promise I won't burn your house down."

"That promise won't mean much if my folks come home to smoldering ashes." She trusted Joey but still felt a tad uncomfortable with those flames. Oh, it was probably safe and she hadn't liked the idea of cooking hot dogs and burgers on the kitchen range at all.

"Incoming!" someone yelled. Ronnie turned to spy Russ Wesolowski's green van creeping up the driveway. There were surfboards in its roof racks.

And the two young men who tumbled out and entered the carport looked rather wet. Their hair, anyway.

"Don't tell me you two were out surfing," said Joey, turning her burner down to where it barely flickered, yellow and blue.

Russ said, "It was way too rough and out of control for board surfing but we jumped in and body surfed a little."

"He body surfed. I rode the little plywood *paipo* I've made myself."

"Pie-poe?" asked Karen, standing in the living room doorway. That put her a couple inches higher than normal. Ronnie had no doubt she liked that. Did she do it consciously? It might have just become a habit of sorts.

"It's a fancy word for a belly board."

"A proper Hawaiian word," sniffed Alan. "Sort of. It wasn't pronounced quite that way originally."

"And it means something like 'head first.' My brother was making them for himself even before he had a surfboard."

"Oh, how is work going on your new board?"

"Slowly." There was a touch of chagrin in Alan's voice. "I keep changing my mind as to exactly what I want."

"That's true of a lot of things in life," Joey allowed.

"Amen," said Ronnie, mostly to herself.

"You're working tomorrow morning, right?" Russ asked Joey. "We can expect you early?"

"Yeah. Darn, I think this blew out again." Both guys bent down to examine the stove. As most guys, they thought they knew mechanical things.

"If you want to surf again, we intend to head for the beach as soon as we're done. All three of us together can make a quick job of it."

"You'll have a wetsuit for me, I hope. Ah, there we go." The flame sprang up.

"And you'll need it," Alan told her.

Did she feel—what, jealousy over the way Joey got along with the brothers? Ronnie had put Alan behind her. He shouldn't mean anything. He and Joey would make a great couple, in fact. Everyone could see that. And Russ, well, there had never been anything there, though she'd had a little crush on him, years ago.

Maybe it was just that she had both of them! And poor Ronnie had no one. She came close to laughing aloud.

"Who's this?" It was getting dark enough one saw headlights rather than the forms of cars. That was as much the result of the increasing storminess as of the approach of sunset. Two figures ran to shelter.

"Hi. Louie!" called Sandy. "Someone to dance with, Jackie!"

Louie. Reggie Dozier's little brother. A senior? Maybe a junior. He did not look overly happy about dancing with anyone, nor even being there. Regina shook water from herself. No one here would be surprised she had no date, not even a fake one.

Reggie looked around. "Hi, Ronnie." She waved toward Joey, at the grill, the Wezzies still hovering near. "Is this it? Or do we expect a late crowd?"

"I wouldn't count on one." But someone could still show up, couldn't they?

"This weather would keep anyone with any sense away. Hi, Russ." She and Penn went inside. Louie stood staring around, uncomfortable with being there. This wasn't his crowd. For that matter, it wasn't his sister's crowd.

And she had already abandoned the boy. He was a rather handsome guy, wasn't he? In a square-jawed conventional sense. The blondish hair didn't hurt either. "Didn't have anything better to do today?" she asked him.

He gave her an uncertain grin. "It wouldn't be polite to say so, would it?"

"Definitely not. I'll assume you dropped your other plans for the evening to be with us. I think Joey has started cooking." She walked over to her friend, expecting Dozier to follow. He did.

"We did include something for our vegetarian friends here, didn't we?" Joey asked, looking up from her grill.

Had they? "Do you guys eat cheese?"

They looked at each other a moment. "We have mixed feelings about it in our house," said Russ.

"We're okay with dairy in general."

"But making cheese means killing calves. For the rennin."

"What's rennin?" asked Louie.

"An enzyme from the lining of their stomachs. It helps them digest their mothers' milk."

"Russ is full of science facts like that," said Joey.

Louie grimaced. Ronnie suspected he might lay off cheese for a while. That sort of thing didn't last, though. Not usually.

"Did you go out today?" Alan asked him.

Ronnie had no idea what he meant by that. Louie did. "Too wild for me! Maybe I'll give it a try in the morning."

Alan nodded. "Us too. And Joey, if she doesn't mind it being bitterly cold."

"Yes," said Russ, taking it up. "The waves are likely to freeze solid and we'll have to ski down them."

Joey only emitted a 'humph' and returned her attention to her burgers. Hot dogs grilled on the other burner. She wouldn't be able to fix many of either at one time. But then, there weren't that many guests.

"Someone else arriving," said Alan, peering toward the darkened drive. "That isn't Gordie's car, is it?"

"We didn't invite him," said Ronnie.

"But that doesn't mean he won't show up," Joey said, not bothering to look. "And it's okay with me, as long as he doesn't bring that Walker girl."

Ronnie didn't think he'd drive that open Moke of his through this weather. Debbie Walker's MG wouldn't be much better. "It's Donna," she announced. She'd actually forgotten they'd invited her, with the distraction of everyone else showing up. "Alone." That last was spoken softly. Maybe no one even heard it.

The Donna she knew, neatly and conservatively dressed, hair carefully in place. There was hair spray involved, Ronnie was certain. Not at all like the boat-rowing girl Kris and Joey had described to her.

"I'm sure you have loads already but I brought chips," she announced, holding up a couple bags as she entered. "And dip. Smoked mullet dip."

"Ooh, stinky," was Louie's comment.

"And delicious," countered Joey. "Bring it over here."

It was unlikely anyone else would show. That was okay. Ronnie had envisioned a small get-together like this. But not one so dull.

Despite the music. Soul. Wilson Pickett, right? That was certainly preferable to hard rock. She wondered who brought the record. It wasn't one of hers. Ronnie went on into the living room to see how things were going. No one dancing? Well, no, not with food starting to appear.

She would have to clean up in the morning. Her parents might or might not be back tomorrow evening but it was best to get it done. Not that this was a rowdy group who would tear the place up or make out in the closets or pee in vases or any of the other things she'd heard of happening.

She almost wished one of them would and liven things up a little. Reggie and Russel had settled down on the hearth of the cold fireplace and were in earnest, hushed conversation about something. They'd been that way since she arrived.

And where was Paulette? Paulette was her friend and she was neglecting her again, wasn't she? Over on the couch with Kris. The two of them had kind of hit it off, hadn't they? Ronnie had noticed it the night they went to the church together.

Yes, Paulette was her friend, but not like Kris and Joey. She didn't feel the same sort of connection. Their friendship just didn't *matter* in the same way. Ronnie thought maybe that was both a good and a bad thing.

And Donna? She seemed to have more of a connection to Kris and Joey than to her. And Kris had barely known her a few days ago. Oh, none of them had really known her. She stood and looked things over. No need to play hostess for a few minutes. Maybe no need later either.

Ronnie decided to look over the rest of the house, just to make certain all was well, that no one had strayed. Through the living room, into the dark hall. Silly, she told herself. Nobody wants to come back here. Around to the back way into the kitchen.

The lights were turned off, to discourage anyway from going in. Not that it mattered. They could be flipped on if she needed to get anything. She looked out the window; from here the view was straight down the screened in walkway that ran to the back yard. At the end, at the screen door, stood two figures, looking out into the stormy night.

Jackie, obviously. She could tell that just from the shape and the height. And—Alan. Yes, that was Alan. The haircut gave him away, if nothing else. The high school boys weren't allowed to grow it that long. Then he leaned down and kissed Jackie Booth.

It shouldn't be surprising, she told herself. Alan was a good friend of Jackie's brother. They had probably seen a lot of each other, long before Ronnie had dated him, when she had barely known Alan Wesolowski existed.

Ronnie had to admit she wasn't bothered at all. Maybe *that* was surprising, despite her claims of being over him. But what of Joey? Did she have feelings for the boy or was that just something her friends had imagined?

She was not going to be the one to say anything to her. Maybe to Kris. Maybe not. Ronnie turned from the window, returned to the living room. "Anyone need anything?" she asked.

Chapter Forty-six
Joey

She had followed Russ's van in her Corvair, rather than riding with the Wesolowski brothers. "We'll check the pier first," she'd been told. "If it's good we won't bother with any other spot."

It was good, or good enough. "Either side should do," felt Alan. Guys with boards were already in the water. Yes, on both sides of the pilings. "I might try those lefts on the north side. It looks to be lining up pretty well."

They had pulled their vehicles into the street south of the pier—Thirteenth—and now stood looking at the water. It looked nice, the sky clear, the waves not too big but rolling in as long, even lines. But damn it was cold! "You'd be better off on this side," Russ said. "Let's get our boards."

Alan helped Joey lift her long board off the roof racks while Russ unloaded theirs. She wouldn't get to use Alan's board today, she suspected. Maybe Russ would let her try out his new 'stick.' That's what he called it sometimes. It seemed to come easy to Russ to use surfer words like those but Alan seemed a little—well, uncomfortable with slang at times.

"Here." Russ handed her a wetsuit, undoubtedly the one she'd used before. "You might as well keep that one for now."

"A loaner," said Alan, "for the rest of the season. You'll want your own next winter."

If she surfed then. If she even surfed again this winter.

"I think you'll want another board too," said Russ.

"Alan will have to make it for me." She'd have to get out of these warm clothes to slip into the wetsuit, wouldn't she? It was a good thing there was a swim suit underneath them. Off came the flannel shirt, the corduroy jeans, and Joey shimmied into the short john. She couldn't help note the speedos the boys wore. Or the boys inside those speedos. Everyone in rubber. Wax the boards. Oil in their ears, as before.

Out she and Russ went into the cool water—though decidedly warmer than the air—as Alan headed up the beach. "You could probably push off the bottom, up here closer to the beach, like you did before," Russ told her. "It would keep you out of the wind." He looked toward the swaying tops of the Australian pines. "Not that it's at all bad. And water will sap the warmth from your body more quickly."

Being the scientist again. Something she both liked and disliked about Wesolowski. "I'll try paddling," she told him.

And she did and the nose of the 'Stretch' board went under the water more than once, spilling her. But she also managed to catch a wave now and again and even to ride them, angling toward shore but not really turning the way the guys did. Joey suspected that was harder with this barge she was riding.

Ah, but what a gorgeous morning it was, after yesterday! A completely clear, intensely blue sky arched above the Gulf. Everything seemed to stand out in sharp relief this day, like a surrealist landscape. Was that someone waving to them on the beach? She shaded her eyes from the glare of the morning sun. Angelica Summerlin.

Joey waved back. She'd go in and talk to her after the next wave. This one? She stroked and thought she'd caught it, only to be left behind. And the one after it was already breaking. Oh well. She paddled and was borne forward by the white water. On your feet, girl! Show Jelly you're a real, honest-to-goodness surfer!

She managed it for a few seconds before hopping off into shin-deep water. Joey as much dragged as carried the big board up onto the beach.

"So you actually do surf," came Angelica's greeting.

"That is open to debate." She turned and looked out across the water. "I may be done for the day."

"If you want to get rinsed off you can come up to our place. Change, too."

That sounded like a good idea. Joey also suspected Angelica would like to talk. Maybe she would herself. "Okay. Let me get this airplane wing onto my roof." Alan had called it that once. She later found out that it was a line from some movie. But it was appropriate for the lengthy surfboard.

Angelica helped her lift it on, hook the retaining straps into place, and then settled into the front seat. She might as well ride back to her house, close though it was. "You look like you just came off a ski slope," Joey told her, as she turned the ignition. The engine didn't catch on the first try. She feared a new battery might be on her shopping list soon. There it went.

"My down jacket? I guess I have worn it skiing." Angelica's seeming detachment gave way to a sudden laugh. "It would get pretty soggy if I went surfing in it!"

"Rubber is better," Joey responded. She hadn't peeled off the wetsuit. The Wezzies had said to keep it, right? They would know she had left. Russ, anyway. She backed around, headed down to Gulf Shore. A few blocks north and she was turning again, to the Summerlin house. She could probably see Alan surfing from the end of the street. Not unless she got out of the Corvair and she didn't feel it was worth bothering. "I'll rinse off outside," she said, to head off any invitation to use an indoor shower. She didn't know whether Angelica might have suggested it or not.

"Okay. You have a towel and everything, right? The hedges give enough privacy you can even change outside."

Joey didn't think being nude in the Summerlin's back yard was the best of ideas. Still, it might be nice to get out of the wet swimsuit. "As long as Gordie isn't lurking anywhere with his camera."

"Yeah, Gordie." She said nothing more but left Joey to find her way around to the outdoor shower.

She was glad Angelica hadn't decided to come with her. A rinse in the cold water, a toweling off in the colder air. It was warming up but she was in the shadows of the many trees. Oh, she might as well change. Even if Gordon Rhein was lurking somewhere with a tele-photo! Out of the top and into a tee. Joey looked cautiously about before slipping off the bottom and stepping into her trousers. The flannel shirt. That was better. She tossed the wet clothes and towel into one of the lawn chairs before going into the house.

"Lumberjack Joey!" exclaimed Jelly, as she entered. "You need a stocking cap to go with that shirt."

"It's in the car." Which was truth. She sat down in the nearest living room chair. "Hey, James. Too late for pan perdu again, I guess."

"Tomorrow," he said. "If you make it to early mass."

"I'll try."

"And I'll look for you." The boy headed up the stairs. He must have come down just to say hello to her. Hey, he could see the shower from his bedroom, couldn't he?

"No pan perdu but I can fill you with hot coffee," said Angelica.

"Sounds good." Quite good. So would bacon and eggs and pancakes but she wouldn't mention those. Sylvie didn't need to be bothered.

A minute later, Angelica returned with large mugs. "I know you take milk," she said, handing Joey one and settling in the chair beside her. "So, tell me about the party. I'll bet it wasn't much fun without me there."

"Oh, it was quite dreary. Everyone sat around moaning, 'oh, why didn't we ask Jelly to come?'"

"Yes, I can see that. We had a very small party of our own. That is, Debbie and Gordie stopped by and hung around most of the evening." A little frown. "I don't know why she has Gordie in tow, when there's obviously nothing between them."

"Maybe to distract you while she worked her wiles on James."

"Maybe! To his credit, James didn't fool around with her. He could have if he'd wanted. I think she wanted to give him a going-away present."

"Better not invite her to his party. Still set for tomorrow night?"

"It is. Gordie is invited, of course. Or maybe not of course. I'm not sure how he became part of our circle."

"You made him feel welcome, as I recall."

"Oh, you would bring that up. We definitely expect Harold Macklin. James insists it will be Mackie's farewell party too.

"Maybe everyone's."

"True enough, though there will be time for another party for the rest of us. Who else? Your friend Reggie? She doesn't have a boyfriend, I take it."

That was a question that required some delicacy. Unless she simply went ahead and gossiped. Maybe there was no reason not to. "It's kind of hard to say. She had one in high school. A very serious one. Pretty much everyone knew they had a sexual relationship and it was assumed they'd get married." Joey rethought that. "Maybe not by Bob. He didn't treat Reggie very good."

Angelica nodded but it was hard to say what her thoughts might be. "Didn't she say she went to the prom with that Mike boy? Somebody said it."

"Yeah. Bob vetoed going and Mike Kelly filled in. They're in sort of the same vein, but Bob's worse. A bad-boy intellectual sort, who saw himself as an updated Kerouac or something of that sort."

Angelica only made a face at that.

"At least Mike does have some talent to back up that sort of persona. To make it short—"

"Too late for that."

"Yeah. Anyway, Bob got himself into trouble. Dealing pot."

"Oh, I've heard of big bales of it coming into Everglades."

"Nothing nearly that large scale. It was the usual thing. A little bit of weed for him and his friends. The courts around here don't care about that. Anyone caught with marijuana is a criminal." They had risked that themselves. It was really kind of stupid to do it. "It wasn't his first scrape with the law."

"So, prison?"

"Nope. He was given the option of having the charges dropped if he went into the military. The last I heard he was in Nam. I don't think he keeps in touch with Reggie." She did not say so but Joey felt this was a good thing.

"I'd say no boyfriend then. We should find her one," Angelica decided—and then changed her mind. "No, you'll have to do it, since I'll be back in Miami."

"I think she kind of likes Russel Penn."

"*My* Russel? I'm not sure I want to share him!"

"I guess you'll have to fight her. But when it comes to Russel it may be more a matter of a sympathetic ear than anything else. He has always been good at providing one."

"The future minister. He should come tomorrow. With or without Miss Dozier." Angelica sighed and shook her head. "Oh, I suppose anybody who wants can come. And we must have guitars this time."

"Why not?" said Joey, and sipped more of her coffee. It was quite good.

Chapter Forty-seven
Ronnie

"I'm afraid my pop disapproves of your surfer friends," said Paulette. "Or hippie friends. That's what he calls them."

"None of them really look much like hippies," objected Ronnie. Well, maybe the Wesolowski brothers. And they were surfers too. Officer Jones might have meant them. "Some of them are downright clean-cut."

"But they, uh, smoke dope, don't they?"

Ronnie managed to keep a straight face. "I've tried it myself a couple times."

"I guess I shouldn't be surprised. You all need to be careful. Especially if you have any more parties. The police might have their eye on you guys."

"I promise if I throw any more they'll be just as boring as last night." There hadn't even been much of a mess to clean up. None the less, she appreciated her friend—yes, Paulette was her friend—coming over to help get things in order before her parents returned.

Paulette smiled. Maybe even smirked. "I don't think you need to worry about a raid."

"But maybe the Summerlins?"

The girl only shrugged. "I don't know. They should be careful anyway."

Had anyone invited Paulette to James's going-away thing tomorrow? Ronnie thought that was going to be more of an inner-circle affair. Still, it was supposed to be Mackie's farewell too. If she asked Paulette to come, she should extend the invite to Carter too.

"The kitchen looks good. Let's move to the dining room." Ronnie hadn't been able to keep her guests out of there, as it was completely open to the living room. She'd given up trying and set out the food on the dining table when it got too nasty outside. "Have you said anything to Carter about college?"

"We've talked to him but he'll only say he's thinking about it.

Maybe you could come over and help convince him. Awful lot of potato chip crumbs in here."

"Okay." Perhaps she would. Or she could talk to him tomorrow night. "There's a farewell party for James and Mackie tomorrow. At the Summerlin place. You would both be welcome." Ronnie couldn't keep herself from snickering and adding, "And you won't be required to smoke any pot."

Though Carter Junior might well be willing. One picked up new habits when they left home. More so if they went all the way to Vietnam.

"One last party, huh? Do tell your friends to be careful."

"Our friends," said Ronnie.

"Uh-huh. I'll run it by Junior."

Why did Paulette seem so reticent? "Does your father think you shouldn't hang with us?"

"He didn't tell me not to." Paulette finished brushing the crumbs off the table and started spraying the Formica top. "And he likes you. He says you're the sort of friend he hoped I'd make in college."

That was flattering. Ronnie Deerfield a valued connection! She couldn't help wondering if being white was part of that. "But concerned, huh?"

"Yeah."

"We'll broom up the floors when everything else is done," said Ronnie. "I'd better use the canister vac on the furniture."

"Good enough. We'll get it done in no time."

"We make an efficient team. If this college thing doesn't work out, we could start a maid service."

"Don't say that," snapped Paulette. "Don't ever say that."

She looked like she was going to burst into tears. What had Ronnie done wrong? "Okay. We're going to be tremendously successful and hire the Summerlins as our domestics."

Her friend grinned. "That's more like it, girl. But today, I guess we are maids, huh? Let's get to it."

By early afternoon, no trace of the party remained—to Ronnie's eyes. "It might even fool my folks," she announced. "How about some lunch?"

"Sure. Nothing fancy. A sandwich is fine."

"Peanut butter and jelly? Fried bologna? BLT?"

Paulette looked a tad exasperated. "Whatever, Ronnie."

"How about I make some grilled cheese? That's always nice on a cold day." She could even do the classic tomato soup to go with it. Nah, too much trouble and she didn't even like it that much.

"Sounds good. Your brother should be back in uniform by now, shouldn't he?"

"Yep." She rummaged through the refrigerator, searching for cheese. Mild cheddar worked nicely. She certainly wasn't going to use the Velveeta if she could help it. "You like Rick, don't you?"

Paulette didn't answer at once. "I do. Pop likes Rick too. But he doesn't approve of dating someone of, um, another color."

"Oh, then your brother can't be my boyfriend anymore?" It was a joke, of course, one they had been making for weeks now. She hoped her quip didn't find its way back to Carter Junior! Ah, there was a brick of Colby. That would work.

"You'll have to meet in secret!"

"The van and its ramp would be a bit of a giveaway." A wide skillet on the largest front burner. Butter. Had to use butter for a grilled cheese.

"Here, I'll slice that," said Paulette, taking the block of cheese. Good, she didn't cut it too thin.

"Then I take it you don't agree with your father," Ronnie continued.

"I don't really know," admitted Paulette. "Especially when it comes to marriage. Inter-racial marriage. That's like—like cutting ties with your community."

It was also jumping kind of far ahead. "Well, you don't have to marry any white guys right now. But you can go over and make out with one of your choice tomorrow night. Smoke pot with him too."

"Oh, you're as silly as your friends sometimes."

"You're just an easy audience. Let's get those in the pan."

She wouldn't mind actually dating a black man, would she? Ronnie didn't think so. Kris and Will hadn't bothered her in the least. She knew Will. He'd been a friend since they were little kids.

Best, maybe, to just avoid the subject around Paulette. And she would not mention Jackie and Alan!

Chapter Forty-eight
Joey

True to his word, James Summerlin was making her French toast for breakfast. He had been, as expected, at early mass. Not Angelica—she was always a bit hit-and-miss when it came to rising before dawn.

But she sat with them now in the kitchen while James busied himself. She had even changed her flannel pajamas for slacks and a sweater.

"Do you really have to leave so soon?" asked Joey. This coffee wasn't as good as what Angelica had served her yesterday. Maybe Sylvie Cooper had a secret way of making it.

James looked up from the bowl where he whisked eggs and cream. "It will take me a little time to get there. I'm going by the scenic route."

"Not by bus?" Not that she would put it past him.

"Nope. Train. You know a passenger train still rolls into Naples. I've worked it out and I should have no problem getting to Boston by rail." James poured his mixture into a shallow ceramic dish. Joey thought it might be a quiche dish, though she had never used one nor made a quiche. Or even eaten one. "I rode trains a lot in Europe."

"Me too," said Angelica.

"Sophisty-kates," Joey muttered, just loud enough they could hear her.

"Yep. You can't be a full member of the club until you ride a train too," Angelica informed her.

James was soaking slices of French bread in his mixture. "Just ride your bike down the tracks sometime and it will count," he said.

"Oh, I've done that loads of times. Awfully bumpy!"

"Good enough," declared Angelica. "You're back in good standing."

She would like to ride a train sometime. Maybe next summer. She could ride—oh, anywhere. New York, and visit Jam and Jelly's sister, maybe. Lin was likely to come down to Naples, though.

"Ronnie says the cops are interested in your dope-smoking ways," said Joey.

"Then they don't care about the beer?" James asked.

"Or the fornication?"

"She didn't mention those. Paulette's father passed along a warning."

"I don't think any of our neighbors would have complained," said James, transferring his soaked slices of bread to a saute pan. "They are old time Naples residents and fairly tolerant."

"And Paulette wouldn't have said anything," added Angelica.

"I don't think she ever witnessed any of us smoking pot."

"Oh, no, I guess not. She wouldn't have said anything, anyway." Angelica turned from her brother to Joey. "She's going to be a teacher, isn't she?"

"I think so. Elementary." Joey wasn't completely sure of that.

"Teachers are a lot like cops," stated James.

"I wonder if Alan hates police too," Angelica replied to this. "He referred to his teachers as jailers."

"Oh? When was this?" James hadn't heard it before but it had gotten around to Joey.

"On the day we will never speak to you about," his sister informed him. "So why are teachers like cops?"

James sighed. Still out of the loop! "Both dedicated to a career of public service, intending to do good for others."

"And in positions of authority," Joey said.

"Like priests," Angelica had to add.

"Oh, yes. Far too eager to order others around."

"I'm certainly not able to do that around here," claimed James.

It was true, Joey had to admit. Jam went out of his way not to assert himself. "Ronnie took it on herself to invite the Jones twins tonight but she thinks it's unlikely they'll show."

"But Ronnie is coming," James said.

"Despite you," his sister told him.

"Yeah, despite me. All that happened last summer made me just want to get away and think things over." He stopped and seemed to think things over again right then. "Which was terribly unfair to Ronnie."

Yes, it was, thought Joey. No point in saying so. "It bothered you more than her, I'm pretty sure. Though—" Maybe there was no point in saying this either. Oh, what the heck. "It may have been a factor in breaking up with Alan."

"I learned about that not long after I left. Via Angelica." He nodded in his twin's direction. "That 's not something you ever wrote to Lin about." He did not sound completely certain but Joey chose not to contradict him. No, she hadn't told his older sister about any of it. James didn't really need to know that.

"These are ready." As he began to slide golden slabs of pan perdu, French toast, onto the three white, earthenware plates, he glanced out the kitchen window into the back yard. "We have a visitor. She looks a bit reluctant to intrude."

Joey stood up to get a look. "Donna. I'll let her in."

"You might as well."

A minute later, Donna was in the kitchen with them. "You're way early for the party," Angelica told her.

"But not for breakfast. Want a plate?" James slid one of them her direction.

"Okay." She settled at the table with them. "I wasn't sure about stopping this early but I saw Joey's Corvair out there."

"It was too cold for the bicycle this morning!" Colder even than yesterday. A little.

"And here I was out rowing at dawn. Anyway—um, anyway, I'm not going to make your party, James, so I decided to come by now and say goodbye. Maybe goodbye to all of you."

"Get a better offer?" Angelica's drawl was hard to read. This didn't prevent James from giving her a disapproving look.

"My father made you sort of off-limits. He thinks you're a bunch of drug users."

Both Summerlins looked toward Joey. "We've heard rumors the police think so too," James said.

"Sheesh. I was afraid he might have said something. He smelled the pot smoke on my clothes." Her grimace shifted to a small smile. "I'm not altogether sure how he recognized it."

"Clients, maybe?" Angelica suggested.

"Maybe. Of course, he didn't think I'd smoked any myself."

"Of course," agreed Joey. "Just bad company."

She had an unexpectedly earnest response to the joke. "The best company I've had in a long time. I get so frustrated trying to be responsible and well-behaved and hang around with other responsible and well-behaved people."

Angelica laughed aloud. "And we're not?"

"At least you're not boring."

"You do have Mike," Joey pointed out.

Donna said nothing immediately but pretty obviously wanted to. She took a deep breath, exhaled slowly. "Sometimes I just feel like breaking loose from him too. He's so—so straight. So upright and do-right."

"Kind of nice to look at, though," felt Joey.

"And kind of nice in bed." Donna snickered in a quite surprising manner. "Upright there too."

There was no good way to respond to that statement. A polite chuckle? A knowing smile? James jumped in. "So we're all out of bounds?"

"Just you Summerlins. And your parties. I don't think he has the least problem with Ronnie Deerfield, if he even connects her to you."

Probably not Kris and her either. It didn't matter that much to Joey. In a week, they would all be somewhere else. Except for her. "So we behave tonight?" she asked.

"It would be best," agreed James. Angelica pouted ostentatiously but nodded agreement. "Our parents will be home, anyway," he continued.

"That puts a damper on any party," said Donna.

"It does," agreed Joey. "And to make matters worse, mine will be here too."

Chapter Forty-nine
Kris

"Jeff was never charged with anything. The police talked to the college and they asked him to go and that was an end to it." Mackie's tone reflected that finality. "So he has no record and could go to some other school or into the military."

"I suppose that's best," said Kris. She wasn't really sure it was but the whole situation seemed complicated.

"I told my parents there was some sort of public disorderly conduct involved, and let them take it as they would." He glanced toward the pier as they crossed Twelfth, before adding, "They liked Jeff."

But had no idea what sort of relationship existed between him and their son. "They're likely to guess fighting or drinking," she said. That was probably just as well too.

"Yeah. And warn me not to get involved in anything of that sort. The Christmas lights are still up?" They had pulled in alongside the Summerlin property in Mackie's car-of-the-day. Not, unfortunately, the yellow Mustang.

"They make a thing of taking them down tonight. Or maybe it's tomorrow. This is Twelfth Night."

"Oh. Like in the Twelve Days of Christmas?"

"Yep. Maria Summerlin is traditional about that sort of thing. So is Joey's mom." There would be adults here tonight. Three or four couples, according to Joey. Mackie's parents should have been invited too. Or even hers! Hadn't anyone thought of that?

But the Macklin family would have their own farewell tomorrow. Mackie parked across the street from the house. "It's warmed up," he noted, emerging from behind the wheel. Kris got out before he could come around and open the door for her. "All the sun today."

Maybe warm enough to hang outside? That would be good. Even better if they fired up the grill. "That's Teri Planter's car," she said, nodding toward the white Valiant. "Joey's mom. I wonder if the Corvair broke down."

"Wouldn't she just get on her bike?"

"Yeah." Definitely. "Here comes Ronnie." The Simca came slowly up the street, stopped as the driver looked things over, then pulled in behind their ride.

"Alone," commented Kris, and went over to greet her. The three crossed the street to the lawn. It was still light out and the Christmas lights twined around the trees added their glow.

"Is Carter coming?" asked Mackie.

"No. Paulette opted for a Sunday night service at her church, and without her to drive him—" She shrugged.

"I could have gone over," Mackie asserted. "Too late now, I guess."

Ronnie could have driven the guy over here, thought Kris. There might be more to it than just a schedule conflict. No point in thinking about that now.

Not only Joey but her parents sat on the porch. That explained why the Corvair wasn't there. Maria Summerlin was with them, at one of the tables. Angelica and James sat nearby, not seeming to pay much attention.

"Oh, welcome," said Maria, rising. "We are glad you could come, Harold, and we could say goodbye to you."

"And I thank you for having me, ma'am." He looked out across the back yard. "Kris explained why the Christmas lights are on today."

"Yes, we turn them all off at midnight. A symbol, one might call it, of the season ending."

"We could do that if we stayed up that late," said Teri Planter.

"Our tree came down this afternoon," Wayne added. "'Bout time. It was shedding needles something fierce."

"I must go in and see to our other guests," Maria went on. "Preston can not manage alone, you know."

Teri Planter got up and followed her into the house. Wayne didn't look like he particularly wanted to but sighed and went with them.

"Guests?" asked Kris, taking a seat."

"Some of them staying a while," said Angelica.

"I've moved back into the library so my aunt and uncle can have my room." James had slept there while Lin visited last summer.

"Tia Tina?" asked Joey. "And your Uncle Whatshisname?"

"Oscar. But neither of our cousins came with them. Rosa thinks she's too sophisticated and Miriam has a husband."

"Miriam married a gringo like her aunt," Angelica let them know.

"The Baileys are here too. I don't know if you've ever met them."

"Mutual friends of my mom and Missus Summerlin," supplied Joey. "There aren't that many."

From church, Kris guessed. Or maybe from when Joey attended the Catholic school. Or something else entirely! "So, do we expect anyone else?"

"No idea," said James.

Ronnie spoke up. "No high school kids. They're all back in school tomorrow."

"I did invite Russel. And Sandy."

His sister might have pretended she didn't hear that. Or maybe her attention was on the little sports cart pulling in at the curb. "Did you invite Debbie Walker too?"

"Not me." He peered toward the MG. "That isn't Gordie with her, is it?"

Kris slipped on her glasses. "Reggie." She slipped them off almost as quickly. "I didn't know they were friends."

"I'm not sure they even knew each other before the New Year party," said Joey. "I did tell Reg to come so I could be held responsible for Debbie too."

"Yes, we'll blame you," Angelica told her. "And if she gets rowdy, you have to be our bouncer."

"She might enjoy that," said Kris.

Chapter Fifty

Ronnie

"No date," murmured Ronnie. "And no brother."

"But a guitar," said Angelica. "That partly makes up for Rusty not coming." She gave a Ronnie a sidelong look. "You expected a date?"

"Not really," she admitted. She hadn't. And she was not going to mention Jackie.

"Hi, everyone," said Alan, placing his guitar case on one of the outside tables. Most of the younger guests had moved from the porch to the yard. "Your parents home, Ronnie?"

"Got back just before I took off. Now I don't have to worry about them! Russ isn't coming?"

"Had to be somewhere else. He does say he'll come over before heading off himself." This he directed toward Angelica.

"He'd better," she remarked. "I suppose James and I must get our instruments out now."

"Later," said her brother. "There's food inside."

Ronnie thought food—and warmth—was an excellent idea. The still air was getting noticeably chillier, as the sun sank into the Gulf. The strands of Christmas lights shone all the brighter against the darkening sky. A few had gone out, here and there.

A car door slammed. "Late arrival," someone said. It might have been Debbie. She was hanging close to James, wasn't she?

"Not too late."

Russ Penn's van. And Sandy was with him.

Angelica had no comment about that. Only, "He doesn't have his guitar."

"He might not want to play this time," came Alan's laconic reply.

This time. Oh, he was referring to the last time the two had played together. With Angelica. Ronnie suddenly realized the statement could be taken more than one way. Did Alan intend that or was she just finding meanings that weren't there?

Anyway, it was good that Sandy had decided to come. The girl avoided looking at Angelica. Maybe Russel did too.

Instead she ran up and hugged James. "I couldn't let you go without saying goodbye!"

He only smiled and returned the embrace. "It's good to have you here. Come on in and have something to eat."

"If our parents haven't wolfed it all down," added Joey.

The tall tree still stood in the living room, still lit, and little the worse for wear. A northern tree, Ronnie assumed. It certainly lasted better than the local pines. They settled around it, adults and—well, they were all adults, weren't they? Except Sandy, and she must be pretty close to it. Ronnie could never be a child at Christmas again. That sucked.

But eventually, the younger guests gravitated to the dining room, leaving their elders to the tree and their conversation. Angelica and James had retrieved their guitars but no one was playing yet. James idly strummed his, adjusted a tuning key. Kris and Joey were whispering to each other about something.

They were as boring as the 'grown-ups' they'd left in the other room. Debbie blundered into the silence. "I hear you're going to be a minister, Russel," she said. "This one—" A nod toward James, at her side. A little too close at her side maybe. "Says he's going to be a priest but I'm not sure I believe him."

"That is what I'm studying," James told her.

"I think it's kind of stupid."

"So do I sometimes."

"You have doubts then?" asked Russ. "I did for, um, a little while but I'm committed again now. More than before." He gave Ronnie a quick look.

He must be thinking of the little talk they'd had in his driveway. Ronnie didn't feel quite comfortable with the idea of her having dispensed spiritual advice.

"I always have doubts." James didn't sound very serious about it but she knew he was. Ronnie thought she knew him pretty well now. "So does my sister but she doesn't let them bother her." More than one pair of eyes turned toward Angelica.

"Not about having a calling, like my brother, but about religion in general. I'm not inclined to take most of Christianity literally."

"I'm not sure you need to," countered Russ. "Just the core."

"That too. The idea that anyone rose from the dead is rather preposterous, really. The idea of it being a symbol of our own eternal life?" She gave the slightest of shrugs. "That might be something I could live with."

"Then you do believe in the soul?" asked Russ.

"Maybe not, or not in the sense you're likely to mean. If we believe in the resurrection of the body do we need a separate soul? Don't give me that look, James. You've had similar thoughts."

He smiled, looking down at the guitar cradled in his lap. "I've admittedly had my reservations about the concept of the spirit."

"Or concepts in general. I know you don't like to confuse ideas with real things."

"We know, too," said Alan. "He's spouted that sort of thing from time to time." Joey nodded agreement.

Russel frowned. "But—if the body will rise, then couldn't Jesus? I mean, if he would eventually. If we all would."

"Not in this finite universe. It must follow its natural laws." Angelica sounded quite positive about this.

Alan added, "So if we do physically rise it will be outside the universe we know." The Summerlin girl nodded an agreement.

"Then we all rise together on the judgment day?"

"Or immediately. It's not like God is limited by time or anything like that," asserted Angelica.

Alan was the one to nod now. "Time's a dimension of this universe."

James strummed a chord. "You see why I don't discuss theology around here. But yes, Deb, I am still on track to become a priest, despite my friends and family and my own misgivings."

"And I still think it's stupid!" After a moment, she shared in the general laughter.

Maybe the girl's feelings had been hurt a little. She was out of her depth with this crowd, with these dazzling Summerlins. So am I, Ronnie told herself. I don't belong here any more than Debbie Walker. And Russ was as out of James's league as she was.

Alan seemed to hold his own. Or he had the wisdom not to say much, most of the time. James launched into a song and then Angelica and Alan took turns.

They were going around a second time when Preston Summerlin came into the dining room and peered out the French doors, closed against the cool air. "I wonder what he wants?" he said, apparently to himself.

Mackie was the one who got up and took a look. "Police?"

The lawyer nodded. "I saw him cruise by slowly and then stop." The two watched a little longer. "Is he getting out?"

It wouldn't be a good idea for them to all crowd at the window. Angelica went over. Debbie looked like she might but chose to stay next to James. Maybe she thought someone would steal her spot.

Everyone else looked undecided but curious. "Back inside," said Mackie. "And there he goes."

"Slowly," Angelica remarked.

"Peculiar," said her father.

"There have been reports of rowdy parties here," Angelica said.

Preston started to chuckle and then saw his daughter was serious. "There have? I can't imagine who might have complained."

"Ben Forrester," spoke up James. It was unlikely any but one of the Summerlin twins would had said anything about it. "He thinks we're corrupting his daughter."

Summerlin considered that for no more than a moment. "Hmmph. Very well." He returned to the living room without further words.

"Okay," said James. "Let's have some more music."

Chapter Fifty-one
Joey

"Not bad," said Angelica, "considering you haven't practiced since summer."

"I bought a cheap guitar in Boston. It's in my dorm room even now." James idly picked a few notes on his Gibson. "It's at least as good as the one I used the last time I busked."

"One of these days you'll have to tell me your stories about that," said Joey.

"So you can steal them?"

"Oh, yes, I'll turn you into a character in a novel. Not the protagonist, of course."

"Of course," agreed Angelica. "The sidekick, there for comic relief. You have something, Alan?"

"Not bluegrass," warned Kris.

"There's nothing wrong with bluegrass," Russel protested.

"Well, I won't do 'Blue Moon of Kentucky,'" promised Alan. "Though I could." He launched instead into something more folk-sounding, gently strumming with a flat-pick. His voice came a bit tentative the first couple lines, then settled.

"I don't know that song," remarked Russel at the finish.

"That's because I wrote it."

"Pretty good reason," felt James. "Pretty good song, too."

"Poetic," said Joey, though she wasn't quite sure why. It just felt that way.

James smiled at that. "We already discovered Alan likes poetry."

"I am *not* reciting Hiawatha tonight," Alan informed them.

Kris casually said, "Ronnie writes poems."

Ronnie did not look at all pleased about that revelation. "Really dreadful ones," said Joey. Of course, she and Kris were well aware of it.

"The worst," added Kris. "I'll bet Russel writes bad poetry too."

"Sure does!" piped up Sandy. She looked to Angelica as if she was going to say something to her but instead turned to Joey. "Do you have a favorite poet?"

Now she was on the spot. Should have kept her mouth closed! "Um, I kind of like Anne Sexton."

"Me too," Angelica said. "My brother prefers to read poetry in Spanish. Borges and Neruda and such." She studied Alan for a few seconds. "You must like someone modern."

He definitely didn't like being put on the spot either, but mumbled, "My tastes run more to Auden."

"Oh, I love Auden," gushed Reggie. She hadn't spoken up much to that point. "Russ, do you remember what really awful poetry Bob used to write? And he actually thought it was good!"

"Whereas I know mine isn't," he replied. "But I'll probably keep writing it."

"Do that," Angelica told him. "Craft requires practice." With that she launched into one of her classical guitar pieces, as if to prove the point.

Alan was closing his guitar up in its case. The musical part of the evening must be ending. Her friends were starting to get up, move around. There was still food wasn't there? Angelica played on as Joey crossed the hall into the kitchen. She was surprised Reg even mentioned the former boyfriend. Only to insult him, true, but he must still be on her mind.

Suddenly, a torrent of abuse was shouted and, a moment later, Debbie Walker stormed past and out the back door. Joey stuck her head out into the hall to watch her go and then toward the other direction. Adults young and old were bunched up there.

"What was that about?" asked someone.

"Nothing much," said James.

"She just saw us making out," further explained Reggie.

"There went your chance at marrying the heiress," said Angelica. "I guess you'll have to be a priest after all."

That brought at least some laughter. Joey certainly added to it. Most seemed satisfied and went back to whatever they'd been doing.

Maria Summerlin gazed toward the back door and stated, "I never liked that girl," before turning to Reggie. "I apologize for the behavior of my guest, Regina."

"Oh, I didn't mind at all, Missus Summerlin. And I guess I'm sort of responsible for bringing her!" More than sort of. They'd all gone out of their way not to invite Debbie. "But now I don't have a ride home."

"I'll take you," offered Russel. "In fact, we should take off right now. It's back to school for Sandy tomorrow." His sister made a face but did not object.

"Then I will say it was a pleasure to have you here, Russel," said Maria. "Do say hello to your mother for me." With that, she returned to her other guests.

And Russel and Sandy and Reggie made their goodbyes and disappeared into the night, their way lit by strands of Christmas lights. Ronnie stood beside Joey on the porch, watching them a moment before saying, "Do you think there is something between those two? James and Reggie?"

"I'd doubt it."

"Yeah, me too. In fact, I wonder if they staged it for Debbie's benefit."

Now that was a thought! "Angelica would probably know."

"Not that we could trust the answer she gave us." Ronnie turned back to the house. "It's time we all said goodbye to James."

"It is," agreed Joey, and followed her friend in.

Chapter Fifty-two
Kris

"I said goodbye to James again after mass this morning. He may be on his train by now."

"I should have gotten up early too," said Kris. She could imagine herself at the station, waving as James's train pulled out. Just like an old movie!

"Last night was enough. I didn't know if I'd see him at church." She paused to look over Kris's shoulder at her sketch. "I didn't even know if I'd be going myself. Epiphany isn't one of the big important holy days."

"But you both showed up."

"And most of his family! Angelica and his mom and his aunt, anyway."

"I didn't really get a chance to talk to the aunt. You met her in Miami, right?" That rock was all wrong. Too big. And it looked like a potato.

"Uh-huh. I still don't know what Tio Oscar does for a living." Joey looked out toward the water for a few seconds before changing directions. "Preston Summerlin was peeved about the police last night. Not *at* the police but at Ben Forrester. He seems to have gone on about it a bit after we all cleared out."

Kris thought maybe she'd say something to her own father about it. More so in that Preston was likely to mention it to him. Sooner or later. Oh, that sucked. She tore the page out of her sketchbook and crumpled it.

"I do not think I've ever seen you do that."

"I didn't realize before how bad my drawings are. I don't know why I think I can be an artist."

"And I don't know why I think I can be a writer. But what the hell, we've gotta do *something*."

"Why?" demanded Kris, with a giggle. Her frustration was already forgotten.

"Oh, don't ask hard questions. You gonna try again or should we ride somewhere?"

"It's too nice to sit and mess with pencils." Maybe that was the problem. "Too bad Ronnie wouldn't come over."

"She wouldn't say exactly why. Something to do with Paulette, I think." Both rose from their seats in the sand.

"We should hang around with brand-new best friends too! You can have Debbie."

"Thank you, no." Joey seemed pretty certain about that. "I was surprised by Debbie's reaction last night. She seems more likely to suggest a threesome than be jealous."

"Don't I know it. That girl is sex-crazy. She'd suggested earlier to me we have a blow job contest with the guys there. I would have assigned her Mackie."

"You're kidding."

"No, I really would have given her Mackie." Kris thought she was pretty funny but it earned only the slightest of smiles. "We could ride down to Port Royal and cruise slowly by her house to taunt her."

"I have nothing against her. I might have been mad too if I'd set my sights on James." Joey looked like she might want to add more to that but said instead, "I wouldn't mind biking down that way."

"Okay. Goodbye, pier! I'll try to draw you some other day." She was never able to get the pier just right. Just the way she wanted it. They went to their bikes and peddled south, along Gulf Shore, following the road as far as it went before jogging over to Second. Which was called Gordon Drive down here.

Or further on maybe. The name changed somewhere. Just like the Gordon River became Naples Bay. One of the entrance roads to Port Royal would come up shortly. She wasn't so sure about going past the Walker house now, even if she had suggested it.

Debbie Walker. She had assumed the girl was only joking. Her plan would not have been at all practical! Not then and there—

But Kris had, for just a moment, visualized it and been a bit aroused. She couldn't help getting horny sometimes, could she? With Will so far away. With all those good looking guys around. James especially, of course. Joey should have jumped him. She knew she liked him. Maybe more than liked.

God, she missed Will. Into the neighborhood of canals and winding roads and mansions they turned, past the Episcopalian church—rather small and unassuming—and over the arched bridge. No time for swans today. No food, either.

"They live on one of the streets named for liquor," she told Joey. "Gin or rum or something like that."

"Rum Row. It's a long ride out to it."

Not that either of them cared. It was nice just to ride. Ride together. They might not get the chance again till summer.

They would get the chance then, wouldn't they? And Ronnie with them.

"We'd be pretty close to the pass if we rode all the way to the end," Joey was saying. "Must be convenient when one has a yacht in their back yard. And, ah, this is it."

It wasn't hard to tell that. Debbie's MG was in the curving concrete drive, partially obscured by exuberant tropical plantings. And Debbie standing next to it, ready to go somewhere. Kris was still reluctant to pull in but she followed Joey.

Riding by and yelling would have been much more fun. Debbie seemed uncertain about this pair of visitors, but Joey jumped right in. "We wanted to see if you were okay," she told her. Was that a fib or did she really mean it? Kris did not care how Debbie was doing at all!

The girl was certainly surprised. Debbie stood there looking stupid for a moment before saying, "Thanks. I'm fine. It takes more than James Summerlin to throw me off my game."

"You only lost your temper," offered Joey.

"Happens to all of us," Kris appended to this. She wasn't sure why.

"Yeah, I guess so." She leaned back against the door of her shiny green MG, open, as usual. Kris didn't think she'd ever seen it with the top up. Even last night. "I'm not really mad at him. But Dozier—that was a *betrayal*." She liked that word. You could tell.

"I'm not sure she even knew you were together," said Kris. Not that they were. It all seemed one-sided last night. Debbie's side.

"And how could she resist James, anyway?" asked Joey. "We all secretly want into his pants."

Debbie broke into laughter. "Damn. I guess you're right about that! I was about to go out to the club to play tennis. Want to come along?" This she had addressed to Kris but deigned to add, "You too, Jo."

"We wouldn't both fit in your toy car," Joey told her.

"We're just going to bike around a little more," said Kris. "Get yourself a bicycle and join us sometime." She knew how unlikely that was or she wouldn't have said it.

"Okay. Maybe I'll see you all before we head off different directions again." With that, Debbie got into her sports car and headed off herself.

Kris and Joey followed somewhat more slowly in her wake. They pedaled some distance in silence before Joey said, "Ronnie thinks the whole thing was faked, just for Debbie's benefit."

Kris considered this and thought it could be true. "That's kind of funny."

"I think it's cowardly."

Chapter Fifty-three
Ronnie

"The newspaper has let me go," announced Ronnie's mom. "Or I should say they canceled my column."

"Oh, that's—did they just tell you?" What a lousy Christmas present!

"I've known for a while and told your father about it. I didn't want to say anything to you until after the holidays. Or anyone else." She busied herself pouring a cup of coffee before saying, "Myra Penn may be in the same sinking boat. She expects the radio station to let her go."

Ronnie wondered if Russel knew anything about that.

"They want younger announcers," Patty Deerfield continued. "You're a friend of her son, aren't you? You should invite him over some time."

Ronnie thought it best not to respond to that. "Use your new-found free time to write a book." Her mom had always threatened to, some day.

"I've given that some thought. Myra and I have also looked at the idea of starting a magazine."

"Get Joey to write for you! Or even—" Hold on. Your mouth is moving faster than your brain. Oh, it would be okay to say it. "Maybe she could get her friend Lin to write something."

Her mom settled across the table. "Lin? I don't think I know her."

"Linda Summerlin. She works for a magazine in New York. Or I guess she uses Linda Salas these days."

"The Naples girl in the big city? That could be interesting." She seemed to muse on the idea for a moment. "Are you seeing her today? Joey, I mean."

"Maybe later. I'm going over to visit Paulette right now." She glanced up at the round clock above the kitchen entry. "I'd better get moving. It's late!"

Mom didn't seem to like the idea of her driving over there. Ronnie could tell. She did feel a little daring going to the Jones house—and neighborhood—on her own. But Paulette had said to come and talk to Carter, hadn't she? It was late morning when she pulled the Simca into their drive.

No other cars in front of the modest frame house. Maybe Missus Jones was working. Ronnie had no idea what she did or if she even had a job. She went up a couple concrete steps to a small stoop with a wrought iron railing. They didn't get Carter and his wheelchair out this way, that was for sure. Ronnie rang the doorbell. Maybe no one was home. She could have called Paulette first.

No, the door swung slowly open. There was Carter balanced on his crutches, looking out through the screen door. "Hi Ronnie. I'm afraid Paulette's gone this morning."

Darn. She definitely should have called. "That's okay. I can talk to her later." It was—at last—getting time to coordinate the drive back to Gainesville. "But can I talk to you now?"

He seemed uncertain. Maybe the fact that he was in pajamas and bath robe played a part in that. "Sure," Carter said, opening the screen door for her and then hobbling to his nearby wheelchair. "I missed a party last night, I hear."

Ronnie settled into a chair beside him. "Paulette says your father isn't big on you guys partying with us."

"Just worried. He's afraid your rich friends are misguiding my sister when she should be concentrating on, um, more realistic goals."

"My family certainly isn't rich. Joey's neither." Nor was Kris's, really, but of course the Carters, both Senior and Junior, meant the Summerlins.

"We're not that well off, you know. My disability only helps some and the van was a big expense. Mom works as a maid, but they expect better things for my sister." He paused before adding, "I guess they expected better things for me, once."

Ronnie frowned at the self-pity in his voice. "They still should," she told him.

He made no direct response to that. "Russ Wesolowski came over yesterday evening." He gave her a rather long look after saying that. "Said goodbye to us. And lectured me like I think you plan to do."

"What, me?" Of course, that was why she was here. "Maybe I simply came to say goodbye too."

"Everyone's gonna be gone again. Just me sitting here." A rueful chuckle. "Feeling sorry for myself."

Ronnie was starting to feel a tad exasperated. "Then you need to get out of here. Out of your pajamas and off to college."

"Edison? How am I gonna get there?"

"That van was meant to be driven. You have lots of friends who could get you up there in it. Alan, for sure." She would talk to him about it, whether she felt comfortable or not. "And you'll be up on that new leg the doctors are going to get you. You'll be able to ride in any car. Shoot," she said, "you might even be driving!"

In her enthusiasm, she had leaned forward and placed a hand on his thigh. His eyes went down to it and hers went to his crotch, where his robe hung open. Carter's erection was obvious through the thin pajama pants, the engorged penis lying along his thigh, straining against the material.

What did it look like? She'd heard all the stories about black men being bigger but she didn't believe them. But Carter wasn't small. She was sure of that. Her hand slid up his thigh, her fingers tentatively brushing the head. The boy gave a little moan and let one of his large hands rest on top of hers.

Holding it there, but not forcibly. Only a reassurance of sorts, for both of them. Her hand moved up the shaft. What now? Ronnie had no idea. They were not going to have sex, that was for sure! But it was okay to, ah, handle it a bit, wasn't it? Would Carter want oral sex? Would she?

She was stimulated too. That was not something Ronnie would deny. But she didn't have any feelings for this guy. Just friendship. Maybe none of that mattered.

"Oh, yeah," he whispered. "It's been so long. Help me feel like a man again."

What? She leaned back, pulled her hand away. "Carter Jones, you are trying to manipulate me," she said. "Make me feel sorry for you. Well I'll tell you, mister, that is not going to work!"

She had half-expected anger but a shamefaced Carter whispered, "I guess that's true. I guess *I* was feeling sorry for myself too."

"And I can see quite well you're a man. Well, I could see." His erection had deflated. Was it normal for that to happen so quickly? Ronnie had no frame of reference.

He pulled his robe around himself. All his excitement had turned to embarrassment. "I'm awfully sorry, Ronnie. There was no excuse for that."

There was plenty of excuse, she felt. And it made her feel—good, to be desired. Sort of desired. Who knows, maybe she would have liked things to go further. But they wouldn't; not now.

Not ever. She was fairly certain. Ronnie rose from her chair. "Tell Paulette I came by, will you? We need to decide when we're leaving for college. And—and do take care of yourself and think about college yourself." She couldn't help giving him a bit of a conspiratorial smile. "A man would want to better himself."

"Okay, Ronnie. And a man would see you to the door." Carter rose on his crutches and accompanied her that far. He stood watching through the screen as she drove away.

She would not say anything of this. Not even to Joey or Kris. And they weren't likely to find out, as they did about James!

Chapter Fifty-four

Kris

Mackie's mother wasn't coming along. She'd already made her goodbyes to her large, athletic, gay son.

Not that she or Dave Macklin knew about the gay part. Mackie was not willing to share that. His parents seemed to think the two of them were an item again. Kris was willing to allow them. It made things easier for Mackie. Maybe it made things easier for her.

And it let her ride along when the boy went to the airport. He would fly into Tampa from Naples and then north. Change planes again before he ended up in Athens. He'd told her where but she hadn't been that interested. Now she and Mackie were in the back seat of a big Suburban. This was Mister Macklin's personal ride, not a car from his lot.

Ronnie sat up front, having accepted her invitation to ride along. Or Mackie's invitation? One of them had suggested it. Ronnie seemed a little preoccupied about something this morning. That was nothing new but the alternate thoughtful reveries and smiles at some private joke were odd.

They pulled left off Airport Road and then left again almost at once. "The terminal is over on the south side," said Mackie. He'd flown in here, Kris assumed, though she'd never asked.

She'd never been to the airport either. It lay across the river and north, some. Just across from where Will's family lived, in fact. "What is with these odd, old buildings?" she asked. Many of them long and narrow and built of block.

Ronnie jumped to supply an answer. "These were barracks during the Second World War. That little building over there was a latrine."

"How do you know?"

"Oh, my dad drove us around once and pointed things out. He was involved in remodeling some of the buildings into workshops and housing." A little frown creased her brow as she remembered. "Gosh, that was a long time ago. Ten years, maybe."

"We lived in one of those remodeled barracks for a while," spoke Mister Macklin. "Do you remember, Harold?"

"I do. I was in the first grade when we moved away." He peered out the window as they took a right. "That was over toward the north side?"

"Just north of where we entered. One of those former latrines lay right across the street. A dairy company was using it then."

"Oh, yeah. I remember the milkmen stopping there in the early mornings." Mackie nodded as it came back to him. "And you had a workshop in the back end of the place."

"Right. I opened up as a mechanic here before I got the dealership. Here we are." A right into the terminal parking lot. A couple hangars, a few small planes, lay beyond.

The four rolled out of the big wagon. Mackie stood a head taller than his father. Maybe his mom came from big folks. "That beacon over there used to keep me awake," he said, pointing. "Round and round all night!"

"Your mother would complain about it too."

She wondered if it shone across the bay into Will's window too. Oh, Will. She missed him so! And everyone else was going away too. Kris started sobbing. She couldn't help it.

Mackie put an arm around her. There was nothing else anyone could do.

Then there was nothing more to do than go in and say goodbye and send Mackie away. She would miss the big guy. She very much hoped he would find happiness.

"Can I take you girls to lunch?" asked Dave Macklin as they climbed back into the Suburban.

Ronnie looked like she might be willing to take him up on it. Best nip that immediately. "No thank you, sir. Dropping us at your house would be fine. Or at the Deerfields." The Macklins lived just north of the old golf course, in a little neighborhood nestled between it and the newer, swankier Moorings. They had walked over from Ronnie's place.

"The Deerfields it will be," he said, cranking the engine. "Can't have you traipsing across the golf course."

They were back on Airport Road before he said, "It was good of you to see Harold off. I was a little disappointed none of his old team-mates came around to say goodbye." A pause. "Maybe he was too, though he didn't say it."

"A lot of them are elsewhere."

"And he has new teammates now," added Ronnie.

"True enough. Both of them."

"You know," Ronnie said, "Kris should write to him every week and tell him how much she misses him. No, twice a week."

Dave caught on. "And run up long distance charges on her parents' telephone bill."

Kris wasn't even writing Will. Not very often. She should. She should write him every day. Suddenly, she felt tears coming again.

"Oh, I'm sorry, Kris," said Ronnie.

"We shouldn't have teased you," said Dave Macklin. "I should have known how much you missed my son."

Kris's tears almost turned to laughter. She managed to control the turmoil she felt, to smile. "It's okay."

God, she wished she were back in Miami, where her mind was on her studies and her everyday routine. Kris thought she hated vacations. She hated this vacation. It would be over soon. She found herself blinking back more tears. Damn, stop that!

Then they were at Ronnie's home, with her bug parked in front, and Mister Macklin drove off. She was unlikely to see him any time soon again.

"Do you want to come in?" asked Ronnie. "Or go somewhere and do something?"

Kris shook her head. "I think I'll just go home now. But you know the triumvirate has to ride together one more time before we split up again."

"Absolutely."

Chapter Fifty-five
Joey

"It's finished?"

"As finished as it's going to be. I need to let it sit a day or two before I try to ride. The fiberglass job needs to cure so it will be stronger."

"Wouldn't want his board to snap in two the first time he rode," said Russ.

Alan laughed. "Unless it rides really bad!"

Joey gave it another looking over. "It's not shiny like the ones you bought." Maybe she shouldn't say that? It sounded like a criticism.

"Went with a sanded finish. It's just as strong and a little lighter."

Joey was willing to believe him. Until someone presented evidence otherwise! "Do you think there will be any surf before you go back to school?" she asked Russ.

"Hard to say. For that matter, I'm not sure what day I'm driving over."

"I was thinking of going too and surfing over there for a day or two," said Alan. "We'd have to take separate vehicles."

"Alan could sack in my dorm room one night and no one would complain. They might not even notice." Russ gave her an appraising look. "You probably couldn't get away with that. But you could come too, if you wanted."

"Definitely," agreed Alan.

"And who would clean up this place?"

"Good point," Alan admitted. "But we should go over and look at the campus sometime. We may both be there in a couple years."

It was possible. More likely for Alan than her. "Okay. We'll both go and sleep on the floor of Russ's dorm room sometime. Right now, I'd better scoot on home."

A few minutes later Joey was in the Corvair, doing just that. Scooting, anyway. She wasn't sure she wanted to go right home. It wouldn't do to waste these last few days of vacation. Gee, why hadn't she invited one—or both—of the Wezzies to do something?

But then, she'd be seeing loads of Alan in the months to come. Maybe Russ too, but they were unlikely to date again. For all she knew, he had a girlfriend waiting over at FAU. Girlfriends! A bevy of future marine biologists, serious girls for a serious boy.

Alan seemed to have found someone too. Cute little Jackie Booth. Too good for him! She'd have to let him know that. He'd missed his chance to date cheerleaders when he was in high school himself. He shouldn't be allowed to make up for it now! Even if he was only a year older than the girl.

Maybe it had taken that year for him to—what was the word she wanted? She should carry her thesaurus with her. Mature? Come into his own? Something along those lines. Blossom? That didn't sound quite right for Alan but was probably closer to what she had in mind. Well, here she was in front of her house. Autopilot. Might as well eat something and then ride her bike.

A half hour later found her pedaling south, pedaling with no destination in mind. All the Christmas decorations were gone along the streets. She hadn't noticed exactly when they disappeared. Probably right after the new year arrived.

Down Third Avenue into the old shopping area. Joey knew every bit as much about 'old Naples' as Ronnie but was less likely to trot it out in conversations. Maybe she could write something about it. She had to remember to research surfing too. It would be nice to have projects. She liked researching things.

Actually writing them, not so much. That was hard work! Lin and she had biked through here one summer Sunday morning and talked about the old buildings. The Summerlin—no, make that Salas—the Salas girl's memories went back further. The old library to the right, a place Joey had hung out a lot when younger. Its location near the middle school was more convenient now but she missed the musty old building. Didn't an artist have his studio upstairs from it? Maybe he still did.

The ugly Quonset hut that housed the theater over on her left. The ancient Seminole Market, where her mom had bought groceries when Joey was very small. Now a boutique. She had seen photos from the

Twenties when it was pretty much the only building on the street. And Preston Summerlin's law offices coming up on the right. Summerlin and Summerlin, not that Conrad was ever in.

Summerlin. As long as she was downtown she would ride by their place. James wouldn't be in Boston yet, she was sure. Joey had no idea how long a train ride north took and he hadn't provided any details. She didn't have as high an opinion of James as once. She doubted her mother was quite as in awe of him either! He had shown himself to be completely human. Not that there was anything wrong with that; Joey felt pretty human herself, most days.

But maybe she had a higher opinion of his sister than she used to. Angelica was, at least, honest. Maybe too honest. She turned right on the next street, Thirteenth, and right again a couple blocks over, cruising down Gulf Shore past the pier.

That car down at the beach end of the street. Was that? Yes. Donna's Lark, not parked next to the Summerlin property but at a slight remove. Joey u-turned back up the street, stopping at the curb. There sat Donna and Angelica at one of the outside tables.

She might as well intrude. They'd already seen her. As she rolled her bike across the lawn, Angelica called, "I was just telling Donna about the cop checking out our party. He could tell we were up to no good!"

The Forrester girl looked at least a little embarrassed. "I'm sorry if it upset your family."

"Oh, don't worry about whatever your father might have said. Daddy expects the worst from Republicans anyway."

"Don't we all?" asked Joey, dropping her bike on the grass and taking a seat.

Angelica leaned across the table to confide to Donna, *sotto voce*, "I think Joey expects the worst from everybody."

"And I'm never disappointed. Especially by you!"

"Oh, you have not seen anything like my worst."

Joey thought she could believe that. "Are you heading back to Gainesville soon?" she asked Donna.

"I considered taking off a couple days early so I could spend some time with Mike." A pause, perhaps thinking of how best to say what she meant to say. "I've been having more fun here."

"But no sex," Angelica pointed out.

"Yeah. That's true."

"I could always proposition you."

By now, Donna seemed to know the Summerlin girl well enough not to be taken aback, saying only, "Um, I don't think so."

"Darn. I'll have to go to my backup. Reggie. She does have rather nice breasts, doesn't she?" The question was apparently directed to Joey, who decided not to have an opinion. "Not the equal of Kris's, of course, but nice none the less."

"I'll let Kris know that."

"Will probably praised them enough already." Angelica turned back to Donna. "So you're hanging in Naples a little longer?

"Leaving Saturday. I'm going to caravan with Ronnie and Paulette."

"Then we can still throw another wild party before you go, with loads of sex and drugs. How 'bout at your place since the police are watching us?"

"Oh, Jel, nobody's interested now your brother is gone. He's the draw," Joey told her.

"Don't I know it? He should give up the priest thing and go into show biz, don't you think? What he lacks in talent he makes up in looks. Just the opposite of me!"

"You're gorgeous!" protested Donna.

"No, I'm just okay looking and maybe seem a little exotic. Joey is the gorgeous one."

"Me?"

"Didn't my sister say so? You're, ah, striking. That's the word. Lin wasn't joking when she said you could model."

Donna nodded to this.

"As long as you don't have to move," added Angelica, snickering. "You walk like a guy."

"That's just the air of a confident woman," Joey informed her. "Now—another party, you were saying?"

Chapter Fifty-six
Ronnie

"I'm driving up on Saturday."

"Me too." Russel was, in fact, busy packing his van when she had ridden up to the Penn house. Sandy seemed to be supervising.

Was that going to be it for their conversation? "I guess we won't see each other again until next summer."

"Hey," interjected Sandy, "your campuses aren't that far apart! You could meet at that beach you like, Ronnie."

"Flagler. And it's not so much me that likes it." Not that she wasn't likely to drive over sometime.

Russel gave that a barely perceptible nod. "It's Alan's place, isn't it?"

"Oh, she doesn't care about him anymore. And—" Sandy gave them an appropriately dramatic pause. "He's got a new girlfriend."

"Jackie."

Sandy seemed disappointed. Russel seemed surprised.

"I have eyes," Ronnie continued. It certainly didn't bother her any to acknowledge it. "You know that might fizzle when she's back in school and has a bunch of cute boys around her."

Sandy snickered. "From sizzle to fizzle!"

"That could be a song," remarked her brother. It was hard to say how serious he was. "Who knows, maybe we *will* run into each other at the beach some weekend. At Stetson we're more likely to drive over to New Smyrna."

"Maybe," she conceded. That wasn't really very far from Flagler. "I get this feeling our mothers are trying to get us together."

"My sister too. She's been dropping clumsy hints."

"Who, me? Hey, here's my ride."

Ronnie didn't know the car. The Jeep. But it was open so she could see Maxie Hall behind the wheel.

"She's bringing you home again?" asked Russ.

"Sure. I'll call if I need rescuing. Or maybe I need to call Angelica to give me another ride on her scooter!" With that she ran out to her friend and rode away.

"That's an astonishing thing for her to say."

Ronnie was inclined to agree. "I guess the Summerlins aren't going to be able to get rid of her, after all." She couldn't resist tacking on, "Or you."

"Ooh. I don't remember you being so candid, Ronnie. Or quite so mean!" They both smiled over that. "I think I got to know you better recently than in all the years we went to school together."

It might be the same for her, though she wasn't about to say it. "We can blame the Summerlins for that too."

"And lots of other things."

Oh, yeah? The remark kind of bugged her. She wasn't sure why but Ronnie felt a need to defend the twins. "You're not so special, you know. Angelica put the moves on me once, too." She grinned—this was fun—and added, "But I had more self-control."

"Ooh, again." He sounded amused. But he was covering his embar-rassment. She should have know better.

"I'm sorry, Russel. I won't mention her again."

"It's okay. I'm okay. I can almost look her in the eye now."

Ronnie laughed at his quip and resisted the temptation to make another joke herself. She might even have felt proud of herself. Yeah, self-control.

Russ said, "And I like James. I think maybe you do too. There's something going on between you two, isn't there?"

"There was something." There still was, in a way.

"There's another James Summerlin, as we saw the other night." Russel seemed to look far away, maybe toward the Summerlin house, maybe toward nothing at all, before saying, "I think you already knew that."

Ronnie felt an unexpected need to unburden herself. An urgent need to let loose all she had been carrying about with her. Who better than this clueless, well-meaning—friend? That's what Russ was. A friend. She almost blurted, 'I had sex with James last summer.'

Her snide remark about self control came back to her. She didn't need to burden Russel either. To his credit, the boy did not intrude but sat down beside her in the open cargo door of the van.

"Did James have something to do with you breaking up with Alan?"

She could only nod her head. Don't cry, you stupid girl, she told herself.

"Alan doesn't know anything about it, of course," mused Russel. "That's best, isn't it?"

Did he actually suspect what happened? "No. I wouldn't want to hurt him worse than I did." She didn't regret being with James, though, just what it did. Actions had consequences. Ronnie had heard that all her life.

And she didn't regret breaking with Alan. It was best for both of them. "I'd better get going," she announced, rising. A minute later she was pedaling hard, with no destination in mind.

Chapter Fifty-seven
Kris

She was not surprised to see Gordie there. She didn't mind it either. As long as he didn't bring Debbie Walker along!

But it was really supposed to be the four of them. The triumvirate-plus-one. Angelica would always be the one added on, wouldn't she? Kris had no idea what one called a triumvirate when it became a foursome. Maybe Ronnie did.

The weather was going to change again. She could tell. Not a big cold front like the last one, just a little wind before it turned cooler. The radio claimed there might not even be any rain.

"I was tempted to drive the Moke up," Gordie was telling Angelica and Ronnie, "but the parents vetoed it. It's in my dad's name anyway."

"Ronnie should drop you on her way north," suggested Kris, taking a seat at the outdoor table.

Her friend clearly did not like that idea. "Or Donna Forrester."

No one offered further comment. Gordie would get to Tampa one way or another. All the light strands had been taken down. Kris kind of wished they'd stayed up till they all left. That she could see the Summerlins' yard lit up one last time.

Oh well, there would be next year! "I'm leaving on Sunday," Angelica announced. "Hey, I can take your bike over for you, Kris. It should fit on my roof rack easily enough." She snickered. "But you might not be tall enough to get it down!"

"I can find plenty of willing guys over there to do it for me. Heeeere's Joey!"

"I didn't expect her to bike," Ronnie almost whispered. "Maybe I should have offered her a ride."

"She rides when she's feeling antsy about something. I know that and you two have known her longer," said Angelica.

Kris knew well that Joey had her ups and downs. She looked to be practically vibrating this afternoon.

"So this is it?" asked Joey, choosing to plop onto the grass rather than take a chair. "One guy for the four of us?"

"I'll give it my best effort," offered Gordie.

"You couldn't handle even one of us," Angelica assured him. "We aren't expecting anyone else, are we? I never know who one of you might invite."

"You told Donna about our get-together," Joey reminded her.

"And she called to say she wasn't coming. Afraid we'd be raided, maybe."

"I'm going to have to go over and steal her little boat. I want to row up and down the bay like she does. Russ already dropped by, didn't he?"

"Rusty, I assume you mean. He did for a moment, yesterday evening. He had the Dozier girl with him. They're dating?"

Joey only shrugged. "They could be. Alan and I are thinking of adding her to our car pool."

"And you can all recite poems to each other to break the monotony of your drive," Kris joked. Maybe she shouldn't have. She knew she didn't really get poetry.

"I'd like to try to set some poems to music," said Angelica. "If Alan can write songs, why shouldn't I? How about your words, Ronnie?"

"She writes free verse," Joey broke in. "Hard to set to music."

"Unless it's plainsong."

"Huh?" asked Ronnie. Kris felt like asking the same question.

"Like Gregorian chant," said Joey. "Prose texts set to music. No meter."

"Oh. Hey, I know some limericks," Kris said. "Some of them I can even recite in polite company."

"We'd rather hear the other ones. The light isn't very good for that, is it?"

Gordie was pointing his camera here and there. She'd heard no clicks of the shutter. "Could be worse," he murmured.

"Yeah, it could be night," said Kris. "School should be out by now. Do you think we might see Sandy?"

"But this is a school night," Ronnie reminded her.

"It's early," she replied. "Lots of time to come over and pine for Angelica."

"Wait, little Sandy likes girls?" Gordie abruptly lowered his camera. "Why haven't I heard any of this before?"

Angelica gave them a deprecating wave of her hand. "I don't know if Sandy is a lesbian or not, and I doubt she knows herself. It is fairly obvious her friend Maxie is."

"Not to me," asserted Joey. "And I think not to her friends."

"Every tomboy isn't a lesbian," Kris said. "Joey is evidence of that."

"Oh, but I've been secretly lusting for your tiny body all these years. Jelly claims you have great breasts."

"And Will has the Polaroids to prove it. Which none of you will ever see!" Not that the three friends hadn't seen each other naked from time to time over the years.

"At least we know Jackie is straight," Ronnie commented. Nods all around. By now, Jackie and Alan was common knowledge. Even Gordie might have heard.

Ronnie didn't seem to mind bringing it up. "Maybe Alan will come," said Kris.

"Nope. He and Russ are on their way to Boca Raton," Joey informed them. "Russ to stay—we aren't going to see him again for a few weeks."

"Maybe *you* won't," said Angelica. "Kris and I aren't going to be so far away from Rusty. We should go look him up, shouldn't we?"

"Whatever, Jel." Kris knew the two of them weren't likely to see much of each other when they got back to Miami, much less socialize. And the only boy she cared about seeing was far away.

Angelica persisted, despite Kris's show of disinterest. "You're in the same dorm room, aren't you?"

"Yeah. My mom is still after me to join a sorority. Sigma Delta Tau, maybe."

"A sorority? That sounds awfully boring. Hey, we should get an apartment together!"

"You know I can't afford that, Jel."

"Yeah, I guess I do. And I won't recommend we be roommates. I practice guitar all night and keep driving my roomies away."

"Oh, you don't have play guitar for that," Joey told her. "Just being yourself is enough."

"Yet you keep showing up here."

Joey left off the wisecracking. "There won't be any point in doing that in a couple days."

"I suppose not." Angelica maintained her seriousness for only a moment. "Even if our moms are best friends now!"

"Yeah, like that's gonna last. Do I hear the roar of a mighty engine?"

The 'roar' was more of a buzzing whine, as Sandy Penn came up the street on her Solex moped. She shut off the little single-cylinder motor perched above the front wheel and came across the lawn toward them.

Gordie scrutinized the new arrival. Seeing Sandy with new eyes? He raised his camera, fired off a couple shots as the girl approached. "She's rather photogenic," he remarked. "Not just another pretty face like you girls."

"All it takes is the long blond hair," said Joey. "Guys are always suckers for that. Hey, Sandy. Any of your friends coming?"

"Oh, they all have things to do. Cheerleader practice and clubs and stuff. Me too! But I had to come and say goodbye, didn't I?" Her eyes went—to the surprise of no one—to Angelica. "I had to make time."

Just how Angelica felt about it was anyone's guess. As with most things Angelica. "And we are glad you did before we we all left."

"Yeah, I'll only have Joey to bug when the rest of you are gone!"

"Anytime," said Joey. That, on the other hand, *was* surprising. Curmudgeon Joey must be taking a temporary break.

If the afternoon got a little boring after that, it was okay. Just sitting with friends was good enough. Who could guess how soon they would again? Gordie slipped off after a while. Yes, they all hugged him before he went. They'd even miss him.

Funny how Kris had tried to avoid him after they broke up in high school. That seemed the ancientest of history. Now she could say she was—what? Fond of him? That seemed a good enough word.

Then Sandy. Hugs all around for her too. Even from Angelica. The girl buzzed off into the dwindling day. "We'd all better get on our way," said Joey. Not that any of them wanted to. Kris would be willing to sit here for at least a couple days more.

The weather still seemed pretty good, the sky clouded over, a modest southerly breeze. Joey would have that to her back biking home. The trio went to their respective rides.

"Remember," said Joey, before pedaling away, "we ride in the morning."

Once more. Once more before going off and doing all the things that were expected of them.

Chapter Fifty-eight
Joey

Third Avenue, like in the old days, the days before they hung around with Jam and Jelly and all these other people whose names she would as soon forget. She was the first there. Joey chained her old bike to a sign post and waited.

Cool, this morning, but fairly bright. A Friday morning. The beach didn't look crowded. Kids all in school, most tourists not out yet. A handful of retirees. Walking the sand was a daily ritual for some of them.

It was a ritual of sorts for her, too. This was important to Joey, more important than it was to her friends. She recognized that. Here came Kris. On the Stingray, not her new bike.

"That's not such a good choice if we decide to ride very far," she told her.

"Oh, let's just walk this morning," came the reply, as Kris chained her bike next to Joey's. Chained it to it, actually.

It sounded like a good idea. The two of them outvoted Ronnie if she would rather bike.

A solitary fisherman cast around the tall pilings. Maybe after redfish. With the sun halfway up the morning sky, he'd probably do better to go home and try some other time. But heck, maybe the guy didn't have anything better to do.

She wouldn't mind having nothing better to do. Ronnie pedaled up. "It looks like you two plan to walk," she said, looking at the chained bicycles. How she felt about it was not clear. The girl wordlessly joined her bike to the others. "North or south?"

"We always go south, don't we?" asked Kris. "Toward the pier."

Toward the Summerlins too. "So north today. Okay?"

"Alright with me," said Ronnie. "Let's go." She slipped off her sneakers and tossed them into the wicker front basket on her bike. No one was likely to steal them.

Off they set, northward along the beach. "How far?" asked Joey.

"All the way to Doctor's Pass?" It was impossible to walk any further along the sand.

"We'd be doing well to reach Lowdermilk Park," Kris felt. "Let's just mosey along and not worry about how far we go."

Good advice, even if it went against her nature. Loads of gulls lined the water's edge this morning. Mostly ring-bills. Those others with the dark bills were young herring gulls, she thought. Russ Wesolowski would undoubtedly know.

The houses up here were more modern. They weren't building much north along the beach yet when the Summerlin house and the others near the pier went up. That one over there had an art-deco look to it. Not that Joey knew much about architecture. Ronnie might be able to say but there was no point in asking.

Still, that might be something interesting to write about, sometime. Joey didn't think she could ever run out of interesting things if she was willing to look for them. She also knew she might feel different about that in a day or two and think none of it was worthwhile.

That was Central they just passed, wasn't it? Not very far yet. "No real waves this morning," Joey remarked, "despite the little front. I'll have to spend my time surfing when everyone is gone."

"Just you and the gulls?" asked Ronnie.

"Boys and gulls," Kris said.

"We need to find her a boyfriend now that Russ abandoned her."

"Yes, wasn't that awful of him? Not that we can blame him for preferring Reggie."

"Sheesh, I should know better than say anything around you two. What is this, Third North?"

"I think so," said Ronnie. "I can see the Beach Hotel up ahead. We should go at least that far."

It would be as good a spot as any to turn around. Joey had no real desire to go as far as Lowdermilk, much less the pass.

But she might well drive to Doctor's Pass now and again in the months to come, with or without surfboard. She liked the privacy there, a partially enclosed space where the jetty wrapped around. And she could fish.

"I see cabanas too," spoke Kris. "Nowhere but the hotel these days."

All three probably remembered when cabana rentals was a thriving business beside the pier. Why had that ended?

At Seventh they halted. Eastward, the golf course could be glimpsed. Golfers, too. A good day for it, almost as good as for walking on the beach. Before them rose the hotel itself, the Naples Beach Hotel. The Beach Club as they were use to calling it and the adjoining course. It looked dated, though it wasn't that old. In unspoken accord, the three turned and started south.

"So what do we do with the rest of the day?" she asked her friends.

"Let's just go hang at Ronnie's house," suggested Kris.

It sounded like a pretty good idea.

Chapter Fifty-nine

Ronnie

"Good morning, Ronnie. Paulette isn't here yet?"

"Her father is going to drop her off." Officer Carter Jones Senior. She wasn't at all surprised to see Donna's Studebaker pull in well ahead of the time they had set.

Paulette would come and they would all head off together for Gainesville. Who knew whether any of them would see each other when they settled in for the new semester?

Hmm, maybe she should let Paulette ride with Donna part of the way. They intended to go up the interstate and she could switch over at one of the rest areas. Nah, she wouldn't mention it. Let Donna offer if she thought of it.

"Oh, I didn't know you played guitar," said Donna. The case was fairly visible, leaning against the rear seat.

"Some. I didn't even bother to take it with me for the fall semester." She was going to practice now. If she didn't drive her new roommate away, like Angelica!

Here came Paulette. Not in a police cruiser today, but her mother's car. Or maybe it was her father's car when he wasn't on duty. She carried the same bag she'd had when they left Gainesville.

Paulette gave them both a wave and then gushed, "My pop loves you now. Junior has decided to enroll at Edison and he says you talked him into it."

"Maybe a little." Ronnie didn't much want to talk about her visit to the Jones house. "Has Alan offered to help?"

"He did! Thanks for that too."

She hadn't needed to talk to Alan about helping. Joey passed things along.

"Are we all ready to go then?" asked Donna. "Last call for restroom visits."

"Not that there won't be places to stop along the way," Ronnie said. "We are going to make stops, aren't we?"

"We'd better," Paulette said.

"If we must." Donna headed for her car.

There was no reason to dawdle. She had said goodbye to her parents and Ronnie didn't expect any of her friends to come see her off. That had all been taken care of yesterday. She and Joey and Kris had sat late in her room, the way they used to.

Not again for a long while. Paulette slipped into the passenger seat of the Simca. Out to the Trail, with Donna in the lead. She was likely to stay in the lead, wasn't she? Donna was kind of take-charge. North on Forty-one, out of Naples.

"Joey offered to help Junior, too," said Paulette. "Or so Alan says. You don't mind talking about Alan, do you?"

"I can't really say I do." Ronnie thought that was the truth. She and Alan were on friends basis now, weren't they?

"Okay, then I can gossip about him!" Paulette giggled a little. "Jackie Booth went out with him last night. I think that was their first real date."

She had assumed they had already formally dated. "Do her parents mind? I mean, he's a little older and he's, um, white."

"So I noticed!" More giggles. "Jackie has been dating white guys ever since she started dating so her parents don't mind Alan. Plus he was a friend of Will." She took a moment before adding, "Can't blame Alan for liking her. She's a cute little thing. But very black."

"She is?" Ronnie had never thought much of it, one way or another. Well, yeah, Will and Jackie were darker than the Joneses.

"I know we all look the same to you," Paulette deadpanned.

"Not true. I can tell you're at least three inches taller than Jackie."

"And considerably bigger around!" Both seemed to think it a subject best not pursued further. Past the street to the high school and the Moorings entrance across the highway.

Paulette seemed more interested in the passing scenery than in talking. Then, "What do you say we ask to be roommates this semester?"

"Only if you don't complain about me playing the guitar," answered Ronnie

Chapter Sixty
Joey

It felt like all of Naples was deserted. Joey biked down the empty way, the dim light of almost-dawn revealing one gray building after another. She would ride along Tenth all the way to the depot, down to where this street crossed the Trail.

A week ago James had boarded a train there. She hadn't heard whether he'd reached his college yet, whether he was once again the serious student at Boston College. Theology studies? Is that what he called it?

Across the highway, to turn right three blocks further along. Alan was back. He might be cleaning kennels at this very moment, though there was no reason for him to be up as early as she was. Tomorrow, they'd be back to their classes, to their commute to Edison.

A more complicated commute, what with Reggie Dozier and Carter Jones in the mix now. She might miss riding with Alan and only Alan. He didn't talk a lot but who needed idle chatter?

Past the rec center, past the front of Saint Ann School. Hey, might as well cut through it. Up the side walk, through the breezeway, and across the field. The playground. Joey had played here herself, for a while. She had first encountered Angelica Summerlin on this ragged grass.

There had been immediate dislike on both their parts, and both had felt drawn to the other. Maybe it was still the same. Out onto the street and down a little to the church, the old rectangular building she had attended as long as she could remember.

The new one being built next to it was circular or octagonal or something like that. Maybe it was too modern for her tastes. Old fogy Joey. That almost rhymed, didn't it? She chained her bike to a railing at the rear entry, where the priests and altar boys went in and out. They wouldn't mind.

Around on the concrete sidewalk, stained rusty-brown from years of sprinklers. The ficus trees loomed to her left, dark masses, but their tops lit golden here and there by the first rays of the sun. Up the steps. Maybe a half-dozen here already. She went to her accustomed pew, about two-thirds of the way back on the left. Not that there weren't plenty of other places to choose from at early mass; the church was rarely even half-full. No crowding.

Joey had always liked that, preferred that. It was as much the reason she attended this early mass as any. Oh sure, she liked to get out and ride in the early morning too, get started on the day.

Someone slid in beside her. She would crowded this morning, just a little.

"I thought you'd be heading for Miami," she whispered.

"Not this early! You should be amazed I even got up in time for mass."

"Okay, I'm amazed."

Mass was brief, as typical. That was partly Father Al, partly the small crowd. As they exited into the cool, already-bright morning, Angelica said, "Come over for breakfast. I can't fix you pan perdu, I'm afraid, but there are certainly some stale doughnuts."

"How can I resist that? Did you walk?" There was no sign of Angelica's Vespa, nor of her Volkswagen. That was undoubtedly packed for the trip to Miami.

"I did. You'll have to push your bike all the way over to our place."

Which was not very far. Joey resisted the temptation to get on the bike and ride back and forth as her friend walked. No, Angelica probably wanted to talk and she should probably listen, and maybe even offer bad advice.

They were maybe halfway there when Angelica stated, "I think being around the triumvirate has made me a better person."

Maybe James too, Joey said to herself and then decided she might as well say it aloud. Not that it was what Angelica wanted to hear. "Maybe James too."

"Ha, I think you three brought out the worst in him!"

"How else can one deal with the worst in one?" Damn, that sounded profound. She had to write it down, but she wouldn't reach for her notepad right now.

"They can just shove it down and ignore it. That's what most of us do." When Joey didn't have a response to that, she went on. "James called last night to tell us he was safely in Boston. Or in Boston, I should say. I don't really know about the safe part."

"Safe from us. You really think we, um, helped you be better?" As soon as she asked, Joey recognized there was some truth in it. Maybe Angelica had even had something of the same effect on them.

"I don't doubt it for a minute. I spent way too much time these last few years being around girls like Debbie. *Becoming* a girl like Debbie."

"God forbid!" Joey suddenly felt the need to chuckle. "I rode down to the Walker home and tried to be a good influence on her."

"I heard something of that from Kris. What gave?"

"To be honest, I felt kind of bad about the way James had treated her. Maybe how we all treated her, a little."

To her credit, Angelica did not make light of it. "We did, didn't we? Leave it to Joey to point it out." After a moment of consideration, she added, "Maybe because you're more removed from her."

"Meaning my family doesn't have any money?" Or class or whatever. She thought she caught what Angelica was intending to say.

"You see people differently than I do. Differently on all sorts of levels." Angelica did laugh then. It might even have been a snicker. "You're the one who will feel sorry for the poor obscenely rich girl."

"I think you would if you thought about it."

"Maybe I would. I guess I have to start thinking more! It seems you are strong in all the places I am weak."

"And maybe vice-versa." Joey certainly knew she had her own weaknesses.

"We're like mirror images, Joey. The same but turned around backwards from each other."

"I'd hate to look in the mirror and see you."

"The feeling is quite mutual, Miss Varney. Here we are."

Joey looked up at the squarish Summerlin home, it's roof aglow in the morning sun, the palms' long blue shadows crisscrossing the white stucco walls. "I think I'll be on my way," she said. "Let me know if you're going to be home any weekends."

The two embraced there on the street and Joey rode away.

Afterword

This second *Women in the Sun* novel continues the stories of the three young women I introduced in "One Summer in the Sun." Might there be more novels? I can promise nothing but do hope to return to Naples in time.

I have endeavored to be accurate on events both in Naples and the world during the time this novel is set. However, the characters are not intended to be accurate, nor even inaccurate, portrayals of anyone. They are quite fictitious and any resemblances to actual persons are coincidental. They are as much inspired by people I have known since as by anyone in the Class of Sixty-eight.

Nor is any character, major or minor, in any sense the author—except that my own memories of that time and place underlie the story. I did attempt to be true to the town itself, and I attempted to be true to my fictional 'triumvirate' of young women. That is what the story is about.

Sienna Santerre